NERO'S NILE

Rowan O'Neill

Published by Old World Publishing.

Paperback ISBN: 978-1-0684773-4-8

Hardback ISBN: 978-1-0684773-5-5

1st edition 2026

About the Author

Rowan Hugh Patrick O'Neill was born in 1987 in Dublin, Ireland. He graduated with a Master's Degree in Materials Science & Engineering from University College Dublin. He now lives in Ireland and works as a mechanical design engineer. He is a part-time novelist. Nero's Nile is his second novel.

Also by Rowan O'Neill:

Gangsters and Demons

Contents

Chapter 1
The Boudican Revolt

Londinium, Britannia, 60 AD. Queen Boudica's revolt against Rome had swept across the province like divine retribution. The Iceni Queen had transformed personal vengeance into a holy war that united tribes across the province. The merchant city that had once been the crown jewel of Roman Britannia now lay in smouldering ruins, its marble forums cracked and blackened.

Two hundred and thirty thousand Briton warriors sprawled across the burning capital like carrion birds feasting on Rome's corpse. Their occupation of the city was a chaotic tapestry of tribal banners, war chariots, painted shields and iron-tipped spears. The River Thames ran dark with blood and debris, carrying the remnants of civilization toward the sea.

On a hill outside Londinium, the last Roman force in Britannia prepared for what many believed would be their final stand. Ten thousand men, detachments from the XIV Gemina and XX Valeria Victrix, along with auxiliary cohorts whose loyalty had not yet cracked under the weight of seemingly inevitable defeat. At the edge of the

Roman camp, two figures stood silhouetted against the distant glow of Londinium's funeral pyre.

General Titus Statilius Taurus V, embodying four generations of Roman ambition and survival. His father had raised him in Egypt to be a general in the Roman army, before dying at the hands of Agrippina the Younger. It was in Africa's crucible that Titus had been truly forged. Tracking leopards through jungles while senators' sons learned rhetoric, mastering survival in lands where only cunning kept a man alive.

Beside him stood Governor Gaius Suetonius Paulinus. A man more suited to governing prosperous provinces through diplomacy and festival planning than commanding armies in desperate battles, he trusted in the military prowess of Titus to get them through this.

"The scouts report their numbers at over two hundred thirty thousand," Titus said.

Paulinus studied the enemy encampment through narrowed eyes.

"Two hundred thirty thousand barbarians, and Rome sends us ten thousand men? I've seen better odds in arena fights where they feed prisoners to hungry lions. Something about this doesn't feel right, Titus. We should withdraw to Gaul, regroup, wait for reinforcements."

"Retreat? What do you think Emperor Nero will do when word reaches Rome that we fled from barbarians and farmers with pitchforks? I suspect our next campaign might involve entertaining crowds from the sand rather than commanding from the hills."

Paulinus considered this, his expression cycling through various stages of dismay as he contemplated the creative punishments Emperor Nero devised for those who disappointed him.

"The boy does have a theatrical streak, doesn't he? What would you suggest then, General Taurus? Intervention of the gods? A plague of locusts? Perhaps the Britons will spontaneously combust from excessive enthusiasm?"

"I'm going to walk over there and kill their Queen."

Paulinus raised his eyebrows and stared at Titus.

"Ten thousand versus two hundred thirty thousand? Those odds would make Mars himself consider early retirement. How exactly do you propose we overcome this minor numerical disadvantage?"

"We use their lack of civility against them. The Britons are barbarous, they have no order, no ranks, no uniforms. All they possess are numbers and a willingness to die for their Queen. So we infiltrate them. We don the clothes of their fallen, blend into their chaos. Then we walk among them. When I reach the centre of their camp, I'll eliminate the source of their unity."

"Queen Boudica."

"As long as she breathes, every tribe in Britannia will flock to her banner. When she dies, they'll fragment back into the squabbling chieftains they've always been."

Paulinus shook his head as he looked back at the enemy encampment.

"Half our senators would sell Caesar himself for the right price, but these Britons will die for a Queen they've never met simply because she shares their hatred of tax collectors. Very well, General Taurus. At dawn, we'll execute your plan. But I'll create a distraction to improve your odds."

"What do you have in mind?"

"I will send a legion to Watling Street to engage the enemy. I'll keep them occupied for as long as I can."

"You're coming too, Paulinus."

"Can't I stay in the general's tent and guard the wine supply?"

"I need someone I can trust by my side, there is no telling what madness awaits in that barbarian camp? We leave at dawn."

Titus gazed once more at the enemy camp, where a quarter million barbarians prepared for what they believed would be their final, triumphant victory over Roman oppression. But the general's resolve never waivered. His father had taught him that impossible odds were simply another form of terrain to be navigated.

At dawn, Paulinus had summoned his senior officers to his command tent. Maps of the surrounding terrain lay spread across the campaign table, weighted down with stones and daggers. He traced his finger along the line of Watling Street, the great Roman road that cut through the heart of Britannia.

"The Fourteenth Gemina will march at first light. Tribune Agricola, you'll take eight cohorts and establish a defensive position here. The terrain favours us. Narrow frontage, elevated ground, thick forest to protect your flanks."

Agricola studied the map.

"What is our objective, Governor?"

"Hold them. Bleed them. They'll expect us to flee, to abandon the province. Instead, you'll stand like a wall of iron across their path."

"How long must we hold, sir?"

"As long as flesh and sinew allow. Every hour you stand is an hour we gain. They fight with fury but no discipline. Let them dash themselves against your shields until their arms grow weary and their hearts grow cold."

Agricola nodded slowly.

"A battle of attrition."

"Precisely. The Britons have numbers, but numbers mean nothing if they cannot bring them to bear."

"And if they overwhelm us?"

Paulinus met Agricola's gaze.

"Then you die as Romans die. Standing, shields locked, facing the enemy. But you will have given us the time we need. Your names will be remembered when we grind Boudicca's revolt into dust."

The orders were given, the dispositions made. Centurions roused their men, armour was donned in the predawn darkness, standards were raised. The Fourteenth Gemina formed up in marching order, as they prepared to march on Watling street.

By morning's light, Titus and Paulinus had transformed themselves into something unrecognizable. They wore the rough-spun tunics and woolen cloaks stripped from British corpses, their bronze torcs and iron arm rings still warm with the blood of their former owners. Mud caked their faces and arms, turning their pale skin mottled brown.

As the sun climbed weakly through the morning mist, Titus adjusted the rough British cloak around his shoulders. Beside him, Paulinus looked equally uncomfortable in his barbarian disguise.

"Ready?" Titus asked.

"As ready as a man can be for walking into his own death," Paulinus replied.

“Look on the bright side, Paulinus. If this fails, at least we'll die creatively.”

They began their descent toward the enemy, hearts hammering against ribs as they approached the outer edge of the barbarian encampment. Titus felt every muscle tense, expecting at any moment to hear the war cry that would signal their discovery, the clash of bronze on iron that would mark their final moments.

But no challenge came.

The first Britons they encountered barely glanced at them, too focused on sharpening weapons or preparing for battle. A group of Iceni spearmen nodded as they passed, taking them for fellow tribesmen from some distant clan. A Trinovantes chieftain eyed them suspiciously but said nothing as they walked past.

Titus and Paulinus exchanged a look of barely concealed amazement. It was working. The very chaos that made Boudica’s army so dangerous in battle had become their fatal weakness. They separated with silent nods, melting into the crowd like wolves among sheep.

The camp was a labyrinth without logic, a sprawling maze of tribal sections that reflected ancient alliances and blood feuds. There were no checkpoints, no sentries demanding passwords, no officers maintaining order. Every warrior was his own commander, every tent his own kingdom. The only authority that mattered belonged to the flame-haired Queen whose fury had united them in common cause.

Queen Boudica's royal tent stood at the heart of the camp, a magnificent pavilion of red leather decorated with gold thread that caught the firelight. Four warriors of her personal guard stood watch, their painted shields and iron-tipped spears marking them as the elite of the British army. Titus and Paulinus walked to a neighbouring supply wagon, speaking in hushed voices while pretending to examine Celtic weapons. Titus shifted his gaze to Queen Boudica's tent.

"I need to get into the royal tent. I overheard the Britons say they are making ground on Watling Street. We can't hold them off for much longer."

Paulinus looked at the neighbouring supply tent.

"I'll create a distraction. That supply tent across from the royal pavilion, it's full of grain and oil. When it goes up in flames, her guards will rush to help fight the fire. That's your moment."

"May the gods protect you."

They separated again, Paulinus melting back into the crowd while Titus positioned himself near the food preparation area. He selected a wooden tray and arranged it with apples and bread, transforming himself into just another servant attending to the Queen's needs.

The supply tent erupted in flames with a roar that shook the ground, tongues of fire leaping twenty feet into the sky. Shouts echoed across the camp as warriors rushed to form bucket brigades, the Queen's guards among them. In the chaos and confusion, no one noticed Titus carrying a tray of refreshments into the royal tent.

The interior of Queen Boudica's tent blazed with luxury. There were silk hangings from distant lands, carved furniture that spoke of royal wealth, silver cups and golden ornaments that reflected the lamp flames like captured stars. It was almost a different realm to the chaos and grit that surrounded it.

Queen Boudica lay in repose on a couch draped in wolf furs, her flame-red hair cascading over shoulders bare except for the golden torcs that marked her royal status. Even in repose, she radiated the fierce charisma that had united warring tribes, her green eyes holding depths that spoke of both wisdom and bottomless fury. In front of the Queen stood two royal guards.

Titus approached the guards, holding the fruit tray at chest level as if presenting refreshments for inspection. The first guard leaned forward to examine the offering, and in that moment of distraction, Titus swung the tray upward with brutal force. The tray struck the guard's jaw with a sickening crack, and he crumpled to the ground unconscious.

Before the second guard could cry out or draw his weapon, Titus had already pulled the fallen guard's sword from its sheath and cut the second guard's throat. Blood sprayed across the tent's silk hangings as the guard fell backward, clutching uselessly at the mortal wound. Titus turned the bloodied sword on the unconscious guard, driving the iron point through his chest to ensure he would never wake. Only then did he face Boudica, the weapon still dripping crimson in his grip.

The Queen continued to lay in repose, showing neither surprise nor fear.

"Very impressive, General Taurus."

"You speak Latin?" Titus replied in surprise.

"Tell me, General, do you even know why you are killing us?"

"Your husband, King Prasutagus, made an agreement with Emperor Nero. He wrote in his will that the emperor would inherit these lands upon the King's death. But you failed to honour this agreement."

"Nero had my husband assassinated days after he signed that document. The agreement was supposed to bring us peace, not death. Why should I honour Rome when you have no honour yourselves?"

"Because we have more swords than you do."

Boudica exploded to her feet in anger.

"Your chauvinistic arrogance will be your downfall. Do you even wonder, General Taurus, why Nero would send only ten thousand men to fight two hundred thirty thousand?"

Titus's eyes darted side to side. He had considered this but never wanted to think too much about it. He looked back at the Queen and straightened to his full height.

“Do you ever wonder, Queen Boudica, why ten thousand Romans could defeat two hundred thirty thousand Britons?”

Boudica sat back down in her couch, her defiance crumbling.

"Let's get this over with then. Do what you must."

Boudica drank deeply from her wine cup as she eyed the general. Titus approached the Queen and raised his sword above her head. He was all but assured of victory. But suddenly, she spat the wine directly into his eyes, the alcohol burning like liquid fire across his vision.

Blind and staggering, he fell to the floor as he felt the sword torn from his grasp. Through tears and wine, he saw the Queen’s silhouette advancing, his own blade now in her hands. He rolled desperately as she struck, the iron point striking the ground where his head had been a heartbeat before.

Again and again she swung the sword at him, driving him backward through the tent until his shoulders struck the leather wall. Trapped, blinded, weaponless, he could only watch as she raised the sword for the killing blow.

"You will never defeat the Britons, Roman. We are more than just a people, we are a spirit. When your empire has crumbled to ash, Britannia will rule this realm far better than you ever did."

The Queen’s sword hovered above Titus like the sword of Damocles; its point aimed at his heart.

"Goodbye, General Taurus."

Before the sword could reach Titus, steel burst through the Queen’s chest in a spray of blood and bronze, the point of a blade emerging between her breasts like a deadly flower. She looked down in shock, then crumpled to the ground, revealing Paulinus standing behind her.

"They know we've infiltrated. We have to leave. Now!" Paulinus said, hauling Titus to his feet.

Outside the royal tent, chaos reigned supreme. Word had spread that Romans had infiltrated their camp, disguising themselves as Britons. Paranoid tribesmen slaughtered their own men, mistaking them for Roman infiltrators. The camp blazed with fires started in the panic. The careful unity Boudica had forged was dissolving into murderous confusion, clan turned against clan as fear consumed reason.

Titus and Paulinus sprinted through the madness, dodging spears and burning debris as they fled toward the distant hills towards their camp. Behind them, the largest barbarian army ever assembled in Britannia tore itself apart in an orgy of suspicion and flame.

The Queen was dead. The rebellion would die with her.

On Watling Street, the enemy began to falter. Word had reached the Britons that their Queen had fallen. Some ran back to their camp. Others fell to their knees. Others fled back into the heartland. Their spirit defeated as the tide turns in their battle into Roman favour. From the elevated Roman position, Tribune Agricola allowed himself a tight smile.

"They're breaking! Form up the cavalry. No mercy. Run them down."

The Roman horsemen surged forward, their spears finding easy targets among the fleeing mob. What had been a battle became a slaughter, then a rout, then a hunt. The tide that had threatened to sweep Rome from Britannia now turned with crushing finality, drowning the rebellion in its own blood.

Meanwhile, Titus and Paulinus stumbled through the perimeter of their Roman camp, their Celtic disguises torn and smoke-stained, their faces streaked with soot and British blood.

Three horses waited at the camp's heart. Sextus Afranius Burrus, the Prefect of Nero's Praetorian Guard, scars webbing across his face beneath the shadow of his helmet. Flanking him were two of his most trusted Praetorians, Marcus and Quintus, younger but equally deadly. The Praetorian's scarlet cloaks hung from their shoulders in precise military folds, its hem stopping exactly at knee height as regulation demanded. Sextus called out as he spotted the approaching figures.

"Governor Paulinus!"

Marcus squinted through the dim light, then unsheathed his blade from its scabbard. Quintus followed suit.

"It looks like they've gone native, Sextus. Let us deal with them."

“Halt!”

Sextus's command stopped the two Praetorians in their tracks. He dismounted his horse and approached Paulinus, eyeing him with suspicion.

"Where have you been?"

"Securing Britannia for the empire."

"By wearing the clothes of our enemy? Do you realize how this appears to Rome?"

"She's dead," Paulinus said.

Sextus froze and stared at Paulinus, looking for any trace of deception.

"Queen Boudica? That's impossible. You were outnumbered twenty-three to one."

"Yes, but we had something they didn't. General Taurus."

Sextus turned to Titus, eyeing him with uncertainty.

"How did you do it, Titus? A quarter million barbarians, and you just stride into their camp and kill their Queen?"

"I used their lack of civility against them. We infiltrated their camp. No uniforms, no organization, no discipline. Their greatest strength became their fatal weakness."

Sextus studied Titus for a moment. Then something crossed his face that may have resembled a smile.

"This may be the greatest military victory since Actium. You could become a senator for this achievement. Tell me what you desire, and it shall be yours."

Titus was quiet for a long moment, his gaze drifting toward the rolling hills that stretched westward from the camp.

"There is a plot of land thirty miles west of here. Rolling hills covered in oak and ash, a stream that runs clear year-round. I wish to retire there with my wife and sons."

"Land? That's all? After what you've accomplished?"

"That's all I want. A place where my children can grow without fear of poison in their wine or daggers in the dark."

"It will be done. The deed will be drawn up before we reach Rome."

"I'll take the senator position," Paulinus interjected with a grin.

"Very well. Come with me, Governor Paulinus. We must debrief in Rome immediately. Emperor Nero will want every detail of this campaign. General Taurus, you are hereby relieved of your command. Enjoy your retirement. You've earned it."

The Praetorians mounted their horses, Paulinus swinging up behind Quintus. Within moments, they were galloping south toward Rome, leaving Titus standing alone in the freshly conquered province.

Dobunni, Britannia, 62 AD. The farm spread across the hills like a piece of paradise carved by Venus herself. Oak trees dotted rolling pastures where cattle grazed contently, while fields of wheat and barley swayed in the gentle breeze. A Roman villa sat at the heart of it all, smoke rising peacefully from its chimney.

Titus was chopping wood, watching his two young sons practice sword work in the yard while his wife tended her herb garden. The boys had his blue eyes but their mother's gentle nature. They would never need to learn the harsh lessons that had shaped their father's youth.

The sound of approaching hoofbeats broke the pastoral quiet. A single rider emerged from the tree line, his scarlet cloak and bronze armour immediately recognizable. Sextus, the Praetorian Prefect, reined in his horse at the garden gate and dismounted.

Titus nodded knowingly to himself, long expecting this visit. He turned to face Sextus, never letting go of his axe.

"Sextus. What brings you to my humble farm?"

The Praetorian's cold eyes swept the peaceful scene: the playing children, the content livestock, the woman humming as she worked among her herbs. He removed his helmet.

“Titus, Emperor Nero would like to speak with you."

Chapter 2
Agrippina The Younger

Antium, Latium, 37 AD. In a seaside villa beneath the seven hills, Agrippina the Younger gave birth. Her screams swallowed by the stone walls, her blood pooling like an offering on the mosaic floor. The infant, Lucius Domitius Ahenobarbus, though history would know him by another name entirely, emerged not with a cry but a gurgle, as though testing the notes of a song yet unwritten.

"A son," announced the midwife.

The child's father, Gnaeus Domitius Ahenobarbus, scanned the child as one might inspect a questionable purchase in the market, his eyes rheumy from last night's excesses. He drank deeply from his wine cup and dismissed the baby with a grunt.

"I hope he brings you what you are looking for."

He took another swig of wine and stumbled from the room. Agrippina gazed upon the infant, not as a son, but as a sceptre, a blade to carve her name into eternity. She held the baby close as she whispered to him.

"You will be the greatest emperor in Roman history. Greater than your uncle Caligula. Greater even than the divine Augustus."

Rome, 41 AD. In the courtyard of their new villa, four-year-old Lucius played alone. He crouched beside the marble fountain, his small fingers wrapped around the neck of a sparrow. The bird's wings ceased their frantic beating as the young boy twisted its neck. He studied the creature with clinical fascination. The tiny body lay still against his palm, and something flickered across his face that might have been satisfaction.

"Lucius."

The boy's head snapped up. Agrippina stood at the edge of the courtyard, her stola rustling in the breeze. Her face betrayed nothing, but her amber eyes flickered between the bird's corpse in his palm and his satisfied smirk. Her brother Caligula had worn that same expression once, in the gardens of their childhood home.

"Come. Dinner is ready."

The boy ran over to his mother and took her hand as they entered the villa. The triclinium blazed with oil lamps, their flames dancing across frescoed walls that depicted scenes of Roman triumph. Ahenobarbus reclined on his couch in his wine-stained toga, his bloodshot eyes drifting to the young slave girl who served their meal. Agrippina watched him with the patient stillness of a viper as she and her son reclined on their couches. Ahenobarbus lifted his cup with an unsteady hand.

"Your son will be a disaster for Rome. Mark my words, woman. A disaster for Rome and for me. He has your brother's eyes. Those same cursed, strange eyes."

Agrippina's jaw tightened at the mention of Caligula.

"He has the blood of Augustus. That is worth more than your family's wisdom."

"Do you really think that little stultus could be emperor? If he ever became emperor, Rome would burn to the ground!"

"If Rome burned to the ground, we would merely rebuild it in his image."

Ahenobarbus burst into a fit of rage and hurled his cup across the room, striking the slave girl in the temple, sending her crashing to the floor.

"Now look what you've made me do! You've made me to spill my wine."

Agrippina remained calm. She looked at the slave girl on the floor and then smiled at Ahenobarbus.

"Don't worry, dear husband. I shall fetch you a new cup of wine. One you will enjoy much more."

Agrippina rose carefully from the table and glided from the room and returned with a fresh cup of wine, its surface dark as blood in the lamplight. Ahenobarbus drained the cup in three long gulps, then fell back against his couch with a satisfied grunt. For a moment, the room was quiet save for the crackle of the oil lamps.

Then his breathing changed. It came in short, sharp gasps at first, his eyes widening as his hands clawed at his throat.

"Enjoying the wine?" Agrippina smirked.

He tried to speak, but only a strangled wheeze emerged. His body convulsed once, twice, and then went still. The silence stretched between mother and son, broken only by the steady drip of wine from the overturned cup beside the couch.

Agrippina moved to Lucius, placing a gentle hand on his shoulder. The boy hadn't flinched during his father's death throes, his blue eyes drinking in the spectacle with the same fascination he'd shown the sparrow.

"Hush now, Lucius. It's all right. He was merely a steppingstone towards your greatness."

Days later, Ahenobarbus's funeral pyre blazed against the grey Roman sky as his body lay wrapped in fine linens atop the wooden platform. Agrippina stood motionless, draped in the deep black of mourning, her face a perfect mask of widowed sorrow. Young Lucius stood at her side, his eyes reflecting twin pillars of fire.

The crowd of dignitaries maintained a respectful distance, their togas fluttering in the wind that carried the smoke toward the seven hills of Rome. Among them moved a figure of unmistakable authority. Emperor Claudius, his slight limp more pronounced as he navigated the uneven ground towards Agrippina.

"My dear niece. I am so very sorry for your loss."

"Thank you, Emperor, it's been so lonely, However, I find it is better to be alone than to share one's bed with a spouse who is unfaithful." Then, after a calculated pause, she added, "But you should know something of that yourself."

"What do you mean?"

"Perhaps I've said too much."

"Tell me."

"Dear Uncle, surely you must know of your wife Messalina's liaisons with Gaius Silius. The whole city whispers of it."

"It cannot be true."

Agrippina moved closer still, close enough that he could smell the subtle perfume that clung to her hair. Her fingers brushed his arm, a touch so light it might have been accidental.

"If I were your wife, Emperor, I would love you and cherish you every minute of every day. I would never treat you as she does. A man of your intelligence, your strength, deserves a wife who recognizes his true worth."

"Roman law prohibits an uncle from marrying his niece." he said, though his voice lacked conviction.

Her smile transformed her face from merely beautiful to devastating.

"The wonderful thing about being Emperor is that you have the power to change the laws."

Claudius turned his gaze toward the crowd, where his wife stood among the other mourners, her attention clearly elsewhere, her eyes scanning the gathering as if looking for someone more interesting than her husband. The sight of her distraction, here at a family funeral, struck him like a revelation.

"You would make a much more worthy Empress, Agrippina. I will do all that is necessary to marry you."

"That would be joyous news indeed, Emperor. Though I confess, I would have but one condition."

"What is it?"

"If we were to wed, I want you to adopt my son, Lucius. So that he too might have the chance to serve Rome as Emperor someday."

"I will consider it. But you must understand that my son Britannicus is next in line to be Emperor."

"Of course, Uncle. I know the proper order of succession. But surely a woman may dream of her son's future? Besides, think of the dynasty we could build. Lucius could marry your daughter Octavia, providing you with grandchildren who carry your bloodline. Your legacy would be ensured for generations to come."

Claudius smiled as he looked at Lucius.

"I have a feeling your son will bring Rome great fortune. I will adopt him if we are to wed. But first I must attend to the matter of my wife."

Rome, 48 AD. In the palace courtyard, the executioner's blade separated Empress Messalina's head from her shoulders. Execution for treason on a suspected affair with Gaius Silius, although no evidence had ever been found.

The new law allowing Claudius to marry his niece passed with surprising ease. The Senate, ever eager to please an Emperor they had long underestimated, readily agreed that special circumstances might warrant exceptions to traditional marriage prohibitions. After all, the Pharaohs of Egypt had married siblings for centuries, and

Rome had always been adaptable in its adoption of useful customs.

The wedding itself was a magnificent affair, held in the palace with all the ceremony befitting an imperial union. Agrippina, radiant in cloth-of-gold, had never looked more beautiful. Her triumph was complete when Claudius formally adopted her son, bestowing upon the boy a name that would echo through history: Nero Claudius Caesar Augustus Germanicus.

Rome, 53 AD. Nero's family gathered for his sixteenth birthday at the imperial triclinium to celebrate his passage into manhood.

Emperor Claudius reclined at the head of the table, his face animated with paternal pride as he gazed upon his adopted son. Beside him, Agrippina maintained her position of honour, draped in deep wine-coloured silk. Nero, resplendent in a gold-bordered toga, accepted the attention with grace. His new wife, his step-sister Octavia, sat in dutiful silence while thirteen-year-old Britannicus fidgeted with barely contained excitement. Claudius raised his silver wine cup.

"My family. On this blessed evening, I am moved to reflect upon the great fortune the gods have bestowed upon our house. Let us raise our cups in a toast. May the Julio-Claudian dynasty reign for a thousand years, bringing glory to Rome and prosperity to all her citizens!"

"To the dynasty!" the table chorused.

Claudius drained the cup and settled back with content.

"Truly magnificent. The gods smile upon—"

His words died abruptly. The cup suddenly slipped from his fingers, striking the floor with a crystalline chime that resonated like a death knell. His eyes widened as comprehension dawned. His breathing became laboured as convulsions wracked his body.

"Father!" Octavia screamed as she rushed to Claudius's side, tears streaming down her cheeks as she tried to rouse him. But his struggles were growing weaker, each desperate gasp shallower than the last until a final, wet rattle scraped from his throat.

"Father!" she screamed again.

"Silence her!" Agrippina commanded the Praetorian Guard.

The guards lifted the sobbing Octavia despite her protests and carried her from the triclinium. Britannicus sat frozen beside his father's corpse, his young face white with dawning terror. Agrippina smiled across the table at Lucius.

"Now you will be Emperor, my son."

"But Britannicus is next in line, Mother."

"Roman law dictates that the emperor must be at least sixteen years of age. Britannicus is only thirteen. Congratulations, Emperor Nero."

Rome, 54 AD. The Roman Senate house stood as it had for centuries, its marble columns reaching toward the coffered ceiling like the pillars of Elysium. Shafts of morning sunlight streamed through the high windows, illuminating the faces of six hundred senators who filled the curved benches in their pristine white togas, each bordered with the purple stripe that marked their senatorial rank. At the centre of it all, upon the ivory curule chair that had seated Emperors before him, sat Emperor Nero.

Behind Nero stood the men who would shape his reign. Sextus, prefect of his Praetorian Guard, stood at attention in his plate armour and scarlet cloak. Beside him stood Lucius Annaeus Seneca, Rome's most celebrated philosopher and now the Emperor's chief advisor. Epaphroditus, Nero's secretary, had risen from slavery to become one of the most trusted men in the palace.

Senator Gaius Calpurnius Piso rose from his position among the senior senators, his silver hair gleaming in the sunlight. His voice carried easily through the marble hall.

"Conscript Fathers, we gather today to hear the first address of our new Caesar, Nero Claudius Caesar Augustus Germanicus. May his words guide us toward a prosperous future for Rome."

Nero rose from the curule chair, his movement drawing every eye in the chamber. The whispers died away until the only sound was the gentle echo of his footsteps on marble as he walked to the centre of the chamber.

"Conscript Fathers of Rome. I stand before you today not merely as your Emperor, but as your servant. As a young man entrusted with the sacred duty of guiding our eternal city toward ever greater glory."

He paused, allowing his gaze to sweep across the ranks of senators.

"I know that some among you may question whether one so young can bear the weight of empire. To you, I say this: youth brings not weakness, but the strength of fresh vision unburdened by the prejudices of the past."

A murmur of approval rippled through portions of the assembly, while others maintained the careful neutrality of experienced politicians.

"We shall rule as Augustus ruled. With justice and benevolence, guided by the wisdom of this august body and mindful always of what best served Rome. The people of our empire, from the merchants of the Subura to the farmers of Gaul, from the scholars of Athens to the soldiers on our frontiers, all shall find in me a protector of their interests and a champion of their welfare."

He extended his hand toward the assembled senators in a gesture both inclusive and commanding.

"Together, we shall write the next chapter in Rome's glorious history. Together, we shall ensure that the empire our ancestors built through blood and courage continues to flourish for generations yet unborn."

A wave of applause rippled through the senators. Senator Piso rose to his feet and put both hands over his heart as he addressed the new emperor.

"Caesar, if these words prove prophetic of your reign, you may yet turn out to be the greatest emperor Rome has ever seen. The wisdom in your address gives this old senator cause for great hope."

A chorus of agreement rose from the benches as other senators nodded their approval, their initial uncertainty giving way to cautious optimism. Here, perhaps, was an Emperor who would respect the traditions and institutions that had made Rome great.

The philosopher Seneca stepped forward, his voice carrying the warmth of a teacher praising a favoured student.

"A tremendous speech, my Emperor. Your words demonstrate not only rhetorical skill but genuine understanding of the principles that must guide a just ruler."

"Thank you for your counsel, Seneca. Without your wisdom, I would be lost in the labyrinth of statecraft. Your teachings have prepared me for this moment, and I pray they will continue to guide me in the trials to come."

The exchange drew more approving murmurs from the senators, many of whom had long respected Seneca's philosophical writings and political acumen. To see the young Emperor acknowledge his debt to such a man spoke well of his character and judgment.

But in the shadows at the edge of the chamber, behind a column that concealed her from most eyes, Agrippina watched the proceedings with very different thoughts. Her calculating eyes missed nothing. Not the senators' growing approval of her son, not Seneca's obvious influence over him, not the way Nero seemed to grow in confidence and authority with each passing moment.

Mother and son, she reflected, ruling together. The partnership she had dreamed of was finally becoming reality. Nero might wear the purple and sit upon the throne, but the true power remained where it had always been.

Later that night, Nero's private triclinium glowed with lamplight as he dined with his family. Agrippina reclined with poise while Nero picked listlessly at roasted peacock and honey cakes. Octavia sat in dutiful silence, and thirteen-year-old Britannicus fidgeted with his silver cutlery.

"That was a wonderful speech in the senate today, Nero," Agrippina said.

"You should know, Mother. You wrote it," Nero mumbled as he pushed a piece of gristly peacock around his plate.

The table fell into an awkward silence. As wine flowed and servants withdrew, Nero sat down his cup.

"Mother, I have a confession. I do not want to be Emperor."

Agrippina's eyes sharpened like a hawk's as she slammed her cutlery on the table.

"I didn't sacrifice everything to make it this far only for you to ruin it now, boy. You are going to be Emperor, and that's final."

"I want to be an artist, Mother. I want to recite poetry, play the lyre, compose verses. Politics is so boring compared to the beauty of creation."

"I will handle the politics, Lucius. All you need to do is give speeches and appear at ceremonies. Leave running the empire to me."

"Very well, Mother. But I want time for music and poetry."

"Of course. But first, I will give you a lesson in power."

"What do you mean?"

Agrippina smirked and turned to Britannicus.

"Are you enjoying the peacock?"

"Absolutely, Mother. It's—"

Britannicus suddenly gasped, his hand flying to his throat. Colour drained from his face as his breathing became laboured, eyes widening.

"I can't—"

His words dissolved into strangled sounds as convulsions wracked his body. A single tear ran down Octavia's cheek as she watched on helplessly as her younger brother died the same way as her father. She knew any attempt to save him would be futile. Britannicus's final breath rattled like autumn leaves as the room went silent.

Agrippina remained perfectly composed. Nero looked at his brother's corpse, tilting his head as if intrigued.

"Why did you kill my brother, mother?"

"He was not your brother, Nero. He was your competition. The throne you sit upon will draw assassins like flies to honey. Some wielding daggers in the dark, others offering poison with a smile. Even the mighty Julius Caesar bled out on the Senate floor, surrounded by men he called friends. No Emperor is ever truly safe. Every Emperor must learn to cut the sapling before it grows into a tree that might overshadow him. One death now prevents a thousand later. Even now, across the Mediterranean, another man grooms his son to take what is rightfully yours."

"Who?"

"Our Proconsul in Africa, Titus Statilius Taurus IV trains his son to take control of the Roman military. Your military. The boy shows remarkable talent with both sword and strategy. He already commands loyalty among the legionaries. Men who might one day proclaim him Emperor over your dead body."

“What would you have me do, Mother?”

"I will show you how to eliminate the threat.”

Agrippina snapped her fingers and the Praetorian Prefect emerged from the shadows.

"Sextus, have the Praetorians investigate proconsul Taurus, everyone is guilty of something. Find out what it is and then summon him to Rome. And deal with this mess while you are at it,” Agrippina said dismissively motioning to the corpse of Britannicus.

Sextus nodded and lifted Britannicus's body, carrying it away as he exited.

Rome, 55 AD. The cobblestones of the Appian Way stretched endlessly before Titus Statilius Taurus IV as his carriage rolled toward Rome. The blood of builders ran in his veins. His great-grandfather had risen from nothing to build monuments that would outlast empires. But that same blood had proven a curse for his father, executed for plotting against Claudius, and now it threatened to claim him as well. He knew why he had been summoned.

In the throne room, three figures awaited him. Nero sat upon the ivory chair of Caesar. Beside him stood Sextus. But it was the woman who drew Taurus's attention. Agrippina, draped in imperial purple. Taurus inclined his head with careful respect.

"Emperor Nero. It is an honour."

"You may speak with me, not my son," Agrippina interrupted.

Nero's jaw tightened.

"I am the Emperor, Mother. I should address him."

"Silence, boy. You shall do as you are told."

Nero stepped back frustratedly as Taurus looked between the two before responding.

"Yes, Agrippina," Taurus said quietly.

"Titus Statilius Taurus IV. I've heard of your son, Titus Statilius Taurus V. You've been training him in Egypt. They say he could be Rome's mightiest warrior, not just strong, but bright and cunning."

"My son has a gift. I don't know where he inherited it, but I hope he becomes a general one day."

"And your daughter, Statilia Messalina, is it true you have been training her in the ways of the imperial palace, so that she may become an Empress?"

"That's right. My daughter deserves the world. This is the only way I could conceive of giving it to her. She would make a great Empress for your son."

"I'm sure she would. But let us dispense with pleasantries. You have been accused of certain irregularities during your proconsulship in Africa."

Taurus shook his head as Agrippina thumbed through the arrest report prepared by the Praetorian Guard.

"By Tarquitius Priscus, a disgruntled subordinate who—"

"Magical practices. Superstitious rites. Communication with powers that Rome has deemed problematic. These are serious charges indeed."

"I have served Rome faithfully."

"You have served your own ambition. Preparing your daughter for imperial marriage? Training your son to be a general without permission from the Praetorian Guard?"

"My son could be the next Julius Caesar."

Agrippina's eyes blazed as she sprung to her feet.

"Julius Caesar!? We don't need another Julius Caesar. Rome has the greatest Emperor in its history, and I am his mother. Are you threatening us, Taurus?"

"No, Agrippina. I would never."

"You trained your son to overthrow the Emperor. You trained your daughter to be an Empress. I know someone who will do anything to take power when I see them."

Taurus felt the trap closing around him. He knew his fate had been decided before he entered the room. He smirked at Agrippina and took on a mocking tone.

"I guess you've learned that from experience."

The silence that followed was profound. Even Sextus seemed to hold his breath.

"The penalty for conspiracy to commit treason is death," Agrippina said.

"Let's get this over with then. Have your lapdog draw his sword and end it."

"No, Taurus. You will not be granted a warrior's death. You will die a coward's death. Sextus will not draw his sword. He will draw you a bath. Then you will get in that bath and take your own life."

"I'd love to know how you plan on making me do that."

"You have a choice, Taurus. Either you take your own life, or we take your children's lives. If you get in the bath, your son will be made a general. Your daughter will be welcomed into the imperial household as my son's mistress. Your family name will be honoured. Or you can choose to fight. In which case, I will ensure your son dies in a distant province, your daughter disappears into prison, your family line ends, and the name Statilius Taurus will be forgotten forever."

The choice was no choice at all. Taurus thought of his son's bright eyes, his daughter's gentle smile, the bloodline that stretched back to greatness.

"My son, you will make him a general?"

"He'll have the opportunity to prove himself."

"And what will become of my daughter?"

"She will be treated with all the honour due to an imperial mistress. She'll want for nothing."

Taurus closed his eyes, seeing his ancestors' faces, feeling the weight of generations. The legacy would continue through his children, even if he could not.

"Very well," he whispered.

As Sextus led him away, Agrippina turned to Nero with satisfaction gleaming in her amber eyes.

"Fear not, my boy. The barbarians in Britannia grow in numbers. We shall deploy young Titus to that savage shore like a lamb to the slaughter. His daughter, however, may make a good mistress. Especially given how Octavia has failed to grant us an heir."

Nero said nothing, his eyes fixed on his mother. Where once there had been childish awe, now embers of resentment began to glow.

Rome, 59 AD. At twenty-one, Nero's true passion remained locked away from the business of empire. In the privacy of his villa, surrounded by lyres and scrolls of verse, he composed poetry that had never graced the public forums, practiced melodies that had never echoed in the great theatres. His hands, meant to wield power over legions, trembled with artistic sensitivity as they plucked strings or guided a stylus across wax.

The morning sun streamed through tall windows as five figures gathered in Nero's private study. Seneca maintained his position near the bookshelves. Sextus stood at attention at the door, while Epaphroditus waited with scrolls and tablets, ready to record whatever decisions emerged from the gathering. Agrippina stood in the centre of the room and began speaking without preamble.

"The Senate grows restless. They question your commitment to governance while you waste time with artists and musicians."

Nero's fingers stilled on the lyre he had been absently tuning.

"Perhaps if I were allowed to pursue my calling, I would find more joy in the duties you insist upon."

"You are Emperor, not some tavern entertainer. You will attend the next Senate session and present the tax reforms we discussed."

"But the people don't like paying taxes, Mother. Let's just dispose of them. It will make me so popular."

"You will do as you are told. You are Emperor because I made you Emperor."

"If I am Emperor, then perhaps I should make the decisions that affect the empire."

"You will do as I say. I sail for Antium tomorrow to inspect the grain stores. When I return, we will discuss your duties further."

She gathered her stola around her shoulders and swept from the room like a storm cloud, leaving tension crackling in her wake. Nero waited for her footsteps to fade before throwing his lyre forcefully against the wall and turning to Sextus.

"I cannot continue to rule my empire under the tyranny of a domineering harpy. My mother is due to sail tomorrow. Ensure her vessel will... encounter difficulties in the water."

Sextus's hand moved to the hilt of his sword.

"Just let me use my blade, Emperor. It will be much quicker."

"Have you no flare for the theatrics, Sextus? Sabotage the boat. We don't want to draw suspicion."

"It will be done, my Emperor."

Sextus raised his right hand to salute the emperor and exited.

The next evening, Nero was composing verse when commotion erupted in the courtyard. Voices shouted, servants scattered, and then Agrippina burst through the door, soaking wet with seawater. Nero rose to his feet in shock.

"Mother! What happened?"

"My boat split apart in the water. Some design flaw in the hull. I managed to swim to shore."

"How... wonderful that you survived."

Agrippina studied his face intensely as she wrang brine from her stola.

"Indeed. We have much work to do when I've recovered. I will retire to my villa to rest."

As she departed, leaving wet footprints on marble floors, Nero felt something snap inside his chest. The final thread of filial obedience, perhaps, or simply the last vestige of fear.

"Enough of this! Sextus, do it your way."

Sextus raised his right hand to salute and strode from the room.

Days later, Sextus returned to Nero's palace. Nero looked at him expectantly.

"It is done, my Emperor."

Sextus showed a lock of Agrippina's bloodied hair.

Nero exhaled a sigh of relief. His tense shoulders suddenly slumped. Overwhelmed with a sense of liberation and euphoria, he started laughing to himself. He picked up his lyre and started playing as he walked around the room with a confident gait.

He moved to the great map that dominated one wall of his study. For the first time in years, he felt truly free to shape his own destiny.

"Now that my mother can no longer hinder me, I am free to reshape Rome in my image."

His fingers traced the borders of the empire around the map. His gaze settled on the southern reaches of the map, where the province of Egypt sprawled along the Mediterranean coast. His finger began tracing the long river that ran through the province.

"What is the name of this river?"

Seneca approached and looked at the map.

"That is the River Nile, Caesar. It provides water to irrigate vast fields of wheat. Without Egyptian grain, the provinces would starve within months."

Nero's finger followed the river's course southward until it disappeared into blank parchment.

"Where does the Nile come from?"

"We don't know, my Emperor. Many have tried and failed to find the source of the Nile. It remains one of the empire's great mysteries."

A glint appeared in Nero's eye.

"I will succeed where they have failed. I need only assemble the right team."

"Who do you have in mind?"

"The African proconsul who took his own life. He had a son raised in those lands, trained as a warrior. Where is he now?"

"General Titus Statilius Taurus V is in Britannia, serving under Governor Gaius Suetonius Paulinus. The native Britons have gathered under Queen Boudica and are in full revolt."

"If I discover the source of the Nile, I shall be remembered as Rome's greatest explorer. History will speak of Nero the Builder, Nero the Artist, Nero the Discoverer. This venture will eclipse even Alexander's achievements."

Nero's eyes gleamed with possibility. He turned from the map, decision crystallizing in his mind.

"Sextus, go to Britannia. Summon Titus."

Chapter 3
Imperium

Rome, 62 AD. The Domus Augusti adorns the summit of Palatine Hill. A palace complex that sprawls across terraced gardens and colonnaded courtyards. Titus approaches through gates flanked by granite sphinxes plundered from Egypt, their enigmatic faces watching him with stone eyes that have witnessed the rise and fall of pharaohs. At the palace entrance, Seneca inclines his head with respect.

"General Taurus."

"It's just Titus now, Seneca. I am retired"

Seneca smiles softly as he motions for Titus to enter the palace.

"The Emperor awaits."

As they walk through corridors lined with plundered treasures from conquered lands, Titus finds himself overwhelmed by the sheer excess on display. Sculptures of impossible anatomical proportions line the walkways, while overhead, the ceiling blazes with frescoes that transform Roman heroes into deities.

"I've never seen such excess," Titus murmurs.

"True happiness is to enjoy the present, without anxious dependence upon the future," Seneca says, though his tone suggests he no longer believes his own philosophy.

They arrive at the throne room where Nero is sitting on his throne practicing the lyre. At twenty-four, he possesses a presence that fills the room despite his unremarkable physical appearance. Average height, with light blue eyes and light curly hair resembling spun copper. His round, prominent chin gives him a petulant expression, while his thick neck and protruding stomach speak of indulgent living. Yet there is something in his gaze that commands attention, a quality that transforms physical mediocrity into imperial majesty.

"Caesar. General Titus Statilius Taurus V has arrived," Seneca announces.

Titus steps forward, his right arm snapping upward and slightly forward in a perfect Roman military salute.

"Hail, Caeser!"

"Welcome, Titus. Thank you for making the journey from your pastoral exile."

"Thank you for having me, Emperor."

Titus's gaze shifts to a woman reclining on a couch beside the throne, her beauty enhanced by silks and jewels that proclaim her exalted status. He bows respectfully.

"Empress Octavia. It is an honour to meet you."

"This is not Octavia. My stepsister has proven... inadequate in providing me with heirs. This is Poppaea Sabina."

Sabina smiles with the practiced charm of one who has learned to navigate imperial favour, her every movement calculated to not offend the Emperor.

Titus's gaze sweeps the chamber, taking in the collection of beautiful women who adorn various couches and cushions like living ornaments. His eyes stop on a familiar face, and his breath catches in his throat.

"Sister? What are you doing here?"

Titus's sister, Statilia Messalina, looks up from the golden chalice she has been examining. She wears silk that costs more than most Romans earn in a year.

"Surviving," she replies.

Titus notes the golden chalice, and her fingers glittering with rings that could purchase entire estates.

"And thriving, it seems."

Nero laughs.

"Brother and sister. Perhaps my empire is smaller than I think."

"Is this why you summoned me here?" Titus asks.

"No. I summoned you because I was told you were raised in Egypt. Is that true?"

"Yes, my father raised my sister and I there."

"Perfect. Then you are familiar with the river Nile."

"Yes, Emperor. It is the lifeblood of the province. All life springs from its waters."

Nero leans forward, his pale eyes brightening with interest.

"Tell me then, where does the Nile come from?"

"I don't know, Caesar. There are five cataracts that prevent our ships from sailing upstream, and beyond the fifth cataract lie the Kushites, who will not grant us safe passage."

"I wish to know where the Nile springs from. I need someone to lead a team to find its source. Someone who knows the land, someone who a knows how to beat impossible odds. I'm sending you on an expedition up the Nile, General Taurus."

"While I am honoured that you would select me for such an important quest, my Emperor, I'm afraid retirement was granted to me as a reward for my victory in Britannia."

"Ah yes, they say you were offered command of Rome's armies, or a seat in the Senate. Yet you chose to live with your family in the middle of nowhere, miles from civilization."

"It's all I've ever wanted."

Nero stands, his voice taking on the passionate cadence of a born performer.

"Noble. Stupid, but noble. When a man is called to greatness, he must accept that call. Which is why I'm giving you one more opportunity. If Rome conquers the source of the Nile, the empire will rule Africa for millennia. You will be remembered not only as Rome's greatest warrior, but as its greatest explorer. They will sing songs of your achievements forever. Discover the source of the Nile, and when you return, you will be Rome's greatest hero. A living God. Our finest sculptors will carve twelve-foot statues in your honour. You will become immortal."

Titus considers the offer, weighing immortal glory against a simple life.

"While you are very generous, my Emperor, I already have everything I want. I would much prefer to go home to my family."

Nero studies Titus and then nods slowly.

"Come, Titus, walk with me."

The Emperor rises and moves toward the garden doors, his silk robes rustling with each step. Titus follows, though something in Nero's tone makes him suspect this conversation is far from over.

Nero leads Titus through bronze doors that open onto the imperial gardens, where terraced slopes cascade down the Palatine Hill. The trees are centuries old, their gnarled trunks bearing witness to the rise and fall of kings and consuls. Ancient olive groves stretch across the hillsides, their silver-green leaves shimmering in the afternoon light. Slaves move between the rows with bronze vessels, collecting the liquid gold that flows from Roman presses. Olive oil so pure it rivals the offerings made to Jupiter himself.

"There is something troubling me, Titus. There is a new sect emerging from Jerusalem. A bizarre cult who believes a carpenter from Nazareth is the son of the Hebrew God. Have you heard of them?"

"I have, my Emperor. In Britannia, some of the men discussed it during the campaign. One of them even seemed to believe it himself."

"It's maddening. They worship a carpenter who never achieved anything. No great conquests. No expeditions. Even his own community cheered his death."

They arrive at a clearing where five figures wait in the shade of a marble colonnade. Sextus stands with Marcus and Quintus, the Praetorian Guards flanking two terrified prisoners. A man and woman whose rough clothing marks them as plebians. Nero looks at them in contempt.

"We caught this man and woman worshiping the carpenter. They were on their knees. Pathetic. He was humiliated and died effortlessly at the hands of our mighty empire, yet they worship him as a God."

Nero nods at the guards. Marcus and Quintus smile as they lower the couple onto the crossed wooden beams that have been prepared for this purpose.

"My empire will not tolerate worship of anyone but the emperor."

The Praetorians hold down the prisoners and begin driving iron spikes through their hands and feet, nailing them to the cross. The man and woman scream in agony. The guards erect the crosses, showing the crucified prisoners to the Emperor. Nero smiles with satisfaction as he watches them writhe in agony.

"If it's good enough for their God, surely it's good enough for them."

The Praetorian Guards all laugh as they turn their attention to Titus, their hands resting on their sword hilts.

"I understand your wife and sons are enjoying life in Britannia," Nero begins. "They tell me—"

The woman's scream interrupts him, a sound of pure anguish that cuts through the afternoon air.

"They tell me—"

The woman screams over Nero again, his patience clearly fraying. Another scream splits the air, and the Emperor's face flushes with rage.

"For the love of Jupiter, cease these unbearable interruptions!"

Marcus drives his spear into the woman's ribs with brutal indifference. She dies with a final, rattling breath. Her husband begins weeping, great sobs that shake his broken body. Nero exhales with satisfaction.

"Much better. Now, as I was saying, Titus, they tell me your wife and sons are enjoying life in Britannia. They tell me your plot of land is even more beautiful than the hills of Rome herself. Is this true?"

Titus forces his voice to remain steady despite the horror before him.

"The privilege of serving the empire's legions has allowed me to see much of its territory. I can assure you; the farmlands of inland Britannia are the most beautiful I have ever seen. I struggle to think what would happen if Britannia ever became its own empire. It might be the only part of the world with more to die for than Rome itself."

"And your wife and sons are happy there?"

"Very happy."

Nero's smile transforms into something predatory. He looks at the crucified prisoners and then back to Titus.

"You are going up the Nile, Titus. Or the Praetorian Guard will pay your family a visit."

Titus looks at the crucified prisoners and then back to Nero, accepting his fate.

"I live to serve the empire. It will be done."

"Splendid. But know this, Titus, you will either return with knowledge of the source, or you will not return at all."

Titus nods as he begins to calculate.

"I can't do it alone."

"You will have as many legions as you need."

"There is no strength in numbers to be gained on the Nile. That is why the empire cannot conquer it. We need a small team, with small boats. Elite men who know how to survive and think on their feet."

"I shall send my best Praetorian Guards with you."

"I have one more condition."

"Which is?"

"I choose my second in command."

The Subura, Rome, later that day. Titus walks through Rome's narrow streets where the afternoon sun struggles to penetrate the maze of insulae that tower six stories above the cobblestones. The air thrums with the chaos of urban life. Merchants hawking their wares from wooden stalls, children darting between cart wheels, slaves hauling amphorae of wine and oil while their masters conduct business in doorways. The smell mingles together in an assault on the senses: roasting meat, human sweat, horse dung, and the ever-present aroma of fermenting grain from the countless taverns that line every street.

He finds the tavern where a weathered wooden sign depicting a wine cup swings from iron chains. The Drunken Gladiator caters to veterans and working men alike. Rough wooden tables fill the space, occupied by men whose scars tell stories of campaigns fought in distant provinces. The floor, covered in sawdust that has seen better days, crunches beneath his sandals as he makes his way through the crowd.

At the bar sits a familiar figure hunched over a clay cup. Paulinus appears to have been here for some time, judging by the slight sway in his shoulders and the way he studies his wine as if it holds the secrets of the cosmos. The former governor signals the tavernkeeper for another drink with the casual gesture of a man who has made this request many times today. Titus slams a silver coin on the scarred wooden counter.

"This one is on me."

Paulinus turns, his face breaking into a rueful smile.

"How long did it take you to find me?"

"This is the first place I looked."

"My reputation precedes me."

"How did Rome's greatest governor end up here?"

"Join me in a drink and I'll tell you"

Titus motions to the tavernkeeper for a cup of wine, noting how the man pours without spilling a drop despite the dim light. Both men drink from their cups, and Paulinus's voice drops to a conspiratorial whisper.

"We weren't supposed to win, Titus."

"What do you mean?"

"In Britannia. They sent us to die."

"How do you know this?"

"Agrippina set the plan in motion before she died. She stoked the revolution in Britannia, made sure it would be big enough to crush us. Then Nero would ride in with a force ten times our size and destroy the survivors. She wanted her precious son to be seen as Rome's greatest warrior. It was impossible for us to win."

"How did we win then?"

"Because of you, Titus. I came back to Rome thinking I'd become a senator. Instead, they exiled me. Dishonourable discharge. Apparently, winning when you're supposed to lose makes you a liability."

"Who will govern Britannia then?"

"Agricola. They are giving him the credit for the victory on Watling street. My days serving the empire are over."

"Unfortunately, not yet."

Paulinus pauses with his fresh wine halfway to his lips.

"Why do I not like the sound of that?"

"I'm putting together an expedition. A small cohort of the best."

"What's the mission?"

"We're going to travel up the River Nile. All the way to its source."

"What's up there? Besides crocodiles, deadly rapids, and hostile natives who don't appreciate Roman tourists?"

"That's what we're going to find out."

Paulinus takes a gulp of wine.

"That sounds like a fun expedition. Be sure to send me a letter."

"You're coming too, Paulinus."

"I'm retired."

"My family's lives are at stake."

Paulinus studies Titus for a moment and finishes his wine.

"Then I guess we don't have a choice. But if we're going on an exploratory expedition into uncharted territory, we'll need a scribe. Someone who knows the history of the region, someone who can communicate with the locals, and document our findings."

"Do you know someone?"

"I happen to know the best scribe in Rome. Gaius Plinius Secundus."

"Who?"

"You probably know him as Pliny the Elder."

Titus and Paulinus climb the winding path up Palatine Hill. Before them stands the imperial library, its façade gleaming white in the afternoon sun, more sanctuary than building. Inside, thousands of papyrus scrolls rest on wooden shelves beneath a ceiling where painted Muses bend toward mortal men, whispering secrets into eager ears. Between the towering archives stand ebony tables, while secluded nooks carved from the walls offer sanctuary to those who commune with the ancient words.

At one such table, surrounded by towers of unfurled scrolls and loose sheets of papyrus, sits Gaius Plinius Secundus. Pliny the Elder to those who know his reputation. The scholar hunches over a massive tome, his stylus moving across the pages with the fevered intensity of a man possessed by knowledge. Around him lie open scrolls detailing everything from military engineering to the mating habits of elephants, all waiting to be catalogued in his great work.

Titus and Paulinus enter Pliny's study, their sandals echoing on polished marble. The sound draws Pliny's attention, and he looks up with the startled expression of a deer caught in torchlight, his stylus clattering to the table.

"By the gods. It's happening, isn't it?"

Titus and Paulinus exchange confused glances. Pliny rises from his chair, knocking over an inkwell in his haste.

"Nero sent you here. I don't care what you threaten me with, torture, exile, crucifixion, I will never compromise on the validity and accuracy of my work. You'll just have to kill me."

Titus raises his hands in a calming gesture.

"That's not why we're here."

"Nero didn't send you?"

"No. Well, yes actually. But not for that reason."

Pliny's shoulders relax slightly, though wariness remains in his intelligent eyes.

"Why then?"

"Is it true you have knowledge of Egypt and the Nile?"

"Yes, it's part of the encyclopaedia I'm writing."

"The what?"

Pliny gestures toward the massive tome that dominates his workspace, its pages thick with cramped handwriting and detailed diagrams.

"It's a collection of all the knowledge of the empire. Every fact, every discovery, every piece of wisdom I can gather from reliable sources. I've been writing it for years."

"Do you have knowledge of the source of the Nile?"

"No. I must admit, I would like nothing more than to document that region. It would make my encyclopaedia the most complete in history, more comprehensive even than Aristotle's corpus."

"Then boy, does fortune smile upon you today," Paulinus interjects.

"It doesn't matter anyway," Pliny continues. "Nero will crucify me if I don't rewrite my encyclopaedia to make it appear he discovered everything himself. My only hope is to disappear somewhere he can't find me."

"Then we'll give you that opportunity," Titus says. "We're traveling up the Nile to find its source. We'd like you to come with us and document everything we discover."

Pliny stares at him as if he's spoken in a foreign tongue. "Are you serious?"

"It will give you the chance to complete your encyclopaedia and avoid Nero during his reign."

"This sounds too good to be true. What's the catch?"

"The catch is we don't know where we're going, we don't know how to get there, we don't know what's waiting for us when we arrive, and we don't know if we'll make it back alive."

"But I hear the weather there is lovely this time of year," Paulinus adds.

Pliny continues staring in disbelief, until his scholarly passion overrides his practical concerns.

"I want to document everything. Not just the source of the Nile. The pyramids, the temples, the customs of the people, the flora and fauna, everything."

"I can make no guarantees, but I'll see what we can arrange," Titus says.

Pliny begins gathering his scrolls with sudden energy.

"All right, I'm in. Shall we depart now? I can be packed within the hour."

"We need to visit one more person before we leave."

"Who?"

"Emperor Nero."

Chapter 4
Pax Romana

Titus, Paulinus and Pliny walk from the marble tranquillity of the Palatine Library toward the Forum Romanum. There, dominating the skyline, stands the Senate House, its columns and pediments a calcified memory of the republic that Rome once was.

The Senate House's bronze doors stand open, revealing the curved interior where heated voices echo off marble walls. The chamber buzzes with the kind of tension that precedes either great decisions or spectacular disasters. Six hundred senators occupy the tiered benches in their purple striped white togas. Nero stands at the centre of the semi-circular space with the energy of a man who loves a crowd. Behind the Emperor, Sextus, Seneca, and Epaphroditus maintain their positions like chess pieces carefully arranged for maximum effect. Nero steps forward, his voice carrying the trained projection of an actor.

"Conscript Fathers, I propose to send an expedition to discover the source of the mighty Nile. This achievement will surpass even the conquests of Alexander, establishing Rome as the greatest power in both war and exploration."

Senator Piso rises slowly from the senior benches, his disposition having grown more frustrated of late.

"Ever since your mother died, your suggestions grow more absurd by the day. How exactly do you plan to finance another one of your pointless adventures when you've abolished the taxes that fund our provinces?"

Nero's eyes brighten with enthusiasm rather than anger. He spreads his arms in a gesture that encompasses the entire chamber.

"Have you no sense of adventure, Piso? What if we discover a kingdom of unimaginable treasure? The wealth of Solomon himself might await us at the river's source."

"The provincial governors will not be pleased. They can barely afford to maintain basic infrastructure as it stands. When they discover this is how you allocate the empire's dwindling resources, their fury will make the Boudican revolt look like a neighbourhood dispute."

"You fail to look on the bright side, Piso. I shall not only be remembered as Rome's greatest artist but also as its greatest explorer. My name will echo through the ages alongside those of the legendary heroes."

At that moment, Titus, Paulinus, and Pliny step through the bronze doors. The assembled senators turn to study these newcomers.

"Ah, here is the expedition now," Nero announces. "Welcome, Titus. Who have you brought to assist in this glorious endeavour?"

"I have summoned one of Rome's most learned scholars to document and understand the regions we'll encounter. Gaius Plinius Secundus, or as you may know him, Pliny the Elder."

"A scholar?" Tell me then, Pliny, what do we currently know of the Nile and the lands beyond our borders?"

Pliny steps forward and produces a large map from his satchel and spreads it across the central table, the papyrus crackling as he unfurls it to reveal the known world in stunning detail. Nero stares at the map in awe.

"Here is the most detailed map of the region we have produced so far, my Emperor. I intend to produce a map so precise it will serve as the standard for all cartographers."

"Fascinating. So much detail. Tell me Titus, how do you intend to traverse this region."

Titus steps forward and stands beside Pliny's map, his finger tracing potential routes.

"The expedition faces several distinct challenges and opportunities. First, we must reach Alexandria. Then we must traverse the Nile's five cataracts. Beyond the fifth cataract lies the Kingdom of Kush, which has remained hostile to Rome, primarily because our previous interactions involved conquest rather than diplomacy. If we approach in peace, seeking passage rather than territory, I believe they will grant us safe transit."

"And beyond Kush?" Nero asks, clearly fascinated.

"The Kingdom of Aksum emerges as a growing power, hostile to the Kushites. With careful planning, we should be able to avoid their territory entirely. Further south, rumours speak of tribes living deep in jungle regions. However, no one who has encountered them has returned to tell the tale."

Nero nods and then turns his attention to Pliny.

"You, scholar, tell me what you know of this new sect from Judea. Will they pose a threat to our expedition?"

"I'm aware of them, Caesar. Their beliefs originated in Jerusalem and have since spread to Egypt and even to Rome itself. However, they seek nothing but peace. They present no military threat to our mission."

Nero's face flushes with sudden anger.

"Anyone who refuses to worship the Emperor threatens the very foundation of our empire. This cult represents an existential threat to Rome itself. They are to be treated as a hostile force. They shall bend the knee to imperial authority or meet the same fate as their carpenter."

He turns to address his Praetorian Prefect.

"I will send Sextus Afranius Burrus to ensure your protection during this expedition."

Sextus steps forward and looks at Titus with disdain.

"How do you expect us to survive this expedition with a retiree leading the group?"

"You're well aware that Titus won us the war in Britannia. He could have had your position if he'd desired it, Sextus. Instead, he chose peace."

"Victory in Britannia has nothing to do with navigating a river."

"His Britannia triumph wasn't the only reason I chose him. He was raised in our African provinces. He knows that region better than anyone in my legions."

Sextus's hand moves to his sword hilt, as he looks Titus up and down.

"Enlighten me then, Titus. What strategy will you employ to achieve victory?"

"A good general studies strategy. A great general studies logistics. We depart from Ostia and sail to Alexandria, where Egyptian Governor Vestinus will provide supplies and rations. There are trading villages along the river where we can rest and resupply."

"And transportation?"

"Small, light boats to traverse the cataracts and navigate shallow waters."

"Small boats? Pathetic. We should use our mighty warships to demonstrate Roman power."

"Trust me, Sextus. When the time comes, you'll be happy we chose manoeuvrability over intimidation."

"And you expect the Kushites to just let was walk in the front door after we razed their capital to ash? What happens when they decide to kill us on sight?"

"Governor Vestinus will recruit a guide from the Kingdom of Kush. He will meet us at Alexandria. If we're lucky, he'll get us through the gates of the Kingdom."

"That's your master plan? Trust an African? I'd rather bring a legion and crush them with overwhelming force."

"Not only can you not bring a legion, but there is also only room for you to bring two other Praetorians."

Sextus turns to Nero in disbelief.

"This is madness, Emperor. Trusting my life into the hands of two retired provincials and an African. Allow me to bring a legion."

"This is Titus's expedition Sextus. You will do as he says. Choose your best men."

Sextus grits his teeth and grips his sword hilt for a moment before exhaling.

“I will bring Marcus and Quintus. They may not be the smartest, but they are loyal and ruthless.”

Nero nods and turns his attention to the former governor.

"And what of Paulinus? What use is he to this expedition?"

"Paulinus fought bravely beside me in Londinium. I can trust him completely, and you know, my Emperor, how rare and valuable someone trustworthy is in Rome."

"Is this arrangement acceptable to you, Paulinus?"

"Not particularly, Emperor. I'd prefer to retire to a vineyard with several attractive mistresses."

Nero smirks at the answer.

"You shall do as Titus commands." His gaze shifts to his Praetorian Prefect. "And that directive applies to you as well, Sextus. Ofonius Tigellinus will take your place as Praetorian prefect in your absence."

Sextus clenches his jaw and grips his sword handle while staring at Titus with barely concealed hostility.

"Upon completion of this mission, you will be hailed as the greatest explorers in Roman history," Nero declares. "Or don't bother returning at all. I shall personally see you off at Ostia."

Dawn breaks over Ostia as the imperial ceremony unfolds along the crowded harbour. Citizens press against one another on the stone quays, necks craned toward the colossal vessel commanding the waters. From bow to stern, nearly two hundred feet of Lebanese cedar stretches across the morning-lit harbour. Above, twin masts stand like obelisks, square sails bound tight against them, awaiting the winds that will propel Rome's explorers across the Mediterranean. The vessel's prow bears the carved head of Neptune, his bronze eyes seeming to scan the Mediterranean horizon with divine authority.

Titus walks up the gangplank with Paulinus and Pliny and stands at the stern. The Praetorian contingent boards next. Three figures in scarlet cloaks. Sextus at the lead, followed by Marcus and Quintus, each man's hand resting on the pommel of his gladius. They position themselves at the bow, creating a deliberate separation between Praetorian Guards and the others. Sextus's hostile gaze bores into Titus from across the ship.

At the harbour's edge, Nero stands behind a marble podium that rises above the crowd.

"Citizens of Rome! Today we witness the dawn of a new age of discovery! When Alexander reached the Indus, he wept because he had no more worlds to conquer. But Rome shall surpass even the great Macedonian! Where others turned back, we press forward. Where others failed, we shall triumph! These brave men sail not merely to explore unknown lands, but to claim for Rome the greatest prize in Africa, the secret source of the life-giving Nile!"

Below, the crowd erupts in adulation. Nero basks in their adoration, arms extended like a deity receiving tribute.

Titus watches the spectacle with a soldier's detachment, his mind already charting courses through desert and jungle, calculating supplies and anticipating threats. Paulinus walks over to Titus's side

"The boy certainly knows how to put on a show. Though I suspect the crowd would cheer just as enthusiastically if he was feeding us to lions in the arena."

The ship's timbers creak beneath them as sailors scurry about, preparing for departure. Salt-laden air carries the mingled scents of fish, tar, and hemp rope. A flock of gulls wheels overhead, their cries almost drowned by the crowd's continuing adulation.

Titus feels the weight of Sextus's stare like a physical pressure against his back. He doesn't need to turn to know the Praetorian's scarred face is twisted with resentment.

Epaphroditus hands Nero his Lyre to play the expedition off.

"Fortune favours the bold. And may Neptune himself guide you safely across his domain!"

The Emperor begins to play a haunting melody that seems to capture both the hope and uncertainty of the moment. The music drifts across the water as dock workers cast off the mooring lines and the great ship begins its slow departure from Ostia.

Three weeks later, The Mediterranean stretches endlessly in all directions, its surface painted bronze by the setting sun. The ship cuts through gentle swells with the steady rhythm that has become familiar to all aboard. Most of the expedition members have found their sea legs, though Pliny continues to look slightly green around the edges. Sextus approaches Titus at the ship's rail.

"Your victory in Britannia was truly masterful, Titus. Tell me, why didn't you choose to be a senator. Why aren't you leading Nero's legions in Gaul or Germania? I know a true warrior would never be content with farming."

Titus continues watching the horizon. The sea breeze carries the scent of salt and impending rain.

"All I ever wanted was a simple peaceful life."

Sextus turns his attention to the horizon.

"I may not be one of Rome's greatest generals, but I'm wise enough to know that such a thing does not exist."

Quintus and Marcus approach, flanking Sextus like wolves joining their alpha. Quintus squares his shoulders and looks Titus up and down.

"Tell me, Titus, how does an African provincial become Rome's most celebrated general? The stories they tell in the barracks paint you as something between Mars himself and Julius Ceaser."

Titus's gaze remains fixed on the darkening horizon where storm clouds gather like bruises against the twilight sky.

"You'll understand after spending time in Africa. The province has a thousand ways to kill you. The sun is hot enough to cook a man alive. There are scorpions the size of your thumb that can kill you with one sting. Snakes glide unseen through the sands, striking before you even know they're there. Beasts living in the waters with jaws so powerful they can bite a man in half. Giant cats stalk the night, hunting Romans like prey. Stray from the path and the desert will consume you. And the locals? They despise us Romans. Turn your back, and a blade finds your ribs. But worst of all, there are older things here, forces no soft-handed city dweller would believe. The land will either kill you, or sharpen you into a warrior."

Quintus and Marcus exchange worried glances, clearly unnerved by Titus's warning. Marcus jerks his chin toward Pliny.

"This scribe. What use is a man of letters in a land that devours warriors?"

"The Emperor demands knowledge, not conquest. The scribe's stylus will serve Rome better than your sword in this endeavour."

"When he collapses in the desert. I won't be the one dragging him."

"You'll carry him on your back if necessary. If Pliny doesn't return to Rome breathing, you can consider our mission a failure."

Paulinus approaches with Pliny at his side. Marcus and Quintus glare at Pliny.

"Why would you agree to this mission, Pliny?" Marcus asks.

"I intend to document the Nile for the book, I'm writing. A collection of all of the knowledge of the empire. There are ancient temples all along the river, their information could be invaluable. I am particularly interested in the Temple of Thebes. There are no writings describing what is inside."

Titus swiftly turns to Pliny, his voice dropping to a register that makes even Sextus pause.

"Forget about the Temple of Thebes, Pliny. We won't be going near it."

"What do you mean? That's preposterous. The temple may contain hieroglyphs that could revolutionize our understanding of human history. Scrolls detailing astronomical observations spanning millennia. Medical knowledge that surpasses even Galen's understanding of the human body."

"It also contains things that should remain undisturbed. I've seen what happens to those who trespass in sacred spaces not meant for Roman eyes."

Pliny scoffs, though his confidence wavers slightly at the intensity in Titus's gaze.

"Superstition. Surely a man of your experience doesn't believe in curses and desert spirits?"

A flash of memory crosses Titus's face, something dark and terrible that he quickly suppresses.

"The Temple of Thebes is forbidden ground. Stronger men that us have entered and never returned."

"So what can I even document then?"

"By the gods..." Paulinus breathes from beside them, staring over the the bow of the boat.

They follow Paulinus's gaze eastward. There, jutting from the horizon like Neptune's spear, stands the Lighthouse of Alexandria. Its colossal form dominates the approaching harbour. Nearly four hundred feet of gleaming marble. The square foundation gives way to an octagonal midsection, then narrows into a circular pinnacle where a massive bronze mirror captures the dying sun, casting its warning light far across the waters.

Even at this range, they can see the flames that burn eternally at its summit, guiding ships safely through the treacherous approaches to Egypt's greatest port. Smaller vessels dot the waters around its base like toys scattered by a giant child. Paulinus stares in wonder.

"I've heard tales of its size, but I thought they were exaggerated boasts from drunken sailors."

"If you think the lighthouse is an architectural marvel," Titus says quietly, his eyes already fixed on the distant shore beyond, "just wait until you see what lies inland."

Chapter 5
Alexandria

The port of Alexandria unfurls over the sparkling blue waters of the Mediterranean. Ships from across the Empire crowd the waters. Grain vessels from Sicily, merchant galleys from Athens, war triremes bearing the eagle standards of Rome. The scent of the Nile mingles with salt air. Rich earth and exotic spices create an intoxicating aroma that speaks of ancient mysteries and untold wealth. The port hums with a symphony of languages: Greek dock workers shouting orders, Egyptian sailors singing work songs, Roman officials conducting business in crisp Latin. Beyond the harbour, the Library of Alexandria towers over a cliff like a mountain of accumulated wisdom.

Waiting at the dock stands the Governor of Egypt, Lucius Julius Vestinus. His face, once the marble-pale visage of Roman aristocracy, has been bronzed and lined by years beneath the Egyptian sun. His toga bears the broad purple stripe of senatorial rank, though his position as governor of Egypt represents the pinnacle of equestrian achievement. Claudius himself had called him 'the jewel of the equestrian order' before appointing him to this most prestigious posting. Vestinus calls out as Titus descends the gangplank.

"General Taurus, welcome back to Egypt."

"I'm not a general anymore, Vestinus. It's just Titus now."

"And Rome is worse for it. But you and your companions are always welcome here."

Vestinus clasps his arm in the Roman manner, but his expression hardens as he notices the Praetorian Guard following Titus down the Gangway.

"Epaphroditus didn't tell me the nature of your visit, but I was provided a list of supplies to prepare. It will be sunrise before everything is ready, but we'll show you proper hospitality tonight."

He lowers his voice as other passengers disembark around them.

"I must warn you, Egypt isn't as safe as when you departed. There's unrest among the population. Nero has abolished taxes, so we lack funds for public services. Worse, there are spies from the Kingdom of Kush everywhere. Assume the walls have ears."

Pliny steps forward, his excitement overcoming the pallor of his seasickness.

"What of the Library of Alexandria? Is it open to visitors?"

"Not normally, but for a friend of Titus, we can make an exception."

Pliny turns to Titus. “There's information in the library that will greatly assist our expedition. I must go immediately."

"Very well, Pliny. But take two Praetorians with you. We're no longer in Rome. You can't be too careful."

Titus nods at Sextus, who nods at the guards.

"Quintus, Marcus, accompany Pliny to the library."

"Aye, sir!" both guards respond in unison.

As Pliny and the guards walk towards the library and disappear into the crowd, Vestinus turns back to Titus.

"I insist you join me for dinner at the governor's residence. I'll instruct my servants to prepare a proper banquet."

"You're most kind, Governor Vestinus, but I must decline. There's a tavern where my father used to take my sister and I when we were young, 'The Golden Ankh'. I've always wanted to return."

"Are you certain, Titus? That area has become increasingly hostile to Romans."

"I'm sure."

"If you insist, then I shall join you."

"I'll take the banquet at the palace if you don't mind," Paulinus quips.

"You're coming too, Paulinus." Titus says.

The group makes their way through Alexandria's labyrinthine markets led by Governor Vestinus. The contrast with Rome strikes them immediately. Here, the people appear hungry and desperate, their clothes patched and threadbare. Merchants thrust inferior goods toward them with pleading eyes, begging them to purchase anything that might bring a few coins.

"Fresh dates! The finest in Egypt!" calls one seller, though the fruit appears withered.

"Papyrus scrolls! Perfect for important documents!" cries another, displaying products that would be rejected by Roman bureaucrats. As the man hoists his papyrus scrolls towards the group, a small wooden crucifix around his neck slips from his tunic. Sextus notices it and turns to Vestinus.

"Why does that man wear a small crucifix around his neck?" he asks, pointing to the wooden symbol that hangs from a leather cord.

"It represents the carpenter from Nazareth," Vestinus explains quietly.

“Does he wear it to mock him?”

“Far from it. He wears it to worship him.”

Sextus shakes his head in disbelief.

"How can he worship a man who achieved nothing and died effortlessly at the tip of the mighty Roman spear?"

"I don't understand it either. The carpenter apparently said when your enemy strikes you on the cheek, you should just present your other cheek."

Sextus laughs harshly.

"By Mars, have you ever heard anything so insane, Titus? How can they be so meek?"

"It doesn't sound like an effective battle strategy," Titus agrees. Sextus laughs, but then Titus adds: "But what would the world look like if everyone adopted that message?"

Sextus's laughter slowly dies as he studies Titus as they approach the entrance of The Golden Ankh.

Pliny walks along the cliffs toward the Library of Alexandria accompanied by the two Praetorian Guards, their iron armour gleaming under the Egyptian sun. The scholar's excited pace contrasts sharply with the predatory swagger of the two Praetorians . Quintus mutters to Marcus, his voice low but not quite low enough.

"Why would the Emperor insist on such a weakling joining us on this expedition? He'll only hold us back."

"Don't worry. I suspect he'll have an accident before he can impede our progress."

Both guards share a laugh. Pliny pretends not to notice, his eyes fixed on the approaching wonder ahead.

The Library of Alexandria appears before them, a colossus of knowledge hewn from white stone. Towering columns support a structure that seems to stretch endlessly in all directions, its walls lined with countless windows that allow natural light to illuminate the treasures within. The building sprawls across several acres, its various wings connected by covered walkways where scholars can be seen moving between reading halls like pilgrims in a temple of wisdom.

They enter through bronze doors adorned with relief carvings depicting the Muses inspiring mortal scholars. Inside, the main hall soars overhead, its ceiling painted with constellations that guide both earthly and intellectual navigation. Reading tables stretch in organized rows, while scholars in simple tunics pore over texts that represent the accumulated wisdom of centuries.

A woman approaches them from behind a wooden desk laden with catalogs and scrolls. She speaks in Coptic, the language of Egypt that has evolved from ancient hieroglyphic roots.

"How may I help you?" she asks in Coptic.

Marcus and Quintus exchange a confused look.

"I've heard this is the largest library in existence. I would like to walk its halls," Pliny replies in fluent Coptic, drawing a surprised look from the librarian. Her expression shifts from wariness to intrigue.

"A Roman who speaks Egyptian? I always thought Romans were too chauvinistic to spend time learning the language of foreigners."

Pliny gestures toward the praetorians with wry humour.

"My friends here think every problem can be solved by driving a spear into it. I believe the Roman Empire has much left to learn."

The librarian's expression softens into a warm smile.

"And what specifically would you like to learn?"

"I've heard there are ancient scrolls here from the civilization that originally built Egypt's greatest monuments. Scrolls containing ancient wisdom about the Nile. I would like to see them."

The librarian studies him for a long moment and then leans forward conspiratorially.

"Normally I would never tell a Roman about the secret collection, but something seems different about you. Walk down the main hall and take the last corridor on the left. You'll see a large black book that has less dust than the others. I suggest you examine it carefully."

As she reaches under her desk to activate a hidden mechanism, a small wooden crucifix slips from beneath her clothing, catching the attention of the Praetorians.

"Ask her why she's wearing that crucifix," Quintus demands.

"Why do you wear a crucifix around your neck? Don't you know that represents a method of torture and death used by the empire?" Pliny asks in Coptic.

The woman's eyes grow distant with something that might be peace or defiance.

"Once I trembled beneath tyrants, but his message freed me from fear. Though Nero rules Rome, Christ reigns as King of Kings."

"What is she saying?" Marcus asks suspiciously.

Pliny studies the librarian before smiling at the guards.

“She said she wears it because she's so impressed by the Praetorian Guard that she wants to honour you."

The Praetorians smile smugly at each other, adjusting their uniforms.

"Now let's go."

Pliny and the Praetorians advance through the labyrinth of knowledge, their footfalls breaking the sacred silence. Scrolls climb from floor to ceiling like the walls of a paper fortress. The thoughts of Aristotle, the geometries of Euclid, the mechanical wonders of Archimedes captured in ink and parchment. Languages from Parthia to Hispania crowd the shelves, while hunched scholars bend over reading tables, oblivious to all but the ancient words before them.

At the last corridor on the left, they find the shelves exactly as the librarian described. Among the ancient volumes, one large leather-bound black book stands out, its surface noticeably cleaner than its neighbours.

"This is it," Pliny breathes.

He grasps the book and pulls, but instead of lifting a tome, he's activated a mechanism. The entire shelf section swings inward like a door, revealing a stone corridor that disappears into darkness beyond.

They follow the passage into a circular chamber dimly lit by bronze oil-lamps. Scrolls of yellowed papyrus and cracked leather line cedar shelves, their edges curling and brittle with age. Texts that predate even Alexandria itself. At the room's centre sits an old blind man on a three-legged wooden stool, his withered frame draped in an unbleached linen tunic.

"Who goes there?" The blind man asks in Coptic.

"My name is Gaius Plinius Secundus. I'm a scholar from Rome," Pliny responds in the same language.

"How did you gain access to the inner sanctum?"

"The librarian directed me."

The blind man considers this and nods.

"If the librarian trusted you, there must be reason."

“I seek ancient knowledge of the civilization that came before us. The builders of the great temples. I want to know what they understood about the Nile."

"You'll find what you seek in that book."

The blind man points toward a large black book on the stone shelf. Pliny walks over and picks up the book, its surface covered with hieroglyphic symbols that seem to dance in the lamplight. He opens the book and flips through the pages, his eyes dart side-to-side as he tries to make sense of it.

"Be careful. That is the Book of the Dead," the old blind man explains as Pliny studies charts with images of ancient Egyptian deities.

“What are these charts?”

"Those are navigation charts for the afterlife. Spells to guide souls through the Duat, past serpent guardians and lakes of fire. But be warned. The forty-two judges who weigh hearts don't care if yours still beats. Ma'at's feather is light, but justice is heavy, and her scales tip for the living just as easily as the dead. When you speak words meant for those crossing into the underworld, you announce yourself to powers that hunt in darkness. The threshold guardians won't ask if you belong there. They'll simply assume you do. And once you've called their attention, once you've opened that door with the breath still in your lungs... well. Some journeys don't allow for a return ticket."

Pliny stares sceptically at the blind man, wondering if sitting alone in this chamber has driven him insane. His finger traces the serpentine paths on the charts depicted in faded gold and ochre.

"These navigation charts, they follow the Nile's course southward. Look. Here are the cataracts, here the confluence of tributaries. This isn't merely religious symbolism. It's a map."

The blind guardian tilts his head, unseeing eyes fixed on some point beyond the chamber's walls.

"The ancients believed geography and theology were the same science. Every bend in the river reflected a bend in the cosmic order. Every cataract was a trial, every marsh a test of worthiness. What you call a map, they called instructions for survival."

Pliny looks up at the blindman, whose milky eyes seem to fix on something beyond the chamber's earthly confines.

"The source of the Nile isn't shown as a lake. It's shown as two gods," Pliny says.

"Horus and Set. The eternal twins, locked in perpetual struggle. Where their conflict began, so too did the waters that give life to Egypt. You seek the physical source, but the ancients sought the spiritual source. It is said that Horus and Set themselves watch over those waters, guarding secrets older than hieroglyphs themselves."

"What's he saying? We're wasting time with this nonsense," Marcus says impatiently, the leather of his armour creaking in the silence.

Pliny slams the book shut.

"We have what we came for. Let's go," Pliny says to the two Praetorians.

The three Romans turn to leave the chamber. The blind man's voice follows them as they approach the exit of the inner sanctum.

"Heed my warning, Roman. The Nile harbours many ancient deities. Should you seek the river's source, petition whatever deity holds your faith that you do not encounter Set. And should you encounter the god of chaos, do not allow him to lure you into his temple. For those black stones have stood before the pharaohs, and they hunger for the blood of men who believe themselves beyond the reach of older gods."

Pliny hesitates at the threshold, then steps through without reply. The concealed door swings shut behind them with a whisper of ancient hinges, sealing the guardian back into his timeless vigil.

Outside, Pliny nods respectfully to the librarian before leading his companions into Alexandria's blinding sunlight. They descend toward the harbour, the limestone cliffs flanking their path, the vast Mediterranean spreading before them in shimmering azure.

"So we have the texts we need?" Marcus asks as they walk along the cliff's edge.

"Yes."

"Excellent. Then we don't need you anymore."

Both guards suddenly grab Pliny's arms, dragging him toward the precipice where waves crash against rocks far below. Pliny frantically struggles against their grip

"What are you doing? If the Emperor discovers you sabotaged his expedition, he'll crucify you both!"

"He won't crucify us if you have an unfortunate accident," Quintus replies.

They hold him at the cliff's edge, his feet scrambling for purchase on the loose stone.

"Now give us the book," Marcus demands.

"It will be of no use to you."

Quintus wrestles the book from Pliny's grasp and opens it, his expression immediately shifting to confusion.

"What is this? Where are the words? It's just a bunch of pictures."

"I don't suppose either of you can read hieroglyphics?" Pliny says.

Marcus lowers Pliny closer to the edge.

"Tell us what it means. Now!"

"And give up my usefulness? That wouldn't be very wise."

The two guards share a frustrated look. Marcus growls but pulls the scholar back from immediate danger. Pliny extends his hand expectantly. Quintus reluctantly returns the book.

"I guess you are useful..." He maintains his grip as Pliny tries to take it. "For now."

When he finally releases the book, Pliny begins walking back toward town, his heart still racing from the encounter. The two guards follow, their earlier camaraderie replaced by calculating silence.

The Golden Ankh tavern falls silent as Titus leads his party through the creaking doorway. Oil lamps throw uncertain light across mud-brick walls and the suspicious faces of Alexandria's working men. Dock labourers pause mid-drink. Merchants and locals shift uneasily on their benches. The Roman's polished armour and straight postures stand in stark contrast to the hunched shoulders and weathered skin of men who earn their bread through sweat rather than conquest.

They claim a table near the back wall, its wooden surface scarred by countless knives and stained by years of spilled wine. Vestinus gestures toward a serving girl, who reluctantly approaches to take their order. Her eyes remain downcast as she scurries away to fetch food and drink. Sextus, still brooding, continues to press Vestinus.

"Tell me what you know of this new sect, Vestinus. Emperor Nero has declared it a threat to the empire."

"It originated in Jerusalem. There was a carpenter there who claimed there was only one God, and that he was his son. He gained a small following among the locals, particularly twelve close associates who became his inner circle," Vestinus replies.

"Then what happened?" Sextus asks.

"He was arrested and forced to face the consequences of his claims. The authorities tortured him publicly in the most brutal fashion imaginable."

"It must have been entertaining to watch him crack."

"That's the remarkable thing. He never did. Even when they nailed him to the cross and left him hanging for hours, he never flinched, never recanted his message."

Sextus shakes his head in disbelief.

"So they worship a dead carpenter who was skilled at maintaining lies under torture. It boggles the mind. What could they possibly be thinking?"

The serving girl returns with clay cups of wine and platters of bread, cheese, and dates. Vestinus takes an indulgent swig before responding to Sextus's question.

"The people throughout the provinces feel abandoned. The outer territories starve while the wealthy in Rome live in impossible luxury. In the capital, senators gorge themselves on peacock tongues and dormice stuffed with honey while children here beg for crusts of bread. Acts of depravity are spreading through the empire like a plague."

He pauses to drink again, then lowers his voice.

"From the provinces, you can see clearly what Rome has become. The people believe it's spiritual. They believe that if such concentrated evil exists in the world, there must be an equal force of good to balance it. They see this carpenter, Christ, as the opposite force to Nero, whom some have begun calling the anti-Christ."

Sextus laughs harshly.

"To compare our divine Emperor to some poor carpenter from a backwater province is absurd. What do you think, Paulinus? Do you believe Nero is the anti-Christ?"

Paulinus pauses with his wine cup halfway to his lips, considering the question seriously.

"I don't know if any of it's real, but I'm certain that if the anti-Christ exists, it isn't Nero." He takes a long drink. "It was his mother."

At that moment, Pliny enters the tavern with Marcus and Quintus flanking him. The scholar's face appears pale, though whether from the sea voyage or recent events remains unclear. He joins them at the table, settling onto a wooden stool with relief.

"Did you get what you need from the library, Pliny?" Titus asks.

“I found an ancient text that will help us navigate the river's mysteries. They call it the Book of the Dead."

Pliny slams a large black book on the table. Vestinus laughs dismissively.

"I've been through that library countless times. Such a book is pure myth. If it existed, it would have been shipped to Rome long ago for the emperor's collection."

Pliny gives Titus a knowing look but says nothing further.

"What do you know of this Book of the Dead?" Titus asks Vestinus.

"Ancient Egyptian superstition. They believed it contained spells and guidance for navigating the afterlife, instructions for the soul's journey through death to rebirth. Primitive religious thinking, though it held great significance for the builders of the pyramids."

Sextus shakes his head.

"When will the world learn that words will never compare to the tip of a spear?"

Paulinus signals the serving girl.

"I'll take another wine and make it a double."

“Sextus,” Marcus says while smirking. “Apparently we have fans.”

“What do you mean?”

“The librarian was wearing a small crucifix around her neck. She is an admirer of our work.”

Sextus adorns the look of a father whose son has just done something particularly stupid.

“That’s not what it means, Marcus. It means she is part of the new cult who worships that carpenter from Nazareth. She is mocking us.”

“But the scholar told us she was wearing it to honour us.”

Pliny shrugs indifferently.

“That’s what I thought she said. My Coptic is a bit rusty.”

The three Praetorians exchange a look, then an imperceptible nod. Vestinus drains his cup and stands.

"There's a room upstairs where you can retire for the evening. Meet me at the harbour tomorrow morning and your boat will be ready and waiting."

"Thank you for your hospitality, Vestinus," Titus replies, rising from the table.

As the group prepares to retire, the tavern's other patrons watch their assent up the wooden staircase to the sleeping quarters. In the cramped upstairs chamber, each man claims a narrow cot. One by one, they surrender to sleep.

Dawn breaks over Alexandria as Titus opens his eyes, wincing at the shaft of light piercing through wooden shutters. His back protests as he rises from the thin straw pallet. Nearby, Paulinus grunts awake while Pliny appears almost ghostly in the morning glow. The silence strikes Titus before he fully understands why. The Praetorian Guard's beds lie vacant, military-neat, as if they'd never been disturbed.

Suddenly, a scream pierces the morning air. A raw, inhuman scream, unlike anything in the normal chorus of Alexandria's awakening. Titus locks eyes with Paulinus, then Pliny. Without a word, they snatch their swords and thunder down the wooden staircase. The tavern door crashes open under Titus's shoulder, and the three Romans freeze at the threshold.

"By the gods," Titus breathes.

The man who had been wearing the crucifix now stood crucified in the street. The small wooden cross around his neck, the symbol of his faith, now mirroring his method of execution. His wife kneels at the base of his cross, her hands bloody from trying to work loose the iron spike that pins her husband's feet to the wood. Her tears mix with his blood as she whispers prayers in broken Greek.

Marcus saunters over to the woman and draws his gladius in a single fluid motion. The blade finds her throat before she can cry out, and she crumples beside the cross where her husband slowly dies.

"Marcus! What are you doing?" Titus barks.

"Just following orders," Marcus smirks.

"Where is Sextus?"

Marcus nods towards the harbour. Titus, Paulinus and Pliny break into a run. Near the water's edge, Sextus stands with Vestinus and Quintus, their conversation casual despite the gathering Alexandrian's hissing at them for their crucifixion.

"Sextus! What have you done?" Titus shouts.

"I have defended the empire," Sextus responds with pride.

"By crucifying an innocent man?"

"The Emperor has declared this sect his enemy. He is not innocent."

"These people are poor and starving! This man look to the carpenter for hope in a world gone mad, and you crucify him for it?"

Sextus looks at the crucified man and then back to Titus with a satisfied smile.

"The only place the world will find hope is standing on the right side of Roman spears."

Suddenly a woman's scream pierces the morning air.

"What was that?" Titus asks.

"You didn't think that man was the only person we crucified did you?"

At the dock's far end, another cross bears a figure Pliny recognizes. The librarian who had shown them kindness the day before. Pliny gasps, breaking into a run. His sandals slap against the bloodstained wood of the dock as he reaches her.

"By the gods, what have they done to you?"

The woman lifts her head with enormous effort, her face pale from blood loss but her eyes still holding the look of serenity he had noticed the day before.

"I forgive you," she whispers.

"Take her down! She has done nothing wrong," Pliny demands, turning to face Sextus.

"She is an enemy of the empire."

Titus wrenches his attention to Vestinus.

"How could you allow this to happen, Vestinus?"

"It is the will of the Emperor, Titus. Besides, it solves the problem of the province having too many mouths to feed."

Vestinus waves his hand as if brushing away a fly. Paulinus jaw clenches tight enough to crack teeth.

"Brilliant strategy, Governor. I'm sure Nero will be tremendously popular with the people now."

"Roman politics is not my concern. I merely follow the orders handed down by the Emperor. My concern is preventing my province from starving to death. My concern is making peace with the Kushites so we can end the constant skirmishes."

A vessel of bound papyrus reeds ports next to them, its prow angled toward the heart of Africa. Burlap sacks of bread bulged against the gunwales, while sealed clay amphorae promised water for the journey ahead. The craft's broad deck offered ample room for men who would soon find any distance between them insufficient.

Aboard the boat is Kashta, a dark-skinned man from the Kingdom of Kush. He wears colourful, flowing robes adorned with gold and jewels. His hair is styled in intricate braids and beads, and his face is decorated with tribal markings. He turns to assess the Romans with eyes that reveal nothing of his thoughts about these strangers he must now guide into the heart of his homeland. Vestinus gestures toward the boat.

"Speaking of which, here is Kashta. He's a guide from the Kingdom of Kush who has agreed to help you travel the Nile toward his homeland. This is his boat, equipped with the supplies you requested."

Pliny's fists clench as he stares at the librarian.

"She needs our help! We can't just sail away!"

“No,” Vestinus says firmly. “There is nothing you can do. These are the Emperor’s orders. Leave now and quickly, before the family of the crucified decide to take matters into their own hands.”

Sextus laughs. He turns to Titus and motions toward the boat with mock courtesy.

"After you, Captain."

Titus, Paulinus, and Pliny step into the papyrus craft first, feeling it dip beneath their weight. The boat rocks precariously as Sextus, Marcus, and Quintus follow, their armour clanking against the wooden gunwales. Kashta settles at the boat's stern and grabs the steering oar.

"We need two men to row. I will guide you from here," he says in accented Latin.

Titus nods to Marcus and Quintus. The two Praetorians look to Sextus who also nods causing them to take up the oars reluctantly.

As they pull away from Alexandria's dock, the wails of the crucified fade into the rhythmic splash of oars cutting through murky water. Titus watches Alexandria's harbour recede, the Lighthouse growing smaller against the azure sky. The crucifixes as thin black lines from this distance, their human cargo reduced to mere specks. Pliny clutches the book of the dead to his chest like a shield and turns to Titus.

“This is madness. Those people posed no threat to Rome.”

Titus turns away from the diminishing shoreline, his jaw clenched tight enough to ache. The sun beats down upon his neck, the same sun that will scorch the crucified until their lips crack and their skin blisters. He focuses instead on the river ahead. The mighty Nile stretching before them like a brown-green serpent, its waters thick with silt and ancient secrets.

"It may be madness, Pliny, but it is nothing compared to what awaits us upriver."

Chapter 6

S.P.Q.R.

Rome, 62 AD. The Roman Senate House buzzes with tension as senators fill the curved marble benches, their white togas bright against the polished stone. At the chamber's heart stands Nero, flanked by his inner circle. Seneca maintains his position as chief advisor, though worry lines have deepened around his eyes in recent months. Epaphroditus waits with scrolls and tablets, ready to record imperial decrees.

But today a new figure commands attention. Ofonius Tigellinus, the new Praetorian Orefect whose capacity for ruthlessness was legendary throughout the empire. Senator Piso occupies his customary position among the senior members, his silver hair more ruffled than usual as he surveys the proceedings with barely concealed disdain. Nero's voice carries the trained projection of a natural performer as he addresses the Senate.

"Now that my policy of ending taxes has greatly improved the lives of Roman citizens, I will move forward with my greater agenda."

Piso springs to his feet in anger.

"Your policy to end taxes is crippling the provinces. They will revolt if you continue this madness!"

Tigellinus steps forward, his hand moving to rest on his sword hilt.

"Silence while the Emperor speaks!"

Nero spreads his arms in a gesture that encompasses the entire chamber.

"I shall inaugurate the Neronia festival. A celebration unlike any other, where art, song, poetry, and contests of strength unite to honour both the gods and the greatness of our empire. In these games, every Roman will witness that true excellence lies not only in the sword or the Senate, but also in the lyre, the voice, and the chariot. Did not the Greeks crown their victors for both wisdom and might? So too shall Rome, under my reign, surpass even Olympus in splendour. And I, your Emperor, do not sit idle in shadow but take the stage myself—singer, poet, charioteer—to show you that your Emperor is not merely ruler of men, but master of the arts, a shining model of divine harmony between body and spirit."

"And how do you intend to pay for these games when you have abolished the empire's tax revenue?" Piso asks.

Nero's face brightens with the enthusiasm of a man who believes he has solved an impossible riddle.

"I have devised the most ingenious monetary policy any Roman Emperor has ever conceived. Our mint currently produces denarii containing pure silver, one hundred percent. I have instructed them to reduce the silver content to merely ninety percent, replacing the remainder with base metal. The coins will look identical, weigh the same, bear the same stamp, but for every ten pounds of silver, we can now mint eleven pounds of coin. Genius, is it not?"

Piso stares at him in disbelief.

"Are you economically illiterate, Caesar? Debasing the currency achieves nothing but inflation. Merchants aren't fools. They'll weigh the coins, test them, and raise their prices accordingly. The denarius will lose its value throughout the empire. You cannot simply conjure wealth from thin air with no tangible support. This will destroy the Roman economy and impoverish the very citizens you claim to serve."

Nero waves the concerns away as if discussing trivial details.

"Furthermore, the month of April shall be renamed Neroneum."

Seneca shifts uncomfortably.

"I'm not certain that is wise, my Emperor."

"And furthermore," Nero continues, his voice rising with excitement, "Rome itself shall be renamed Neropolis!"

"This is madness," Piso yells.

"Silence!" Tigellinus barks.

"You know this is insanity, Seneca," Piso says, turning to the philosopher. "You must speak up!"

Tigellinus draws his sword halfway from its sheath.

"You will not be warned again, Senator Piso. Bite your tongue, or I will remove it."

Seneca clears his throat carefully.

"Emperor Nero, your vision for the Neronia festival is truly remarkable. We will begin preparations immediately. However, renaming a month and the eternal city itself requires careful consideration. Too many changes at once could cause chaos among the citizenry. Perhaps we should witness the success of the games before implementing your other proposals."

Nero's expression darkens.

"It appears that once again, you have sided with Piso against your Emperor. Do I need to question your loyalty, Seneca? Or perhaps I should have Tigellinus question you."

"No, my Emperor. I am eternally loyal and grateful to you. I merely wish to ensure the successful implementation of your agenda. Only fools rush in. You are very young. We have many decades to achieve all your magnificent goals."

Nero stares at his former tutor for a long moment, his blue eyes unreadable.

"Perhaps, you are right, Seneca, for now we will just proceed with the games. Epaphroditus, begin preparations for the Neronia festival."

"Yes, Emperor." Epaphroditus says dutifully.

"Tigellinus," Nero continues, "how progress the Praetorian Guard's efforts to investigate this new sect from Jerusalem? What do we know of them?"

"We have discovered why it spreads so rapidly, Emperor. The carpenter had twelve close followers who have been spreading his message throughout the empire. They travelled through Egypt and have now arrived in Rome itself. One of his associates, a man named Peter, is building a temple to worship their dead leader right here in the capital, with assistance from another called Paul."

"What do we know of this Paul?"

"He used to go by the name Saul of Tarsus. He initially helped us deal with this cult. But while traveling to Damascus, he claims he saw a vision of their risen carpenter that converted him into one of his followers. Since then, Paul has been spreading their message, particularly among non-Jews throughout the empire."

"So he went mad, then."

"It appears so. Shall I bring them to you, my Emperor?"

"Not yet. Let them build their temple. We shall observe who flocks to their gathering place. It will serve as a honey trap for our flies."

Tigellinus smiles, truly impressed.

"Great strategy, my Emperor."

"Thank you Tigellinus. But now I grow bored with politics. I shall retire to compose new verses for the festival."

Piso rises to his feet, his voice thick with disgust.

"Retire? The provinces fall apart while their governors lack funds for basic administration, and all you consider are games and poetry? This cannot continue."

"You should learn to enjoy life, Piso. You'll live longer."

As the Emperor moves toward the exit, Piso's voice follows him.

"Perhaps I am not the one who should worry about how long I'll live."

Nero freezes mid-stride. His shoulders rise beneath the purple-trimmed toga, then fall. The chamber grows so quiet that the scratch of Epaphroditus's stylus against parchment sounds like thunder.

Nero turns slowly as his gaze sweeps across the senators in the tiered benches. The senators shift uncomfortably under his scrutiny, their eyes darting between the defiant figure of Piso and their increasingly unpredictable Emperor. The ancient chamber, which had witnessed centuries of Roman debate and decision, holds its collective breath as each man calculates the cost of his next move.

"How many of you agree with Senator Piso's sentiments?" Nero asks.

The question hangs in the air. Then, slowly at first, then with gathering momentum, hands rise across the chamber. Four hundred of the six hundred assembled senators lift their arms in a silent declaration of dissent. Nero subtly takes note of which senators have raised their hands, his expression unreadable.

"Conscript fathers, all this talk about games has given me the most wonderful idea. The Roman people love song and spectacle, yes, but they also crave something more primal. The raw might of gladiatorial combat, the clash of steel, the thunder of the crowd baying for blood. I shall commission one of the greatest gladiatorial spectacles in Roman history."

Piso's voice cracks with barely restrained fury.

"More games? The empire crumbles beneath the weight of your incompetence, provinces teeter on the edge of rebellion, and all you can conceive of is spectacle? The senate will not condone this madness!"

"The senate will not only condone the games, they will participate as gladiators."

The chamber erupts in confused murmuring. Piso stands frozen, his voice strangled with disbelief.

"How do you expect senators of Rome to stand in the arena? They will never agree to this."

Nero turns his gaze back to the crowded benches, letting his eyes linger on the still-raised hands, then pivots back to Piso.

"Four hundred of them just volunteered."

Rome, 63 AD. A mammoth wooden arena stands newly erected on the Campus Martius. Its tiered seats packed with one hundred thousand spectators. The structure groans under the weight of the crowd. merchants and slaves, soldiers and freedmen, all pressed together in a rare moment of equality, united by their hunger for spectacle. Banners bearing Nero's name snap in the breeze above the uppermost seats, while below, the sand of the arena lies pristine and golden, soon to be baptized in blood.

A fanfare of trumpets cuts through the cacophony, and the crowd's roar softens to an expectant murmur. From the western entrance, Nero emerges, resplendent in imperial purple edged with gold thread that rustles in the breeze. He walks with the measured gait of an actor who knows every eye is upon him, his arms outstretched as if to embrace the entire assembly. The mob erupts. Some in genuine adulation, others in the reflexive cheering that accompanies imperial presence. He reaches the centre of the arena and turns slowly, a complete revolution to acknowledge every section of the vast amphitheatre.

"Citizens of Rome! Today you witness something unprecedented in the history of our eternal city. These games are absolutely free to every man, woman, and child of Rome!"

The crowd roars its approval, a sound like thunder rolling across the Campus Martius.

"For too long, Rome has crumbled while those entrusted with her care have abdicated their sacred duty. Our provinces cry out for leadership, our citizens struggle under burdens that should never have been theirs to bear, and why? Because the men who sit in the Senate House, the men who promised to serve you, to protect you, to guide our empire toward greatness, have failed!"

He turns toward the eastern gate and raises his arm.

"Behold! your senators!"

The gate groans open, and they emerge. Four hundred senators, stripped of their dignified togas and clad in the simple tunics of arena fighters. The Praetorian Guard flanks them on all sides, a wall of armour and steel ensuring none can flee this public humiliation. They shuffle into the sand like condemned men walking toward execution, which perhaps they are. Some hold their heads high, clinging to the last vestiges of patrician dignity. Others stare at the ground, shoulders hunched.

A chorus of boos erupts from the crowd, so forceful it seems to shake the wooden structure itself. Rotten fruit and vegetables rain down from the upper tiers, spattering against senatorial tunics and the sand below. The jeering intensifies, a hundred thousand voices united in condemnation. Nero raises his hands, and gradually the tumult subsides enough for him to be heard.

"Together, we will remind these senators that they are public servants, not public masters. They work for you, and it is long past time that the Roman people held them accountable for their failures!"

The crowd erupts into something beyond mere cheering It becomes a primal roar, a sound of vindication and savage joy. The wooden benches shake as thousands stamp their feet in rhythmic approval.

"Furthermore," Nero continues, waiting for the noise to crest and fall, "I have furloughed the wages of these negligent servants in order to provide you, the true heart of Rome, with lavish gifts. Behold!"

At his signal, imperial servants emerge from tunnels around the arena's perimeter, their arms laden with cloth sacks. They reach into the bags and begin hurling handfuls of coins into the crowd. Gold and silver flash in the sunlight like a metal rain, and the amphitheatre descends into beautiful chaos as spectators scramble and fight for the imperial largesse.

The senators stand clustered together in small groups, their faces pale as death masks. Some tremble visibly. Others stand rigid, as if by remaining motionless they might somehow become invisible. One elderly senator near the front has lost control of his bladder, a dark stain spreading across his tunic and pooling in the sand beneath his feet.

A smirk plays across Nero's lips as he surveys them, savouring this moment. Then he pivots back to face the crowd, raising both arms high above his head like a priest preparing to invoke the gods.

"Let the Senatorial Games begin!"

The roar that answers him seems to rise from the very bowels of the earth itself, a sound that will echo through Roman history long after the temporary amphitheatre has been dismantled.

Nero reclines on his cushioned couch in the imperial balcony, a position of perfect elevation from which to survey the arena below. The awning above provides blessed shade from the afternoon sun, while the roar of the crowd washes over them in waves. Piso occupies a chair to the right, his knuckles white as he grips the armrests, unable to tear his gaze from the four hundred senators standing in the sand below. Men he has served alongside for decades. Tigellinus looms behind them all, a silent presence whose hand never strays far from his weapon. Seneca stands to Nero's left, hands clasped behind his back, as he leans forward to Nero.

"My Emperor, what are your intentions for these senators?"

"Just some fun, Seneca. Or at least, it will be fun for me," Nero says as he smirks at Piso.

Seneca clears his throat.

"It would be unwise to execute these senators in the arena. While they may seem to obstruct your vision of greatness, they have been effectively maintaining the machinery of Rome while you pursue your artistic endeavours."

Nero turns his head lazily, a smile playing at the corners of his mouth as his eyes find Piso.

"What do you think, Piso? Should I be merciful to your followers?"

"They are not my followers," Piso replies. "They seek only to maintain the empire while you abdicate your duties as Emperor."

"I am the Emperor, Piso. The empire is mine to maintain as I see fit."

"You are truly descending into madness if you think executing four hundred senators will maintain anything. You will tear Rome apart from within."

Nero's smirk widens. He rises from his couch and strides to the edge of the balcony, his purple cloak billowing behind him. Below, the four hundred senators stand clustered in the arena's centre, ringed by Praetorian Guards who have formed a wall of shields and spears with their backs pressed against the arena's perimeter. Nero's voice cuts through the ambient noise like a blade.

"Citizens of Rome! Prepare yourselves for one of the greatest gladiatorial contests in Roman history, as your Senate prepares to defend itself in mortal combat!"

The crowd's roar shakes the wooden structure, a hundred thousand voices united in bloodthirsty anticipation.

"But wait—" Nero pauses, his hand raised in theatrical surprise. "The senators are unarmed! Do you think we should provide them with swords to defend themselves?"

Nero theatrically raises his hand to his ear. The crowd's response is immediate and unanimous.

"No!"

Nero throws back his head in laughter.

"That would not be very sporting of us, now would it? Praetorians! Give the senators their weapons!"

The Praetorian Guards each reach into bundles at their feet and hurl wooden swords toward the terrified senators. The crude training weapons clatter across the sand, some landing at feet, others bouncing off shoulders and backs. The crowd erupts in laughter as senators scramble to retrieve them, their dignified bearing completely abandoned in their desperation for even this pathetic means of defence.

The senators lift their weapons and stare at the wooden blades with expressions of mounting horror and disbelief. Some test the weight, as if hoping the swords might somehow be useful. Others simply hold them limply, already resigned to their fate.

"Don't say I didn't give you a fighting chance!" Nero calls down, his voice dripping with mock sincerity. The crowd's laughter reaches a new pitch, cruel and delighted.

"Now, let me introduce to the arena those who will battle the senators!"

Nero gestures grandly toward the side gates. The massive wooden doors begin to swing open, their hinges groaning. From the darkness beyond comes a sound that chills the blood. The clank and rattle of metal, the shuffle of many feet. The senators turn as one toward the sound, their wooden swords trembling in their grips.

Out they come. Perhaps a hundred slaves and prisoners, their bodies wasted by starvation and disease. Their hands and feet are bound with rope and iron, forcing them to shuffle and stumble. They are unarmed. Rags hang from skeletal frames. Some can barely walk, supported by their fellow condemned. Their faces are hollow, eyes sunken, lips cracked and bleeding. They look less like opponents and more like victims already half-consumed by death.

The senators stare at them in shock, confusion replacing fear on many faces. Nero leans forward on the balcony railing, his expression eager, expectant. The senators look up at him, mouths opening as if to protest or question, but no words come. The Praetorian Guards at the arena's edge suddenly stamp their feet in perfect unison. As one, they level their spears at the senators. The senators all look up at the emperor and speak in unison.

"We who are about to die, salute you."

The phrase comes out ragged, unenthusiastic, spoken by four hundred voices that have lost all hope of dignity. Some senators barely whisper it. Others spit the words like poison.

At some unseen signal, the prisoners and slaves surge forward, a desperate wave of humanity driven by guard's whips and the promise of freedom or mercy that will never come. They have no weapons, no strength, barely any will, but they throw themselves at the senators nonetheless. Some collapse before they reach their targets. Others manage feeble strikes, their bound hands making pathetic fists that wouldn't harm a child.

Nero reclines back on his couch, settling into the cushions with a satisfied sigh. He plucks a grape from a nearby tray and watches the spectacle below with the detached amusement of a man observing an entertaining play. Beside him, Seneca's face has gone carefully blank, his philosopher's mask firmly in place. Piso stares straight ahead, refusing to look down.

In the arena, mathematics asserts its brutal logic. Four hundred senators against one hundred dying slaves. The outcome is never in doubt. The senators, even untrained and armed only with wood, easily overpower their pitiful opponents. Wooden swords crack against skulls. The slaves crumple to the sand, their bound limbs making resistance impossible. Within minutes, all one hundred lie motionless or groaning in the blood-stained sand, while the senators stand over them, breathing hard, their tunics spattered with blood and dirt. Nero rises from his couch and returns to the balcony's edge.

"It appears the senators have been victorious in combat!"

The crowd boos lustily, disappointed by the one-sided contest.

"Now the question remains... what is to be done with the losers?" Nero pauses, letting anticipation build. "I will let Senator Piso decide." He turns and gestures elegantly toward Piso. "Senator, join me."

Piso remains frozen in his chair, every muscle rigid. Behind him, Tigellinus's sword whispers from its sheath, just an inch, just enough for the sound to carry its implicit threat. Piso rises slowly. He walks to the balcony as if approaching his own execution and looks down at the broken bodies scattered across the sand. Nero's voice is conversational, almost friendly.

"What say you, Senator Piso? Thumbs up or thumbs down?"

Piso's hand rises. His thumb extends sideways for a long moment. The gesture of indecision, of mercy withheld but not yet denied. Then, slowly, inexorably, it turns downward. Signalling his wishes for the losers to receive death. The crowd's booing intensifies, a wall of disapproval that makes the wooden structure shake.

"In honour of Senator Piso," Nero announces, "I will let the prisoners live. A reminder to the senator of where his place in Rome belongs."

The crowd's mood shifts instantly to wild cheering. Piso stands at the balcony, his arm still extended, his thumb still pointing down at nothing. After a moment, he lowers his hand and returns to his seat like a man in a trance.

Below, guards drag the defeated prisoners from the arena. The senators watch them go, and relief floods their faces. Their shoulders sag. Some drop their wooden swords. A few even laugh nervously, shaking their heads as if to clear them of a nightmare. The purpose of this spectacle, they now believe, was merely humiliation. A cruel lesson taught, but one they will survive. Nero's eyes glint with something sinister as he addresses the crowd again.

"And now, for the senator's true test!"

An excited murmur ripples through the crowd, the sound of a hundred thousand people leaning forward in anticipation. Nero turns his head slightly, speaking just loud enough for Piso to hear.

"You didn't think you were getting off that easy, did you?" Piso's fists clench as Nero turns back to address the arena. "The senators will now fight for their lives against wild beasts!"

The crowd erupts in a mighty roar of excitement.

"At least give them real swords," Piso says.

"Silence," Tigellinus growls.

"And as a special treat to the people of Rome," Nero continues, "this battle will be accompanied by music performed by your Emperor himself!"

The crowd's roar reaches its highest pitch yet, a sound of pure ecstasy. Some spectators weep with joy at the prospect of hearing their emperor play. Epaphroditus hands Nero his lyre. The instrument is inlaid with ivory and gold, its strings perfectly tuned. He cradles it lovingly and begins to play, his fingers dancing across the strings to produce tense, martial music that sets the blood racing.

"Release the beasts!" he calls out, never pausing in his playing.

The Praetorian Guards in the arena move to large chains embedded in the sand. They pull in unison, muscles straining, and slowly—agonizingly slowly—trap doors begin to open with grinding, ominous scrapes. Dark holes appear in the arena floor, and from them rise sounds that freeze the blood: snarls, roars, the scrape of claws on stone.

The senators abandon all pretence of courage and huddle together in the arena's centre, a tight knot of four hundred terrified men. Their wooden swords point outward in trembling hands, aimed at the mysterious sounds emanating from the opening trap doors. Some pray audibly. Others simply whimper.

In the imperial box, Piso's knuckles have turned bone-white against the chair's armrests. Sweat drips down his temple, tracing a path through the dust on his face. He leans forward despite himself, every nerve screaming in anticipation of what horror might emerge to slaughter his colleagues. Suddenly, from the largest trap door, they come.

Pigs.

Dozens of pigs, their pink bodies smeared with their own excrement, squealing and snorting as they charge into the brightness of the arena.

Piso exhales explosively, not realizing he had been holding his breath. The crowd erupts in hysterical laughter, the sound rolling through the amphitheatre in waves. Beside Nero, even Tigellinus allows himself to smile.

Nero plays his lyre with exaggerated intensity, his music now comic rather than martial, matching the absurd scene below. The pigs run in frenzied circles between the senator's legs, smearing them with feces and mud. The dignified leaders of Rome dance and hop, trying desperately to avoid the filthy animals while maintaining some shred of composure. Their white tunics become brown with filth. The smell rises even to the imperial box.

The senators, one by one, lift their eyes to the balcony where Nero plays his lyre, a beatific smile on his face. His message is clear in every note, every plucked string: I am in control. You live or die at my whim. Your dignity exists only as long as I permit it. The crowd finds its rhythm, a chant building from the lower sections and spreading like wildfire through the entire amphitheatre, a hundred thousand voices united in worship:

"Nero! Nero! Nero!"

The emperor plays on, his fingers never faltering, his smile never wavering, as his senators stand covered in the excrement of pigs and their own shame.

Chapter 7
The Pyramids

The shallow river boat cuts through the muddy waters of the Nile Delta with steady rhythm, its papyrus hull riding low under the weight of men and supplies. Marcus and Quintus pull at the oars in synchronisation, sweat beading on their foreheads despite the morning cool.

At the boat's prow stands Kashta, motionless save for the occasional gesture toward hidden sandbars or treacherous currents. His dark skin gleams with perspiration as he points the way through channels that shift with each season's flood. Years of navigating these waters show in his confident gestures and the way his eyes read the subtle signs of current and depth that remain invisible to Roman eyes.

Behind him, Pliny peppers the Kushite guide with questions about river navigation, seasonal patterns, and the ancient civilizations that once flourished along these banks. His scroll case rests open beside him, ready to capture any detail that might prove valuable to their mission or his encyclopaedia.

At the boat's stern, Sextus lounges with the arrogance of man accustomed to being the deadliest presence in any room. The Praetorians pass a wineskin between them while making crude jokes about Egyptian women and speculating about the exotic pleasures awaiting them upriver.

Titus and Paulinus approach them, their footsteps causing the boat to rock slightly on the gentle current. Titus squares up to Sextus authoritatively.

"Let's get one thing straight, Sextus. This is my mission. You are here to assist. I am in charge."

Sextus looks up from the wineskin with a cold smile.

"You are wrong, Titus. The Emperor is in charge. You aren't the only one who received specific orders before departing Rome."

"The purpose of this expedition is intelligence gathering, not slaughtering people whose only crime is worshipping a man who preached peace."

"The purpose of this mission is to serve the Emperor and advance the glory of the Roman Empire. Or do I need to bring your loyalties into question?"

Marcus and Quintus stop rowing, their hands moving to rest on their sword hilts. The casual atmosphere transforms instantly into something predatory and tense. Titus, realising he is outnumbered, responds through gritted teeth.

"Next time you decide to embark on an impromptu killing spree, inform me first."

"If you continue speaking to the Praetorian Guard in that tone, Titus, you'd better learn to sleep with one eye open."

The two men lock eyes in a stare that carries the weight of competing authorities and incompatible philosophies. Marcus and Quintus begin rowing again. The boat continues its steady progress through waters that have witnessed the rise and fall of pharaohs, while tension thick enough to cut hangs in the humid air.

Titus turns his back on Sextus, jaw clenched, and nudges Paulinus with his elbow. Titus's hand remains near his sword hilt until they reach the bow where Pliny continues his animated conversation with their guide.

"What's our next destination?" Titus asks Kashta.

"We must port at Memphis. It's a seven-day journey from here. There we can rest and resupply for the journey ahead."

Pliny's eyes light up.

"Kashta has been telling me about the pyramids near Memphis. I must document them, Titus. Such monuments represent irreplaceable historical knowledge."

"Ancient tombs are of no interest to us or the emperor," Titus replies dismissively.

"This is an expedition for knowledge. Why limit ourselves to information merely about the river? With the research we conduct here, I will write the greatest encyclopaedia ever compiled by Roman scholarship."

Titus pauses, considering the scholar's words while watching the succession of mud-brick villages that line the riverbank.

"What difference will it make?" Pliny continues. "We have to port there and resupply regardless. A few hours of additional research could yield invaluable insights."

"Very well," Titus concedes. "But make it fast."

The expedition drifts up the Nile for what seems like weeks, their papyrus boat cutting through waters that range from muddy brown near the delta to crystalline blue in the deeper reaches. Along the banks, date palms sway in the desert wind as reed beds whisper secrets to the flowing current. Temples emerge from the green strips of cultivation like monuments to forgotten dreams, their sandstone columns carved with hieroglyphs. The infernal African sun tanning their skin to a rich brown.

They guide the boat to a wooden dock where other boats bob gently in the current. The familiar sounds of a working port, shouting dock workers, creaking ropes, braying donkeys, create a symphony of human industry that contrasts sharply with the eternal silence of the river behind them. Titus delivers instructions as they disembark.

"Paulinus, you and the Praetorians remain here to gather supplies. Pliny and I will examine those monuments."

"You aren't going alone, Titus," Sextus interjects.

"What's the matter, Sextus? Don't you trust me?"

"How can I trust a man who chose to live on a farm instead of serving the empire? How do I know you won't simply disappear and establish yourself as a farmer somewhere in Egypt?"

"So be it. We'll meet back at the tavern in town before sunset. Paulinus, have Kashta show you where to obtain the supplies we need."

"Understood," Paulinus replies.

Titus leads the way across the ancient sands, with Pliny and Sextus following in single file. Their elongated shadows rippling over dunes once pressed by the sandaled feet of pharaohs and high priests. The pyramids appear from the desert plateau, their limestone faces gleaming white as polished marble in the afternoon sun. Each massive structure towers over four hundred feet into the cloudless sky, their surfaces so perfectly smooth they appear to have been carved by the gods themselves. At their peaks, capstones of electrum—an alloy of gold and silver—catch and scatter sunlight like captured stars, creating brilliant points of radiance visible from miles away.

The Great Pyramid covers more than thirteen acres. Smaller pyramids flanking it seem modest only by comparison, though each would dwarf the greatest temples of Rome. Between them, causeways paved with granite connect the monuments in patterns that mirror the constellations above.

Sextus shakes his head with the impatience of a soldier who sees no tactical value in ancient stonework.

"Why are we wasting our time examining some giant triangles?"

"We are here to answer some fundamental questions," Pliny replies enthusiastically.

"What questions?"

"Who built them? How did they build them? When did they build them? And most importantly why did they build them?"

Sextus stops in shock.

"You mean we don't actually know what these things are? Why doesn't the empire send its most learned scholars to simply figure it out?"

"That's precisely why I'm here."

Sextus turns to Titus.

"You know these lands, Titus. You and your father spent most of your lives here. Surely you must have learned their purpose."

"The locals say it's impossible to build them. Even with our most advanced engineering, we could not replicate their construction."

"Surely the inhabitants have theories."

"They have theories. Nothing you would believe, though."

"Try me."

Titus pauses, choosing his words carefully.

"The elders in Alexandria once told me a tale, one the priests of Egypt guard like sacred treasure. They spoke of ancient magic, of gods descending from the sky and breeding with human women, creating a race of giants to construct their stone monuments. They call them the Nephilim. Born of heaven's rebels and mortal women, they were not only giants of war but also builders of wonders. They hauled the massive stones across the desert and shaped monuments so vast no ordinary human could have conceived them. The priests swear it was not slave labour but the strength of these half-divine giants that raised the pyramids. They believe the desert still keeps their secrets buried in the sand, waiting for the day their blood stirs again."

Sextus laughs harshly.

"You were right, Titus. I don't believe a word of it."

They clamber up the rough-hewn steps toward the Great Pyramid's entrance. Little more than a gash in the limestone face. As they duck inside, the desert heat falls away, replaced by cool stillness and the primordial scent of stone.

The walls are etched with hieroglyphics. Pliny approaches one wall, running his fingers across the carved symbols with reverent care.

"Well then, Pliny," Sextus says. "Enlighten us."

Pliny opens the Book of the Dead, comparing the ancient papyrus with the wall carvings.

"According to these writings, the pyramid was not a tomb but served a far more complex purpose. These symbols describe the structure as a place where earth's energy was captured and transformed. The passages and chambers were designed to channel natural forces through the stone itself, what they call the 'breath of the gods'."

They descend through the Descending Passage, a four foot high narrow corridor that plunges at a precise twenty-six degree angle into the pyramid's heart.

"Notice the angle," Pliny says, "Twenty-six degrees precisely. The same angle appears throughout the structure in the ascending passages, in the gallery, in the shaft alignments. This is no accident of construction."

The passage opens suddenly into a rough-hewn chamber carved directly from the bedrock beneath the pyramid. The chamber feels deliberately unfinished, its ceiling low and irregular, its floor uneven. Pliny translates as he runs his finger along the walls.

"The hieroglyphs speak of this as the 'Chamber of Chaos'. A place where the energies of the underworld—the Duat—could be accessed and controlled. See here, these symbols describe waters flowing through channels we cannot see, creating pressures deep within the earth."

They retrace their steps and find the junction where the Ascending Passage branches upward into the Grand Gallery. Pliny kneels to examine rectangular holes in the floor, running his fingers along the precise edges.

"The texts speak of great stones that once slid along these channels. Not to seal the passage, but to create... I'm not certain of the translation. 'Resonance barriers'? 'Sound gates'? The symbols here describe vibrations traveling through the stone, controlled and directed by mechanisms we don't understand."

At the gallery's upper end, they crouch again to pass through a low antechamber, constructed entirely of red granite. Blocks weighing up to eighty tons each, transported somehow from quarries five hundred miles away. In the chamber's western end stands a lidless granite sarcophagus.

"The hieroglyphs call this the 'Chamber of Resurrection," Pliny says. "But not resurrection of the body, resurrection of something else. These symbols speak of the king's ka—his spiritual essence—being transformed here, elevated, merged with the divine energies channelled through the structure."

They climb further still, finding a chamber that lies at the pyramid's exact horizontal centre. A large niche in the eastern wall once held something, removed long ago.

"The granite chambers were positioned to resonate with vibrations from deep within the earth. The gold capstone served not just as decoration but as a focal point for these energies, broadcasting them across the land. They describe waters flowing through hidden channels, creating pressures that would generate what they call 'divine fire'. Perhaps some form of energy we don't understand. The entire structure functioned as a great machine, drawing power from the earth and sky to serve purposes we can only guess at."

Titus pauses in a narrow corridor and examines a carving in the stone. A jackal headed god carrying a pharaoh into the underworld. He squints intently at the carving, noticing an uncanny resemblance between himself and the pharaoh. His head tilts as if listening to something the others cannot hear. For a moment, he hears whispers echoing from the stone itself, a voice speaking in languages that predate human memory. A whispering voice of someone who calls themselves Anubis.

"Did you hear that?" Titus asks.

"Hear what?" Pliny says.

Titus shakes his head.

"Never mind."

But Anubis's voice grows clearer, no longer a whisper but a presence that fills Titus's mind's eye. The jackal headed god communes with Titus, not with words but with knowledge that flows directly into his mind.

Visions of the Nile's source, glimpses of a golden chest hidden deep in African jungles where the river begins its journey toward the sea. Then the vision shifts to a vast black temple overlooking a lake, its scale defying reason. From the temple's balcony, a canine-headed god uncorks a vial of viscous black poison and pours it into the Nile. The waters darken, spreading like ink across the land.

"Titus?"

The scholar's voice snaps the Roman general out of his trance. Titus gasps for breath as he looks at Pliny and Sextus, a bead of sweat cutting through the dust on his cheek. Pliny and Sextus exchange a concerned look. Titus catches his breath and straightens himself, his soldier's discipline reasserting itself.

"It's time to go."

They emerge from the pyramid's depths to find the sun lower in the sky. As they walk back toward Memphis, they pass the Great Sphinx, its lion's body carved from a single massive block of limestone, its human head gazing eternally eastward toward the rising sun.

"By the gods," Sextus breathes. "What is that giant cat?"

"They call it the Sphinx. They say it represents the union of human wisdom and animal strength," Pliny explains. "But some texts suggest it guards something far more significant. A chamber beneath the sand containing the complete records of the civilization that built these monuments."

"That's a great many words. Tell me, how is any of this supposed to expand the might of the Roman Empire?"

"The Greeks understood that knowledge itself is power. They learned from Egyptian wisdom and used it to build their own empire. Alexander conquered the world not just with swords, but with the accumulated learning of generations. If we can understand how these monuments were constructed, imagine what we could build. If we can comprehend the forces they harnessed, imagine what we could accomplish. The empire that masters such knowledge wouldn't just rule the Mediterranean, it could rule the world."

Sextus smirks.

"Worlds aren't conquered with scholarly musings, Pliny the Elder. They're conquered with the tip of a spear."

As they walk back toward Memphis, the pyramids behind them catch the last rays of sunlight, their golden capstones blazing like beacons in the gathering dusk. Whatever secrets they contain remain locked within their stone hearts, waiting for minds capable of understanding mysteries that have endured for millennia.

As they approach the harbour and find their boat, Titus's blood turns to ice. Paulinus lies sprawled across the deck, his face a mass of bruises and cuts, blood seeping from a gash above his left eye. Titus breaks into a sprint toward the vessel.

"Paulinus! What happened?"

Paulinus spits blood over the side, wincing as he tries to sit up.

"I tried to stop them. They're mad dogs off their leashes."

Behind Titus, Sextus approaches with unconcealed satisfaction gleaming in his eyes.

"What are you talking about?" Titus demands.

Paulinus nods weakly toward the town centre.

"Go see for yourself."

Titus turns and runs toward Memphis's main thoroughfare, dread building in his chest with each step. There, in the centre of the town square, an old man and a young woman stand crucified. Each with a small wooden crucifix hanging around their neck. Marcus and Quintus observe their work with a satisfied smile. Sextus arrives behind him, surveying the scene with pride.

"More threats to the empire dealt with. Another productive afternoon," he declares cheerfully.

"Have the gods stripped you of your sanity, Sextus? These are innocent people!" Titus roars.

"Anyone who would worship a dead carpenter over the Emperor is not innocent. They represent a clear and present danger to our glorious empire."

Titus looks up at the young woman in her early twenties, her face pale with blood loss but her eyes still holding desperate hope.

"Please. Why?" she whispers.

Titus moves to her cross and begins pulling out the iron spike pinning her feet to the wood.

"This madness ends here," Titus yells.

"Guards, seize him!" Sextus commands.

Marcus lunges first, reaching for Titus's sword arm, but the general pivots and drives his elbow into the Praetorian's solar plexus, doubling him over with a strangled gasp. In the same fluid motion, Titus catches Quintus's grasping hands and uses his momentum against him, throwing him into the dirt. Marcus recovers and charges again, but Titus ducks under his wild swing and delivers a devastating uppercut that snaps the Praetorian's head back and sends blood spraying from his mouth. Quintus staggers to his feet, drawing his dagger in desperation, but Titus seizes his wrist and twists until bone grinds against bone, forcing him to drop the blade before driving his knee into the man's ribs. Both Praetorians collapse into the dust, gasping and broken. Titus goes back to freeing the crucified woman.

"Stop him now!" Sextus shouts.

Sextus tackles Titus from the back. Marcus and Quintus stand up and overwhelm Titus through sheer numbers, wrestling him to the ground and pinning his arms behind his back. They drag him before their commander, who smirks at having finally gained the upper hand. Sextus draws his gladius ceremoniously.

"Aiding enemies of the Emperor constitutes treason, Titus. You know what the punishment is for treason."

"I know what punishment the gods reserve for those who massacre innocents."

Sextus inches his sword to Titus's throat. He leans closer, savouring the moment as he presses the metal against flesh.

"Any final words, General?"

Titus spits blood onto the dirt.

"I should have killed you back in Alexandria."

Sextus smiles.

"Goodbye, Titus."

Suddenly, another blade appears at Sextus's neck. The Praetorian Prefect turns to find Paulinus standing behind him, blood still dripping from his battered face but his sword hand steady.

"Killing the Emperor's chosen expedition leader would also constitute treason, Sextus. If Nero discovers you sabotaged his mission by murdering its commander, what do you think will happen to you?"

Sextus's eyes move to the blade at his neck, then to Titus, then back to Paulinus. After a long moment, his cold smile returns as he slowly withdraws his blade from Titus's throat.

"I suppose you still have some use, for now." He sheathes his sword. "Marcus. Quintus. Let's find a tavern. Listening to scholarly lectures about triangles all day has made me hungry."

Sextus and his men walk away laughing, their voices fading as they disappear into the town's winding streets.

Titus, Paulinus, and Pliny stand in the town square. The man and woman hang limply, their parched lips moving in silent prayers or curses. Flies buzz in great black clouds around the crosses, and ravens perch on the cross-beams like dark omens, their cawing the only sound that breaks the terrible silence.

Titus walks over to the crucified old man whose beard is matted with blood. The man's eyes flutter open, revealing clouded irises that search Titus's face with fading recognition.

"Water," the old man whispers.

Paulinus limps to Titus's side, wincing as he kneels. He offers his waterskin, and Titus holds it to the dying man's cracked lips. Most of the liquid spills down his chin, but he manages a few swallows before coughing weakly.

"Why did they target you?" Titus asks.

The old man's breathing comes in shallow gasps.

"We refused to kneel for the Emperor. We only kneel for one man," he whispers.

"The carpenter from Nazareth," Titus mutters.

The old man's rheumy eyes fix on Titus, but despite his condition, he looks at peace. A look of serenity washes over him as he takes his last breath.

“What do we do, Titus?” Pliny asks.

Titus looks at the crucified woman, knowing the spikes in her hands and feet are the only thing stopping her from dying of blood loss.

“There is only one thing we can do."

Titus walks over to the woman and draws his gladius. He looks deep into her eyes. A tear runs down her cheek as she nods at the Roman General. Titus drives his sword directly into the woman's heart, granting her a quick and painless death. Titus sheathes his sword, his expression never wavering.

"We need food and rest. Tomorrow at first light, we continue upriver.”

The three Romans walk in silence towards the tavern. Villagers who've escaped the Praetorians wrath press themselves against buildings or flee into alleyways as they pass.

Titus, Paulinus, and Pliny enter the local tavern to find Sextus and his guardsmen already occupying the largest table as they share wine and crude jokes about the afternoon's crucifixions. Kashta sits alone at a table across the room. The tavern's interior offers little respite from the horrors outside. The locals stand frozen against the wall, terrified to even make eye contact with the Praetorians.

Sextus looks up as they enter, his cold eyes locking onto Titus with predatory intensity. Neither man breaks the stare as Titus leads his companions to Kashta's table. They settle onto wooden stools.

"How long do you think before they kill us?" Pliny asks quietly.

"They'll keep us breathing as long as they need us. Just make certain you don't lose that book," Titus replies, never taking his eyes off Sextus.

"So we simply wait until we reach the source of the Nile, then they murder us."

Paulinus raises two fingers to the tavern keeper. A serving girl approaches, setting down a wooden platter heavy with bread, olives, and roasted meat, followed by a clay jug of wine. Paulinus slips a gold coin into her hand and she pauses, startled, before murmuring her thanks and moving on. Pliny picks listlessly at the bread before dropping his voice to a whisper.

"Perhaps we should return to Rome. When darkness falls, we could simply sail away."

"If you think Sextus is dangerous, imagine what Nero will do if we return empty-handed," Paulinus replies while filling his cup with wine.

Titus turns to their guide, who sits silently observing the Roman dynamics with the patience of a man accustomed to foreign madness.

"Where do we port next, Kashta?" Titus asks.

"Aswan."

Pliny's eyes brighten.

"Titus, I know you've said it is off-limits, but the Temple of Thebes is close to Aswan. May we please stop to explore it?"

"No."

"It would only take a moment, Titus. The inscriptions there could provide invaluable historical context."

"The answer is no. Men have ventured into that temple never to return."

"I'll go alone. I'll be brief and careful."

Titus finally breaks his stare with Sextus to look directly at the scholar.

"I would only enter that cursed temple if my life depended on it."

“Why? What’s in there?”

“The locals call it the City of the Hungry Dead. Tombs were violated by grave robbers centuries ago and something was disturbed that should have remained sleeping. Those who venture into its depths do not return.”

“Maybe we should just send Sextus inside then,” Paulinus says.

Across the room, Sextus raises his wine cup in a mocking toast. Titus holds Sextus's gaze for a moment before turning back to his companions.

"We leave at dawn for Aswan. The sooner we reach the source, the sooner this ends."

"And if the Praetorians murder more innocents along the way?" Pliny asks.

"We cannot save everyone. But we can complete our mission and ensure these deaths weren't meaningless."

Kashta, who has remained mostly silent throughout their exchange, suddenly speaks.

"The river grows treacherous beyond Aswan. The First Cataract marks the boundary of Roman control. Beyond the Fifth Cataract lies the Kingdom of Kush, where your Emperor's name carries no weight."

"Will your people welcome us?" Paulinus asks.

"My Queen is not fond of Romans. She remembers how your legions burned our villages and enslaved her people. The memories of Petronius's campaign still haunt our elders."

"But you agreed to guide us," Titus says.

"I guide you because my Queen commanded it. She wishes to understand the purpose of your journey. Knowledge is power, and my people have learned to gather intelligence about potential enemies."

Paulinus drains his cup.

"So we'll be walking into hostile territory with a guide who serves a Queen that hates us. Splendid."

"Queen Amanitore is wise. She will not harm you without cause. But she cannot protect you from the biggest threat you face."

“Which is?” Titus asks.

Kashta's eyes flick toward Sextus.

“Your own men.”

Chapter 8
Incendium Magnum Romae

Rome, 63 AD. Nero arrives home at his palace from the Senatorial games, still laughing to himself as he remembers the senators struggling to dodge pigs. He enters his private chambers to find two women awaiting him, their contrasting expressions immediately drawing his attention.

His wife Octavia sits on a marble bench, tears streaming down her cheeks, while Poppaea Sabina stands with radiant joy illuminating her beautiful face. The Emperor pauses in the doorway, unsure what drama has unfolded in his absence. Sabina's voice trembles with excitement as she makes an announcement to Nero.

"It has finally happened, my Emperor. I have provided you with an heir."

"You are with child?"

"Yes. Your bloodline shall continue through me."

"This is the most joyous news I have ever received!"

Nero enthusiastically embraces Sabina, his eyes gleaming with happiness. Octavia looks up through her tears, her voice breaking.

"How could you do this to me? How could you do this to us?"

Nero turns his attention to his wife, his expression transforms from joy to anger in an instant.

"Us? There is no 'us'. For nine years you have failed to provide me with an heir."

Octavia's sobs grow louder, her composure crumbling completely.

"And now you weep, Making this moment all about your self-pity, always playing the victim. Sabina has given me what you could not. Your barren womb has failed the empire."

Octavia bursts into tears and flees the chamber, her cries echoing through the marble corridors. Nero opens his arms to embrace Sabina, pulling her close against his chest.

"I will marry you, my love, and make you Empress of Rome."

"Oh, my Emperor. You make me happier than Venus herself."

Nero's expression grows calculating as he holds her.

"But first I must deal with Octavia."

The divorce proceedings unfold with indifferent efficiency. Roman law, manipulated by imperial will, dissolves the marriage that had once symbolized dynastic stability. Octavia, daughter of Claudius and sister-wife to Nero, finds herself stripped of title, status, and protection in a single afternoon.

Three days later, a messenger delivers news to the Senate that Octavia was found dead in a hot bath on Pandateria, the island of her exile. No witnesses are mentioned. No investigation follows. Only a brief notation in the imperial records, filed between tax collection reports and appointments to provincial offices. The official records will state that Octavia chose death over dishonour, though those who knew her understand that such choices are rarely voluntary when emperors grow tired of their wives.

Within days, new ceremonies transform the palace. Nero takes Sabina as his bride in a celebration that emphasizes rebirth, renewal, and the promise of legitimate succession. The guests who attend speak of love triumphant and imperial happiness, though some notice how quickly servants have removed all traces of the previous Empress from the halls where she once walked.

The empire has a new Augusta, and soon it will have a new heir. In Rome, such transitions are measured not in sentiment but in political necessity.

Rome, January, 63 AD. The cries of a newborn pierce the winter air in Nero's private chambers as Poppaea Sabina delivers the child that will secure the imperial succession. Nero's daughter, Claudia Augusta emerges into the world amid silk cushions and golden lamplight, her tiny lungs announcing her arrival to an empire that has waited years for this moment.

Nero paces outside the birthing chamber like a caged lion, his imperial composure abandoned in favour of raw anticipation. When the midwife finally emerges with news of a healthy daughter, his face transforms with pure joy. He enters the chamber and takes the swaddled infant from the midwife, cradling her with a tenderness that surprises even his closest advisors.

"A daughter! Perfect and beautiful, like her mother."

The child's face is red and wrinkled, her eyes squeezed shut against the harshness of the world, yet to Nero she appears more perfect than any marble statue crafted by the finest sculptors of Greece.

"Claudia Augusta," he whispers, pressing his lips to her forehead. "You shall be the greatest empress Rome has ever known."

Poppaea watches from her birthing bed, her face still flushed with exertion but glowing with triumph. Her golden hair clings to her sweat-dampened brow, yet she has never appeared more beautiful to Nero. She has accomplished what Octavia could not, provide him with an heir.

In a gesture unprecedented in Roman history, Nero grants both mother and child the title of Augusta, elevating them to the highest rank possible for imperial women. The baby Claudia Augusta becomes the youngest person ever to bear such an honour, while Sabina finds herself elevated from mistress to Empress to now the mother of Rome's future. Nero cradles his daughter, his blue eyes bright with paternal love.

"She shall have everything. A palace worthy of divine blood, gardens that rival those of Venus herself."

Seneca, summoned to witness this historic moment, watches with the careful expression of a man who has learned to temper imperial enthusiasm with practical reality. When Nero begins describing his vision for the Domus Aurea. A golden house that will span hundreds of acres and house his family in unprecedented luxury. The philosopher clears his throat diplomatically.

"Unfortunately, there is no available space in Rome for such an ambitious infrastructure project, my Emperor."

"There must be somewhere."

"You would need to build outside the city limits. The only way to create sufficient space within Rome itself would be if a significant portion of the existing city burnt to the ground."

Nero nods absently, his attention focused entirely on the tiny life in his arms.

"Whatever it takes. She deserves perfection."

As the weeks go by, the joy that fills the palace proves as fragile as winter ice. Sabina, weakened by a difficult birth, struggles to recover her strength. Her face grows pale and gaunt, while fever makes her delirious for days at a time. The baby, too, shows troubling signs. She feeds poorly, cries constantly, and her breathing often sounds laboured.

Nero, however, seems oblivious to their condition. He visits daily, not to comfort or console, but to share his artistic visions and plans for their future. He describes the Domus Aurea in exhaustive detail. Its rotating dining rooms, its artificial lakes, its walls covered in gold leaf that will reflect light like captured sunbeams. He visits them one afternoon, producing his Lyre.

"Listen. I've composed a lullaby for our daughter."

As Sabina lies trembling with fever and baby Claudia breathes slower than normal, Nero plays elaborate melodies, his voice rising and falling with dramatic flourishes. He seems genuinely puzzled when neither responds with enthusiasm, interpreting their silence as appreciation rather than exhaustion.

"Art heals all wounds. Music soothes even the gods themselves. I shall play you another song."

He begins playing his Lyre again as tears run down Sabina's pale, gaunt cheek.

Rome, May, 63 AD. Nero bursts into the chambers with unusual energy, carrying scrolls covered in architectural drawings. His face glows with excitement as he prepares to share his latest revisions to the golden palace plans.

"Sabina, my love, you must see what the architects have designed for Claudia's nursery. The ceiling will be painted to show the constellations at the moment of her birth, and there will be a fountain that—"

The words die in his throat.

Sabina sits motionless on her couch, her face streaked with tears that have dried into salt tracks on her cheeks. In her arms lies Claudia Augusta, Nero's daughter, dead at three months old. The baby's face, once flushed with life, has taken on the waxy pallor that marks the end of all earthly concerns. Sabina whispers, her voice barely audible.

"She's gone. She stopped breathing an hour ago. I... I couldn't save her."

Nero stares at his dead child, his architectural plans sliding from nerveless fingers to scatter across the marble floor. The silence stretches until it becomes unbearable, broken only by Sabina's quiet sobs.

"You did this," he says, his voice low and dangerous. "You killed her. My only child. The Empire's only heir. You killed her."

"Nero, please—"

"I run the greatest empire in history. I compose the greatest art ever written. All you had to do was mind my daughter... and you killed her."

Sabina looks up at him with tears streaming down her eyes.

"Please, Nero. She was sick from birth. The physicians said—"

"The physicians are fools! And you are worse than a fool, you are a failure! You killed our child!"

He storms from the chamber, leaving Sabina alone, trembling with their dead child in her arms.

In the months following his daughter's death, Nero transforms from Emperor to ghost haunting his own palace. He wanders the marble corridors in the same soiled tunic for days at a time, his unwashed hair hanging limp around hollow cheeks. The man who once preened before mirrors now avoids his own reflection, unable to bear his own sight.

The palace staff whisper about their Emperor's decline. Meals sit untouched outside his chambers, wine cups gather dust on tables, and the golden lyre that once provided daily entertainment lies silent in its case. The vibrant court life that characterized his early reign dissolves into oppressive quiet broken only by Nero's aimless footsteps echoing through empty halls.

Meanwhile, Rome itself begins to mirror its ruler's deterioration. Without imperial attention, the city's problems multiply like weeds in an abandoned garden. The grain supply from Egypt grows irregular, causing bread shortages in the Subura. Public works projects halt mid-construction, leaving half-built aqueducts and unfinished roads as monuments to imperial neglect. Crime increases as the Urban Cohorts receive no clear directives, and fires burn longer because the Vigiles lack adequate funding for equipment.

Seneca enters the private chambers to find Nero sprawled across a silk couch, eyes fixed on the middle distance, seeing nothing. Servants linger at the periphery of the room, exchanging nervous glances, unsure whether to approach their Emperor or flee. The lines etched into the philosopher's face have deepened in recent months. The cost of maintaining an empire while its master retreats into the labyrinth of his own mind.

"My Emperor, there are matters requiring your attention. The grain ships from Alexandria are three weeks overdue, the aqueduct repairs have stalled without funding, and tax collection in Gaul has virtually ceased."

Nero struggles to lift his head and turn it towards Seneca. His voice is barely audible, carrying the flat tone of a man who has stared too long into an abyss.

"What does any of it matter? We build, we plan, we achieve, and death takes it all anyway."

"The people depend on your leadership—"

"The people will die regardless of my leadership. Everyone dies. Everything ends. Tell me something that will matter in a hundred years, Seneca. Tell me something death cannot steal."

Seneca shifts uncomfortably, recognizing the dangerous territory of imperial despair.

"There is another matter, Caesar. Peter has completed construction of his church in Rome."

Nero's lethargy is suddenly penetrated like a blade through silk. He sits up slowly, his pale eyes focusing with sudden intensity.

"How is there room for Peter to build a church that spits in the face of my empire, but no space for the Emperor to build a home for his daughter?"

"The Christians gather in increasing numbers—"

"And what do they worship in this church?"

"A large wooden crucifix with a dead body nailed to it."

Nero rises from his couch with explosive energy, months of suppressed rage finally finding a target.

"These people are insane! Why would anyone worship a man with no accomplishments at his moment of greatest weakness? How dare they disrespect me with such madness! Burn their church to the ground!"

"Emperor, a fire in that location could very easily spread throughout Rome. The buildings are closely packed, the wood is dry—"

"Then we will finally have room to build my golden palace."

"I must strongly advise against starting a fire in Rome," Seneca warns.

"In order for a phoenix to rise, we must first create a pile of ash."

Nero walks over to Seneca, and eyes the philosopher up and down, his voice drops to a dangerous whisper.

"It sounds like you've been talking with Senator Piso again."

"My Emperor, I would never betray you."

Nero raises a finger to stop Seneca.

"Set a blaze at the heart of the church. Let what happens happen."

Seneca stares at his former pupil, seeing in those pale eyes the complete absence of the young man he once tutored in philosophy and virtue. With a heavy heart, he bows and exits the chamber. Several Praetorian Guards follow him into the corridor, their armour clanking as they disappear into the night.

Hours later, Nero stands on his palace balcony watching a small glow appear in the distance where Peter's church stands. The fire spreads hungrily, leaping from building to building as the dry wood and close quarters create perfect conditions for conflagration. Seneca returns, his face grim with the weight of what they have unleashed.

"My Emperor, we must organize efforts to contain the fire. Shall I summon the Vigiles Urbani?"

Nero doesn't respond. Instead, he walks to where his golden lyre rests and lifts it with reverent care. His fingers find the strings, and a haunting melody drifts across the night air. The lullaby he composed for his daughter during those brief, shining weeks when he believed happiness was possible. He plays the lyre as his eyes reflect the distant flames.

"Claudia used to love this song."

Chapter 9

The Sarcophagus of Amun-Ra

The pyramids fade behind into heat shimmer on the horizon as their boat cuts through the Nile's muddy waters toward Aswan. The current runs stronger here, forcing Titus and Paulinus to pull harder at the oars. The rhythmic splash of wooden blades creates a hypnotic cadence that mingles with the distant calls of ibises hunting in the papyrus reeds.

At the boat's stern, Quintus lounges with the arrogance that has marked their entire journey. He leans backward over the gunwale, trailing his hand in the water while his companions share a wineskin and make jokes about the crucifixions in Memphis. Kashta fixes his eyes on the Praetorian's reckless position and calls from the steering oar.

"Do not lean over the boat. You must respect the river."

Quintus laughs harshly.

"Or what? Will the water get angry and complain to Caesar?"

"Or the Nile will come alive and eat you."

Marcus and Quintus burst into disrespectful laughter. Marcus mimics Kashta's accent while Quintus pantomimes falling overboard, arms flailing. They sprawl back against the gunwales, legs splayed wide, heads tilted skyward. Quintus leans even further over the boat's edge and slaps the water's surface with mocking enthusiasm.

"Wake up, river! Time to come alive and eat some Romans!"

Marcus roars with amusement at Quintus's wit.

Suddenly, the water explodes upward in a geyser of spray and fury. A massive Nile crocodile erupts from the depths like a primordial nightmare given flesh. Twenty feet of armoured death that strikes with the speed of the gods. Its jaws, lined with teeth like iron daggers, chomp at Quintus who dives to the other side of the boat to avoid them.

The crocodile thrashes on the boat its jaws snap at Quintus who has wedged one sandaled foot against the beast's snout and braced the other on its lower jaw. Marcus hacks at the crocodile's armoured flank, but the ancient scales deflect the blow with a dull clang.

Titus strides towards the crocodile with the calm precision of a veteran and drives his sword deep into the reptile's unblinking yellow eye. The beast hisses, before slipping beneath the Nile's surface, leaving only ripples and bloodstained water.

Everyone aboard immediately scrambles toward the boat's centre, suddenly understanding that the Nile's waters hold more than fish and mud. The casual bravado that marked their journey evaporates like mist before the dawn.

As the days go by, the boat drifts through the ancient heart of Thebes, where colossal ruins line the riverbank. Massive stone blocks, weathered by millennia but still defiant against time, form walls that once enclosed the greatest city in the ancient world. Granite obelisks reach toward the sky like fingers of Pharaohs, their hieroglyphic inscriptions worn smooth by desert winds. Palm trees grow wild among the ruins, their roots breaking through temple floors where pharaohs once worshipped.

"Where are we?" Paulinus asks.

"Thebes," Titus replies, his eyes scanning the familiar landmarks.

"Have you been here before?"

"Unfortunately, yes."

As they round a bend in the river, the Temple of Thebes towers above the water, its pylon gates flanked by seated statues of pharaohs that dwarf even the tallest trees. Beyond the gates, rows of sandstone columns march into the temple's depths like an army of stone giants, each one wide enough to hide a dozen men.

Titus stares at the temple, his gaze drawn to the dark space between the massive columns. For a moment, he hears something. A whisper that seems to come from inside his own mind, speaking in a language he doesn't recognize but somehow understands. The voice of Anubis, beckoning him towards the temple.

Pliny interrupts, breaking Titus out of his trance.

"Titus, just let me take a quick look at the temple. I'll quickly transcribe the hieroglyphics, and we can continue."

"No, Pliny. It would take an act of the gods to make me enter that temple."

Suddenly, a strange sound reaches them from the south. A distant roar like wind and shifting earth growing steadily louder. The air begins to taste of dust and electricity. Paulinus turns towards the noise and furrows his brow.

"What is that?"

Sextus peers over the boat's edge, his eyes widen with recognition.

"Sandstorm!" he yells.

Everyone on board scrambles to their feet. On the southern horizon, a wall of sand rises like a tidal wave of earth, stretching from ground to sky in a curtain of brown fury. The storm advances with terrifying speed, swallowing the landscape as it approaches. Kashta shouts over the growing wind.

"We must find shelter. Dock the boat!"

Titus and Paulinus begin paddling frantically toward shore. The storm towers towards them now, blotting out the sun and turning day to twilight.

"Row like your lives depend on it!" Sextus commands.

They reach the muddy bank as the first gusts of wind-driven sand begin to sting their faces. The guards start gathering supplies from the boat.

"Leave it! Run!" Sextus shouts.

They leap from the vessel and sprint toward the temple, the only substantial shelter visible. Behind them, the sandstorm's roar grows deafening.

"Get to the temple!" Sextus commands.

"No, we can't enter!" Titus protests, even as he runs.

"We have no choice!" Paulinus shouts back.

They race across the sandy ground toward the temple entrance, the storm's leading edge beginning to overtake them. Titus notices something wrong with the ground ahead.

"Watch where you're running! Don't step on the wet sand!"

Pliny suddenly plunges knee-deep into what appears to be solid ground, his momentum carrying him forward into the trap.

"Help! I'm stuck!"

"It's quicksand!" Titus shouts, grabbing Pliny's arms.

"Help, I'm sinking!"

"Don't struggle or you'll sink faster," Titus warns, pulling with all his strength.

The sandstorm bears down on them, only moments away. Sextus sees the approaching wall of destruction.

"Abandon him! We must reach shelter!"

The Praetorians sprint towards the temple. Pliny looks back at the approaching wall of sand and then back at Titus.

"Go, Titus. Leave me."

Suddenly Paulinus grabs Pliny's other arm.

"Go limp, Pliny," Titus yells.

Pliny goes limp as they heave him out of the quicksand with a wet reluctant sound, the three men falling onto the sand. They scramble to their feet and sprint towards the entrance of the temple. Sand fills the air, stinging exposed skin and choking breath from lungs.

They reach the temple entrance as the sandstorm's full force arrives, throwing themselves through the massive doorway and slamming the ancient doors shut just as the desert's wrath engulfs the world outside.

In the sudden darkness of the temple's interior, they huddle together while the storm rages beyond the stone walls, their breathing heavy with exertion and fear. Before them stretches a vast darkness, broken only by thin blades of light cutting through wall cracks. The dim illumination reveals hieroglyphics crawling across every surface. Titus turns to the group.

"Not one step further. We wait here until the storm passes, then we leave immediately."

Kashta closes his eyes and begins chanting in his native tongue, his hands moving in protective gestures as ancient as the temple itself. Sextus eyes the Kushite guide with suspicion.

"What's he saying?"

Pliny begins translating Kashta's ritual.

"He's warding off the spirits of the temple. He says they're trying to lure us deeper into the temple's heart to consume us."

Paulinus raises his eyebrows.

"Well, I don’t feel like getting consumed. Why don't we just remain here until the storm passes?"

"Indeed," Titus agrees, though his eyes keep drifting toward the dark corridors that branch off from the entrance hall. Quintus approaches one wall, studying the intricate carvings with a soldier's practical curiosity.

"What do these markings mean?"

Pliny moves closer to examine the hieroglyphs and opens The Book of the Dead to translate them.

"These inscriptions describe the temple as a dwelling place of Amun-Ra, where the god's ka resides in physical form. The priests believed the temple's architecture itself was designed to channel divine energy through specific pathways. These corridors aren't just hallways, they're conduits for power that flows from the inner sanctum like blood through arteries."

Quintus, fidgeting with impatience during the lecture, runs his fingers along the hieroglyphs until he encounters a stone that yields slightly beneath his touch.

"Don't touch anything!" Pliny's warning comes a heartbeat too late.

The stone depresses into the wall with a soft click, then begins moving of its own accord, sliding deeper into the ancient masonry. The sound of mechanical gears begins. The entire temple begins to shake. Dust falls from the ceiling like snow while the walls themselves groan with the sound of bronze wheels turning.

"The walls!" Paulinus shouts.

The corridor walls begin closing inward. The space between them shrinks steadily, promising to crush anyone caught within.

“Run!" Titus commands.

They sprint down the narrowing corridor, sandals slapping against worn limestone as ancient gears grind behind them like the teeth of some colossal beast. Dust billows in choking clouds as the walls continue to close in.

Kashta stumbles and sprawls face-down on the stone floor. Titus skids to a halt, his sweat-soaked tunic clinging to his back. He seizes Kashta's forearm and hauls the Kushite upright. Together they dive through the narrowing gap just as the massive walls slam together with a thunderous boom that reverberates through the temple's chambers.

Titus stands and looks around, his heart pounding from the close escape. They find themselves in a circular chamber lit by shafts of light from hidden openings high above. The room stretches about fifty feet across, with multiple corridors branching off in different directions like spokes on a wheel. Hieroglyphic inscriptions cover the curved walls, depicting scenes of Anubis carrying souls to the underworld. Suddenly a new mechanical sound of turning gears fills the chamber.

"Now what?" Paulinus asks.

The floor begins opening in the centre of the chamber, ancient stone sections grinding apart to reveal a circular pit. From the pit rises the unmistakable sound of hundreds of scales rasping against stone and each other. A dry, papery susurration punctuated by venomous hisses. Cobras, asps, and vipers of every Egyptian variety writhe below, fangs dripping with milky poison as they twist around each other in a living knot of death.

The floor continues its mechanical transformation, triangular stone sections sliding outward toward the walls like the petals of some monstrous lotus blossom. Paulinus feels his section tilt precipitously and scrambles for purchase as his sandaled feet slip toward the snake pit. He falls but manages to catch the crumbling edge with white-knuckled fingers, his body dangling mere feet above the undulating mass of serpents. A cobra rises up, its hood flaring wide, obsidian eyes fixed on his exposed ankles.

"Titus!" Paulinus shouts.

Titus immediately drops to his knees and grabs Paulinus's arms, pulling with all his strength. But the floor sections continue their inexorable movement, and soon there will be no edge left to grip.

"Pliny!" Titus calls.

The scholar leaps across the widening gap to their side of the chamber and adds his strength to the rescue effort. Together they haul Paulinus up just as his handhold crumbles away.

Now the chamber floor exists in two halves separated by a twenty-foot chasm filled with writhing death. Sextus, Marcus, Quintus, and Kashta stand on one side, while Titus, Pliny, and Paulinus occupy the other. The central pit continues to widen, forcing each group to choose a different corridor through the ancient maze.

"We'll find another way around," Titus calls across the pit.

"As will we," Sextus replies, though his expression suggests he sees opportunity in their separation.

Both groups turn toward their respective corridors, the temple's ancient designers having achieved their purpose. Separating intruders, forcing them deeper into the sacred space.

Titus, Pliny, and Paulinus inch forward through the narrow stone corridor, each footfall releasing puffs of ochre dust that hang suspended in the stale air like ancient ghosts. The stone walls, loom no more than an arm's span apart, every surface crowded with hieroglyphs. Falcon-headed deities and ankh symbols that appear to undulate in the wavering light that filters through hairline cracks in the ceiling.

"Watch your step. Don't touch anything. Look for an exit," Titus says.

A whisper echoes through the stone passage, seeming to come from within the walls themselves. The whispering voice of Anubis.

"*You are leading them to Amun-Ra, Titus. Soon we will be united in the Duat.*"

Titus freezes mid-step. "Did you hear that?"

"Hear what?" Paulinus asks, his eyes darting nervously between the shadows.

Titus shakes his head, unsure if the voice exists outside his own mind. The passage narrows further, forcing them to turn sideways to continue, their shoulders scraping against limestone. The air grows thicker with each step, laden with the scent of natron, the ancient preservatives of mummification. The walls depict the jackal-headed Anubis bringing the dead to the underworld.

“I hear whispering,” Paulinus says.

“I hear it too. Someone calling themselves Anubis has been whispering to me since Memphis,” Titus responds.

“What’s he saying?” Pliny asks.

“He speaks of someone called ‘Amun-Ra’. What do you know of him?”

Pliny opens the Book of the Dead.

"According to ancient texts, Amun-Ra was the supreme deity of ancient Egypt during the New Kingdom around 1600 years ago. When his earthly reign ended, Anubis mummified his body but preserved his ka—his spiritual essence—within these walls. The book claim he remains conscious, luring souls into his temple to harvest their life force until he grows strong enough to rule again."

"Well, at least he couldn't be worse than Nero," Paulinus mutters.

The floor beneath their feet suddenly fractures with a sound like breaking pottery. They slide down stone a chute through absolute darkness, bodies scraping against ancient stone that feels cold as a tomb and smooth as oiled marble. The descent seems endless until they crash onto the unyielding granite floor of a vast chamber below, the impact driving the breath from their lungs in pained gasps.

They stand and look around in awe and horror. The room stretches nearly a hundred feet in each direction, its ceiling supported by massive columns carved to resemble palm trees. At the chamber's far end, against the wall, stands a sarcophagus of impossible proportions. Designed for a being thrice the height of any mortal man. The golden surface gleams with inlaid jewels that catch what little light penetrates the sacred space.

Lining both walls, leading toward the giant sarcophagus like an honour guard, stand rows of human-sized sarcophagi. Each one bears the image of a warrior in ancient Egyptian armour, their painted faces stern with eternal vigilance.

The massive sarcophagus vibrates, sending dust cascading from its seams. A voice emerges, deep and powerful, speaking perfect Latin:

"Welcome, Titus Statilius Taurus V. I have waited centuries for a soul of your quality. The ka of a warrior who has faced death and survived, who carries the weight of command. Such essence will provide the strength I need to become whole and reclaim my divine throne.

"Who are you?"

"I am Amun-Ra, King of Gods, Lord of Karnak, He Who is Hidden and Yet Revealed in the Sun's Glory."

"We mean you no harm. We're merely taking shelter from a storm. We wish to leave in peace."

"You speak of peace while you conquer and rename everything you touch. You stand in my temple, built when your ancestors were still painting themselves blue and worshipping trees, and speak of peace. You should have heeded the warnings carved at my threshold and never entered this sacred place."

"I need no warnings from dead gods. Your time has passed. Egypt belongs to Rome now."

"Tell me, Roman, when Anubis guided you through Memphis, did that feel like the touch of dead gods? We do not die, Titus. We merely wait. Egypt has risen and fallen and risen again across three thousand years. Rome is an infant playing with weapons it doesn't understand."

"What do you want from me?"

"I offer you what no mortal has been offered in a thousand years. Fall upon your sword. Surrender your ka willingly, and I will preserve your consciousness within mine. Together we shall rule, not as god and servant, but as merged divinity."

"I don't seek transcendence or divinity. I only want to return to Rome, to complete my mission and serve my Empire."

"The Empire you claim to serve sent your father to his death. The same is Empire ruled by a mad boy who thinks himself an artist while Rome crumbles. What has the Empire brought you other than death and suffering. You would serve that rather than become a god?"

"I serve my empire for one reason alone. It is where my family has the opportunity to live peacefully.

"Then you have made your choice. If you will not surrender your essence willingly, I will take it by force."

Paulinus draws his gladius, the blade ringing as it clears the scabbard.

"First you'll have to get through me."

"I won't need to. My eternal guardians will handle that task. They have waited sixteen centuries for fresh meat."

The sarcophagi lining the walls snap open all at once, revealing the desiccated remains of royal guards wrapped in yellowed linen that crumbles at the edges. Their hollow eye sockets seem to follow the living. But worse than these preserved corpses is what pours from the opened tombs. A living carpet of iridescent blue-black scarabs and bone-white scorpions with stingers raised like tiny spears. Their chittering bodies flow across the stone floor like a tide of death, the clicking of thousands of legs echoing off the walls in a sound like rattling bones.

Titus feels the floor vibrate as they approach. Just as the first wave reaches within arm's length of the three Romans, a thunderous crack splits the air. A section of wall explodes inward in a cloud of limestone dust and debris, crushing dozens of the creatures beneath jagged chunks of falling stone. Their bodies burst with sickly yellow fluid.

Sextus appears through the breach, his face streaked with dirt and sweat, wielding a flaming torch that he sweeps back and forth. The insects retreat from the fire as he shouts, his voice hoarse with urgency.

"We found a way out! Go!"

Marcus and Quintus emerge behind him, adding their own torches to the defence as Titus, Pliny, and Paulinus sprint toward the opening.

"Move! Move! Move!" Sextus shouts, following close behind.

They enter a corridor with blessed daylight visible at its end. The voice of Amun-Ra follows them:

"Once you enter my temple, you may never leave!"

The walls begin closing with the same mechanical force they experienced before. Behind them, surviving scarabs and scorpions give chase, their legs clicking against stone. They sprint toward the opening as the corridor narrows around them, diving through the gap just as the walls slam shut.

They tumble into the harsh light, lungs heaving as they gulp the scorching desert air. Kashta waits outside, his face showing relief at seeing them emerge alive. The sandstorm has passed, leaving the landscape transformed. Dunes shifted like the ridges of a vast fingerprint, temple columns half-buried in fresh sand.

"Well, that was an eventful rest stop. Where to now?" Paulinus pants.

"We continue to Aswan. We'll rest and gather supplies there."

They trudge back toward their boat, each footfall sinking into sand still warm from the storm's fury. They board their vessel, the wood creaking beneath their weight as they push off from shore. As they sail away from the temple, Titus turns to Paulinus.

"In the temple, when the voices spoke to you, what did they whisper?"

"You don't want to know."

"Tell me."

Paulinus stares at the water flowing past their boat.

"Someone calling themselves Horus told me we should turn back to Rome and depart these lands."

"Why?"

"Because we're all going to die on this expedition."

Chapter 10
The Crucifixion of Peter

Rome, 64 AD. The Senate House echoes with unprecedented fury as six hundred senators rise from their marble benches, their white togas fluttering with rage. Voices blend into a cacophony of accusation and outrage that reverberates off the marble columns. At the chamber's centre, Nero stands alone, his imperial purple a defiant splash of colour amid the sea of senatorial white.

"Conscript Fathers, the new sect from Jerusalem has finally made their move. They sought to burn Rome to the ground in their fanatical hatred of our empire. Thankfully, I was able to organize efforts to contain the fire before greater damage occurred. Never fear, my vengeance upon these enemies will be merciless."

Senator Piso rises from his position among the senior members with fire in his eyes.

"Do you think us fools, Nero? We know it was you who set Rome ablaze!"

The chamber erupts in agreement, senators shouting their support for Piso's bold accusation. Nero calmly motions for the screaming senators to sit back down.

"Trust me, Piso. It was the Christians who committed this atrocity, and I shall deal with them personally. But look on the bright side, at least I now have the space needed to build the Domus Aurea."

"You must have truly descended into madness if you think you'll escape consequences for this act. The people of Rome will not stand for such tyranny. I will not stand for it!"

"You've always been as boorish as you are boring, Piso. Now If you'll excuse me, I'm going to treat the Roman people to a performance from their Emperor at the Neronia festival."

"Now you abdicate your duties when Rome lies in ashes and the provinces collapse without leadership? You will not destroy this eternal city. I will not permit it!"

"I suggest you attend my performance, Piso. A man of your proclivities could benefit from some culture in his life."

"A man like you could benefit from accepting responsibility, son of Agrippina. Being Emperor isn't about winning popularity through songs and spectacles. You are accountable for ensuring Roman lives don't fall to ruin under your rule!"

"I'll see you at the amphitheatre then."

"You burned the amphitheatre down in your fire."

Nero pauses, eyes darting side to side before he smiles.

"Well then, I shall see you at the Theatre of Pompey."

"No, you won't. Someone must remain here to ensure Rome doesn't crumble while you chase applause. Someone must attend to the thousands left homeless by your flames. Someone must correspond with provincial governors who receive no guidance from their Emperor." Piso turns to address his fellow senators. "While our emperor fiddles, Rome requires leadership. We have work to do, Conscript Fathers. The people depend on us now more than ever."

Murmurs of agreement ripple through the assembled senators.

"Nero's empire may be crumbling," Piso continues, "but the principles that built Rome endure in those willing to serve something greater than themselves. Let the Emperor have his songs and games. We have an empire to govern."

Nero's eyes narrow to slits as he watches Piso gain the attention and approval of the Senate.

"You forget yourself, Piso. You forget who rules this empire."

"Do I? Tell me then, Caesar, what have you ruled these past months besides your own grief? While you wallowed in self-pity, who maintained the grain shipments from Egypt? Who negotiated with the Germanic tribes pressing our northern borders?"

“The glory of Rome isn't measured in ledgers and cargo manifests, my dear senator. Rome is the greatest empire because we are the greatest artists. The best sculptors, the best architects, the best painters, the best musicians, the best poets. Rome is a stage and I am her greatest performer.”

“The citizens of Rome are not going to care about your dammed poetry when they are starving to death!”

“The citizens of Rome will be proud to have lived in the greatest empire there ever was or will be, not that I would expect someone of your faculties to understand. Perhaps you should attend my performance. It might elevate that provincial mind of yours beyond ledgers and grain counts.”

Nero turns to exit the chamber, his footsteps echoing hollowly on marble floors, Piso remains standing in the centre of the chamber. He calls out to the other senators, his voice carrying the authority of a man who has served Rome longer than their emperor has drawn breath.

"Conscript Fathers, we convene in emergency session. The city burns, the provinces starve, and our Emperor retreats to his theatre. If Caesar will not govern, then we must."

The bronze doors slam shut behind Nero with a sound like thunder, leaving the six hundred senators alone in their marble sanctuary.

Nero prepares to walk on the stage in the vast stone semicircle in the Pompey Theatre. A place where the greatest performers of the empire have sought immortality through their art. Seneca’s nephew Lucan, an aspiring Roman poet, finishes Nero’s warm-up act. He walks off the stage to half enthusiastic applause. Nero does not acknowledge him as he takes the stage to thunderous applause.

Nero stands at the theatre's centre. Light dances across the strings of his lyre while his imperial robes cascade around his form, a waterfall of regal purple. The crowd falls silent in anticipation, twenty thousand faces turned toward their Emperor who has chosen to entertain rather than govern. Nero's voice carries effortlessly to the highest tiers, trained by years of performance.

"Citizens of Rome, tonight I offer you not laws or taxes, but beauty itself. The divine gift of art that elevates the soul above mortal concerns."

The first notes emerge from beneath his fingers. Murmurs ripple through the audience; those who came to mock find themselves silenced by genuine artistry. Nero begins reciting his poetry:

"Behold, how flames danced through eternal streets,
Like golden serpents writhing through the night,
Consuming all that age and pride completes,
Yet birthing beauty in their sacred light.
I watched from marble halls as fire wrote,
New stories on the city's ancient face,
Each ember like a star, each spark a note
In symphony that time cannot erase.
What was must die that what will be might live,
The phoenix knows this truth that mortals fear:
Destruction is the gift that gods can give
To make the future crystal pure and clear.
So let the old Rome burn in memory,
While new Rome rises in divinity."

The crowd erupts in thunderous applause, their voices raised in appreciation for an Emperor who shares his artistic gifts with the citizenry. Nero basks in their adoration, his face glowing with the satisfaction of a performer who has found his perfect audience.

The applause continues for long minutes, washing over him like a tide of validation. This is what ruling should feel like. Not the tedious burden of governance, but the pure joy of artistic expression shared between artist and audience. Then, cutting through the celebration like a blade, a voice calls out from the crowd:

"Christ is King!"

The theatre falls silent. Nero's expression transforms from joy to fury in an instant, his eyes scanning the assembled masses with dangerous intensity. His voice carries clearly in the sudden quiet.

"Who said that? Who dares interrupt imperial performance with such insolence?"

The crowd divides, leaving a solitary figure exposed at the centre of the theatre. A man stands there, neither young nor old, wearing a tunic frayed at the edges. While others shrink back, he remains upright, his steady gaze locked with Nero's, as though emperor and labourer were equals meeting on common ground.

"And who might you be?" Nero asks.

"My name is Peter. You burnt down my church."

"Ah yes, you were one of the companions of that carpenter from Nazareth. Unfortunately, I am somewhat disposed with artistic matters at the moment. Won't you join me at my palace later. We have much to discuss."

Nero turns and strides from the stage in a storm of fury, his fists clenched at this side. His robes billow behind him as he disappears into the shadows beyond the performance area, leaving twenty thousand Romans staring at the solitary figure who had dared to challenge their Emperor.

Later that evening, Nero enters the marble corridors of his palace, his fists still clenched in anger. Sabina, now seven months pregnant with Nero's second child, waits in the atrium. She rises to greet him, her swollen belly preceding her movement. Her face, once the radiant visage that captured Nero's heart, now carries shadows beneath her eyes and a certain wariness in her gaze.

"How was your performance, my Emperor?"

Nero walks past without acknowledging her, still furious over Peter's interruption. Her hands tremble as they cradle her swollen belly, tears welling in her eyes.

"You barely acknowledge me anymore. I carry your child again. Soon you will have a new heir."

Nero's stops in his tracks, he turns around and looks down at her with disdain.

"How do I know you won't let this child die as well? What is the point of having children if you cannot even keep them alive?"

She begins to weep.

"Do you think it doesn't pain me? I miss Claudia too."

Nero's eyes flash red.

"Do not speak her name!'

His hand lashes out, fingers clamping around Sabina's trembling arm with bruising force. With a savage jerk, he hurls her to the ground, her slight frame collapsing against the cold, unyielding marble. Sabina cries out, a sharp, desperate sound that echoes off the gilded walls, her hands instinctively clutching her swollen belly as she crumples.

She struggles to rise, her breath hitching in pain, but Nero's foot finds her side before she can. The first strike is brutal, a sickening thud that drives the air from her lungs. He kicks again, and again, each blow harder and faster. His face is a storm of torment, his veins bulging from his neck.

Sabina's cries grow faint, her voice fracturing into soft, broken whimpers. Her hands, once protective over her unborn child, fall limp, blood seeping from her lips to stain the pristine marble beneath her. The crimson pool spreads, slow and relentless, as her body stills, her lifeless form curled as if to shield the child she carries. The atrium, once alive with the soft trickle of the fountain, now holds only the weight of silence and death.

Seneca enters to find Nero standing over the bloodied corpse of his pregnant wife. His face shows signs of horror despite years of witnessing imperial cruelty. He stops his lip from trembling and regains his composure.

"Peter is here to see you," Seneca manages.

"Who?" Nero replies casually, as if nothing had just happened.

"The man who was building the church where you started the fi... I mean, the man from the theatre."

"Ah yes. Send him in."

Peter steps into the atrium, his simple tunic stark against the opulence of the palace. His eyes, wide with a quiet intensity, sweep the room and freeze on the grim tableau before him. Sabina's lifeless body lies sprawled across the marble, her blood pooling in the crevices of the intricate mosaic. Nero gestures casually at his pregnant wife's corpse as if it's a trivial inconvenience.

"Welcome, Peter. My apologies for the mess. I haven't yet had time to tidy."

Peter stands still, mouth agape at the horror, but remaining stoic. Nero clicks his fingers, signalling Tigellinus to remove the body, leaving a dark stain on the marble floor. As he passes, Peter makes the sign of the cross. Nero cocks his head in intrigue.

"What is that gesture you've just performed with your hands?"

"It is the sign of the cross. A blessing from God."

"You emulate the method used to torture as a way of blessing people? Your sect truly is bizarre."

"I wouldn't expect someone like you to understand the will of God."

Nero circles Peter like a predator studying prey.

"God? Tell me, Peter, what power does this God possess compared to Jupiter, who commands thunder? What wisdom compared to Minerva, who guides empires? What strength compared to Mars, who grants victory in battle?"

"My God created thunder, wisdom, and strength itself," Peter begins. "Your gods are made of stone and gold, fashioned by human hands. My God fashioned humanity itself."

"That stone and gold you dismiss has built the greatest empire in history. My empire. Your carpenter built nothing but flimsy wooden chairs."

"He built something your empire cannot destroy. Hope for the hopeless, love for the loveless, forgiveness for the unforgivable."

"Hope? Love? Forgiveness? These are weaknesses that make men soft. Rome was built on strength, discipline, the will to conquer. Your carpenter preached submission to enemies."

"He preached victory over death itself. Your empire conquers lands that will one day be dust. My Lord conquered the grave that awaits every Emperor."

"And where was this mighty God when Roman soldiers nailed his son to wood? If he has such power, why did he not save him?"

"Because love sometimes chooses to suffer rather than to strike back. Because true strength lies not in the power to destroy, but in the choice to forgive."

"Riddles and mysticism. My gods give tangible rewards. Wealth, pleasure."

"And where has that gotten you, Caesar? You have all these things, yet you rage against people who preach forgiveness. You rule the empire, yet you fear a handful of believers who own nothing but their faith. Your gods promise you everything except the one thing you need. Peace."

Nero falls silent, Peter's words striking something deep. He stands tall, a look of intensity appears in his eyes, not of an artist, but of a soldier.

“Only a fool would ever think peace exists. The gods give me what I need. Victory against the one thing my empire is guaranteed. War.”

The two men stare intensely into each other's eyes before Nero smiles and begins walking towards the gardens.

"Walk with me, Peter."

They move through the palace into the garden where Palatine Hill overlooks Rome. Tigellinus waits beside a wooden cross prepared for this moment. Nero stands with his hands behind his back, observing the view of the city from the hill.

"I want you to do something for me, Peter. I want you to publicly renounce the carpenter. Your people still listen to you. There is no room in the empire for a sect who refuses to worship the Emperor."

Peter doesn't say a word. Nero continues.

"I will make you one of the richest men in Rome if you help us in this endeavour. I will make you a senator."

Peter looks at the cross and then back to Nero, understanding the threat.

"Although I walk in the shadow of the valley of death, I shall fear no evil."

Nero's voice drops to a whisper.

"If you speak in proverbs one more time, Peter, I will put a 100 denarius bounty on the head of anyone who mentions the carpenter's name."

Peter raises his chin.

"I'm afraid I love my God too much to bend the knee for anyone but him."

Nero's eyes flash red as he nods at Tigellinus.

"If you love your God so much, then you won't mind sharing the same fate as he did."

Peter looks at the cross without fear.

"I am not worthy of the same fate as the Son of God. If you must crucify me, do so upside down."

"So be it."

Tigellinus seizes Peter with rough hands. The Praetorian Guards drag him to the cross, its splintered surface scarred from past use. The ropes bite into Peter's wrists and ankles as they bind him, inverting his body as he requested, his head dangling toward the earth, his limbs stretched taut against the coarse wood. The soldiers drive iron nails through his flesh. First his hands, then his feet. Blood trickles from the wounds, pooling in the dirt below, staining the earth a dark, accusing red.

The cross is hoisted upside down, creaking under Peter's weight. His face flushes with the rush of blood to his head, his cheeks reddening as gravity pulls at his inverted form, yet his expression remains unshaken, his eyes fixed on some unseen horizon beyond the reach of pain or fear. The nails tear deeper into his flesh with every slight movement. His voice rises, clear and unwavering.

"Lord, forgive them, for they know not what they do."

Nero watches with ruthless gratification as blood pools underneath Peter's crucifix. He exhales with satisfaction.

"That will be the last church ever built in the name of Christ in Rome."

Nero walks back to his palace. He re-enters his atrium to find Seneca still standing where Sabina's body had lain, his face ashen.

"I shall need a new Empress. Summon Claudia Antonia. I do so love her name."

Seneca snaps out of his trance and composes himself.

"That may be inadvisable, my Emperor."

"And why is that?"

"You executed her husband some years ago."

Nero's smiles as if Seneca just told a joke.

"Summon her."

Dawn breaks over the imperial gardens, where Peter's inverted form stands crucified in the manicured grounds. Nero watches from his chamber window, fingers tapping against the marble sill. The door creaks behind him. Seneca's reflection appears in the polished glass, face drawn with fatigue. A woman's silhouette follows. Claudia Antonia, Nero's estranged stepsister.

"Caesar, Lady Claudia Antonia, as you requested."

Nero turns from the window, studying the woman with calculating eyes. She stands with dignity despite the circumstances that have brought her here. Nero approaches her with the confidence of absolute power.

"Claudia Antonia, I offer you the honour of becoming my Empress, to share in the glory of ruling the greatest empire in history."

"I must respectfully decline, Caesar."

Her response comes without hesitation. Nero's expression darkens instantly.

"You refuse to do your duty for the empire? This constitutes an act of rebellion."

Claudia's eyes blaze with fire.

“Your mother killed my father and my brother. You killed my sister and my husband. The only worthwhile thing you ever accomplished in your life was sending your mother to Hades. I would rather be fed to a Nile crocodile than take your hand in marriage, even if it made me the richest Empress in Roman history. “

Nero, stunned and silent, slowly turns to Seneca.

"Charge her with rebellion and execute her for treason."

Seneca hesitates, his eyes darting side to side as he appears to be considering a line of argument.

"I grow increasingly suspicious of you, Seneca. First you appear to side with Piso, now this rebel. I begin to wonder where your loyalties truly lie."

"My loyalties are with you, my Emperor, for the glory of your empire. I seek only to counsel you as best I can."

"Your counsel is noted, Seneca. Now have this rebel executed. And bring me my mistresses. I shall choose one to be my new Empress."

"At once, my Emperor."

Seneca nods to the guards, who grasp Claudia's elbows with iron fingers, dragging her from the chamber as she spits curses that would make a sailor blush.

Shortly after, he returns with the Emperor’s mistresses, each one beautiful and refined, arranged like jewels on display. Their eyes, though downcast in practiced submission, dart sideways to assess rivals, each woman's spine stiffened by the knowledge that they may be named Empress.

Nero walks before them like a general inspecting troops, studying each face and form with the detached interest of a man selecting entertainment. He stops before Statilia Messalina, eyeing her up and down like a selection from the market.

"This one will do, I suppose."

"I live to serve the Emperor."

Messalina eyes still fix on the marble tiles. Nero circles her like a predator.

"General Taurus is your brother, is he not?"

"Yes, Caesar."

"And you both spent your childhood years in Egypt?"

"Yes, Caesar."

"How exciting it will be for your brother when he returns from the Nile to discover his sister has become an Empress."

"Yes, Caesar. I eagerly await his return."

"Indeed. I wonder if they are still alive."

"Knowing Titus, almost certainly."

"I can only imagine what adventures Titus faces on the Nile."

Chapter 11
The Temple of Horus

The Nile flows broad and green-brown as the papyrus boat cuts through the ancient waters. Along both banks, the landscape unfolds in bands of vivid contrast. The narrow strips of impossibly fertile black soil, then the abrupt transition to golden desert sand that stretches endlessly toward horizons shimmering with heat. Palm trees cluster at the water's edge, their fronds rustling in the wind.

Pliny stands near the bow, a leather map case open in his hands. He studies the worn parchment, his fingers tracing the winding path of the river southward. His eyes flick between the map and the passing landscape, correlating the ancient cartographer's marks with the reality unfolding before him.

"Titus, the Temple of Horus lies in the town of Apollonopolis Magna. I know you will say no, but I must document it for my encyclopaedia. The architectural details, the inscriptions, the religious practices—"

"All right, Pliny. We'll go there," Titus interrupts calmly.

Pliny blinks, his prepared arguments dying unspoken on his lips.

"I thought you were going to say it was forbidden. After everything that's happened in Thebes."

"We were encouraged to visit the temple as children. The locals and my father both believed that Horus's blessing brought good fortune, protection in battle. My father was never a man to dismiss such things lightly, especially when serving in Egypt."

Paulinus looks between the two in shock.

"You can't be serious. Another temple? After what just happened in Thebes? Have the gods stripped you of your mind entirely?"

"Don't worry, Paulinus. This temple is different. Horus is the god of healing and protection. We will be safe there."

Paulinus raises his eyebrows, his expression caught between incredulity and contempt.

"Egyptian gods? Seriously? You don't actually believe all this nonsense, do you?"

"I know what I see with my own eyes, Paulinus. I've been to this temple with my father. Trust me, it is safe."

Sextus's whetstone makes a rhythmic scraping sounds as he sharpens his gladius.

"You better be right, Titus. Because if you fall into another pit of scarabs and scorpions, don't expect me to save you again."

As the boat approaches the Apollonoplis Magna dock, the usual bustling activity is conspicuously absent. No merchants call out their wares, no children play at the water's edge, no fishermen mend their nets. Instead, a line of armed men stands at the quay, perhaps thirty of them, local militia by the look of their mismatched equipment. The boat bumps against the dock and Titus disembarks to address the mob.

"What is the meaning of this?" he asks, his voice firm and authoritative.

The mob looks at each other in confusion. Kashta steps forward and translates Titus's question into the local dialect. A man steps forward from the militia's ranks, older than the others, his beard streaked with grey, a copper armband denoting his status as their leader. Kashta translates his message to the group.

"We heard what your party did in Alexandria and Memphis. We will not allow you to kill our people. We will not let you defile our sacred places."

Sextus moves forward immediately, flanked by Marcus and Quintus, their scarlet cloaks rustling in the desert breeze. He surveys the militia with a soldier's eye. Counting numbers, assessing capabilities, identifying weaknesses. They outnumber the Roman party five to one, but Sextus's expression shows no concern.

"To threaten a Roman soldier is to threaten the empire itself. If you lay one finger on any of us, I will summon an army from Rome that will raze this city to ash and salt the earth where it stood. Your children will grow up as slaves in distant provinces, and your names will be forgotten before the season turns."

The militia members shift nervously, spear points wavering. But their leader holds his ground, though sweat beads on his forehead despite the cooling evening air.

"We do not wish to harm you. We only wish to defend ourselves. We will give you the supplies you need. Bread, dried fish, water, whatever you require, but you will not enter our town. You will not bring your Roman violence to our streets."

He gestures, and several younger men throw bags of provisions toward the Romans, keeping their distance as if dealing with dangerous animals. The bags land in the dust between the two groups, a no-man's-land of mutual distrust.

"Leave Behdet now. Seek shelter elsewhere. There is the temple to the north, or the desert if you prefer. But you will not sleep within our walls."

Titus surveys the scene for a long moment. The frightened but determined militia, the bags of supplies in the dust, his own men bristling with indignation at this treatment. Finally, he turns to his companions.

"We will sleep tonight in the Temple of Horus, then."

"Titus—" Paulinus begins, but Titus cuts him off with a raised hand.

"We accept your terms. We will take the supplies and trouble your people no further."

The Romans gather the provisions, and with the militia watching their every move, they begin walking toward the massive stone structure visible in the distance, the Temple of Horus. Behind them, the militia remains at their posts, watching until the Romans disappear into the lengthening shadows, making sure these dangerous strangers truly leave their town in peace.

They arrive at the Temple of Horus as the sun begins its descent toward the western horizon, painting the massive stone structure in shades of gold and amber. Its entrance flanked by twin pylons that soar nearly a hundred feet into the air, their surfaces covered with enormous relief carvings of pharaohs smiting enemies and making offerings to falcon-headed deities.

Beyond the pylons, a massive courtyard opens up, surrounded by columns thick as ancient trees, each one crowned with capitals carved to resemble lotus blossoms and papyrus reeds. The hypostyle hall beyond is a forest of stone, its ceiling supported by columns so numerous they create a maze of shadows even in daylight.

They make camp in the inner courtyard. Bedrolls unfurled, a fire pit dug and ringed with stones scavenged from fallen masonry. Soon flames crackle and dance as they roast strips of goat meat on sharpened sticks. As night settles fully over the temple, the group gathers closer to the fire's warmth. Pliny turns to Kashta, who sits cross-legged on his bedroll.

"I've been studying my maps. The townspeople called this place Behdet, but every Greek cartographer marks it as Apollonopolis Magna. It's the same settlement. Why two completely different names?"

Kashta picks up a stick and prods the fire, sending sparks spiralling upward into the darkness.

"Because this town has always been called Behdet—'Place of Horus Behedty.' That name is older than your Republic, older than Athens. Three thousand years it's been called that. The Greeks renamed it Apollonopolis Magna after they rebranded Horus as Apollo."

"What do you mean, 'rebranded'?"

"The Greek Empire rebranded everything the Egyptian Empire built. They tried to make it seem like they created it themselves. Horus became Apollo. Amun became Zeus. Sobek became Poseidon. They took our gods, our stories, our wisdom, and simply changed the names." He pauses, looking around at the Romans who have all stopped eating to listen, their faces intent in the firelight. "But you Romans should know this pattern well. You copied the Greeks and rebranded it as your own."

Sextus drops the stick of meat he's been holding, his face flushing dark.

"Careful with that tongue, African. You're speaking of the empire."

Kashta shows no fear, meeting the soldier's anger with calm certainty.

"You rebranded Zeus as Jupiter. Poseidon as Neptune. Athena as Minerva. Aphrodite as Venus. The list goes on. I wonder if the Roman Empire even knows it is merely a second-hand copy of the Egyptian Empire, filtered through Greek interpretation."

Sextus laughs.

"Rome would never need to copy anyone. We are the greatest civilization in history. We conquered the world through our own strength and ingenuity."

Kashta points upward at the massive columns surrounding them.

"Look at the stone carvings on top of those pillars. The lotus capitals, the papyrus bundles. Have you seen their like before?"

The group follows his gesture, their eyes traveling up the columns to where elaborate capitals display carved lotus flowers and papyrus bundles, each petal and leaf rendered with mathematical precision in stone. Sextus squints at the stonework.

"Similar designs throughout Rome, I suppose. Standard architectural flourishes. I'm a soldier, not a stonemason."

"They're in Greece too," Kashta continues quietly. "In every major temple, every important building. And they're here, in Egypt, carved fifteen hundred years before Athens was even founded. The same designs. The same proportions. The same mathematical principles. It's not different civilizations creating similar art, Roman. It's the same civilization, changing its name each time it relocates."

Sextus leans forward, his expression caught between anger and curiosity.

"Then answer me this, Kushite. If Rome copied Greece, and Greece copied Egypt, where did the Egyptians get the idea from?"

Kashta motions to the walls that surrounds them.

"The answer to that question lies in the hieroglyphs."

The Praetorians turn their attention to the walls, where the firelight illuminates carved scenes of impossible grandeur. Beings of enormous stature descending from the sky in vessels that seem to burn with celestial fire, bending before pharaohs and presenting them with objects of mysterious purpose, teaching them secrets with gestures frozen in stone for eternity.

"Why do the empires keep collapsing?" Pliny asks.

"Look at a map, Roman, and you will see the pattern. Egyptian civilization sprang from the Nile Delta when this region was the most fertile land in the world. Then the temperature became hotter, the rains failed, and it started becoming desert. When Egypt collapsed, the civilization moved northwest to Athens, where the climate was more temperate. When the temperature became too hot there and the land less fertile, the civilization moved northwest again. To Rome, where it stands now."

A heavy silence falls over the group. Even the fire seems to burn more quietly.

"And if Rome collapses, where will the civilization go then?" Pliny asks.

"Take out a map and you will see."

Pliny retrieves his map case and unfurls a large parchment showing the known world. He spreads it near the fire where all can see.

"Draw a line from the Nile Delta to Athens to Rome," Kashta instructs. "It will be easy to predict the empire that will surpass Rome."

Pliny takes a piece of charcoal and carefully traces a line north-west from Egypt, through Greece, through Rome, and then continuing further northwest across the map. The line extends beyond Rome's current territories, pointing inexorably toward lands still considered barbaric and wild. The group leans forward, following the line to its terminus.

"Britannia," Titus says quietly.

Kashta nods slowly.

"When the farmlands in the Roman Empire become drier and less productive, Britannia will emerge as the next great empire. Then you will begin to see the same columns built there that you see now littered across the ruins of Egypt, Greece, and Rome. The pattern continues. The civilization moves. Only the names change."

Sextus's voice cracks like a whip, too loud in the confined space.

"Rome is eternal! We are the greatest empire in history. We will never be so stupid as to collapse like the Greeks. We've learned from their mistakes. Roman discipline, Roman law, Roman engineering, these things are superior to anything that came before."

Kashta and Titus exchange a knowing look across the fire.

"Let's get some sleep," Titus says. “We depart at first light."

The group disperses to their bedrolls, but sleep is slow to come. Above them, the carved gods and giants watch from the walls with their ancient, knowing eyes. The fire has burned down to glowing embers that pulse with fading warmth. The night is deep and still, that dead hour before dawn when the world seems to hold its breath.

A voice cuts through Titus's dreams. Soft as silk, cold as winter wind. The familiar voice of Anubis.

"*Titus.*"

His eyes snap open as he jerks upright. He scans the camp to do a headcount. Everyone is sleeping and accounted for. But one bedroll lies empty. Sextus is gone.

Titus's gaze sweeps across the courtyard again, more carefully now, searching the pools of shadow between pillars. Then he sees a figure standing at the far end of the colonnade, silhouetted against the deeper darkness of an interior corridor. The jackal-headed profile of Anubis rendered in shadow. The figure turns and walks deeper into the temple.

Titus rises from his bedroll and follows the figure through the colonnade, past reliefs of offerings and processions carved in stone. The figure moving just beyond reach, always turning the next corner before he can catch up.

Finally, the passage opens into a chamber he doesn't remember seeing during their earlier exploration. The space is circular, its walls covered floor to ceiling with hieroglyphs. In the centre stands Anubis. Translucent, ethereal, his form flickering like heat shimmer above desert sand. His voice resonates not in the air but inside Titus's skull, bypassing his ears entirely.

"*The living world is a dream, Titus Statilius Taurus V. The Duat is where truth resides. Come. Walk with me through the weighing of souls. See what awaits all men who carry the weight of greatness in their hearts.*"

"Where is Sextus?"

Anubis extends one ethereal tendril, pointing toward another doorway that Titus is certain wasn't there a moment ago.

"He seeks communion with older powers. He opens doors that should remain sealed. Set hungers. And the hungry must be fed."

Titus doesn't remember moving, but suddenly he's running, his feet pounding against stone that feels simultaneously solid and insubstantial. He bursts through the doorway into another chamber, smaller, more claustrophobic. The walls here are painted blood-red, the pigment so fresh it seems wet. At the far end stands a massive statue of Set, the chaos god rendered in black stone. Standing directly before the statue, back turned, is Sextus.

"Sextus?" Titus's voice cracks.

But Sextus doesn't respond. Titus approaches slowly, tentatively reaching his arm out.

"Sextus, what are you doing?"

Anubis glides into the chamber behind him, still in that ethereal state, his form casting no shadow despite the flickering torchlight that now illuminates the space, torches Titus doesn't remember being lit.

Titus reaches Sextus and places his hand on his shoulder. The flesh beneath the tunic feels wrong. Too hot, fever-burning, the muscle twitching with unnatural rhythm.

"Sextus, we need to leave this place. Come back to—"

Sextus turns.

But the face that pivots toward Titus is not the face of his companion. The features are Sextus's. The scarred jaw, the broken nose, the familiar planes and angles, but the expression is alien. The eyes have gone completely black, pupils dilated to consume all colour, and in their depths something ancient and vast moves like storm clouds. He holds two swords, one in each hand. When he speaks, his voice has split into layers. His own rough tones beneath, but riding above them something else, something that makes the torchlight flicker and the painted walls seem to pulse.

"I am Set, son of Nut, brother-slayer and storm-bringer! I am the red desert wind that strips flesh from bone. I am the strength of Ra himself, the violence that keeps the serpent at bay. The Kingship is mine by right of conquest!"

Sextus plunges both swords into Titus's chest.

Titus jerks awake from his bedroll. His hands fly to his chest, clawing at the tunic, expecting to feel the warm wetness of blood, the ragged holes where steel pierced flesh. But there's nothing. Just the rapid hammering of his heart against intact ribs, just the cold sweat that has soaked through his clothes and turned his skin clammy in the pre-dawn chill.

He looks around and sees that everyone else is half-packed, eager to leave an uncomfortable camp. Paulinus notices him stirring and glances over.

"Good morning, sleepyhead. Decided to join the living after all?"

Titus sits upright, his body stiff and aching as though he truly had been run through with steel.

"Why didn't you wake me?"

Paulinus hefts his pack onto his shoulder.

"We tried. Multiple times, in fact. You were in such a deep sleep that nothing could rouse you. Not shouting, not shaking, not Marcus threatening to dump water on your head. We genuinely thought you might be dead for a moment there."

Sextus runs a whetstone along the edge of his gladius.

"Unfortunately, we weren't so lucky. Now that you've had your beauty sleep, let's move. I'd rather not spend another night in this tomb."

Titus pushes himself to his feet, his eyes lingering on Sextus. The same man who seemed to plunge two swords into his chest mere moments ago. He turns to Kashta, who is rolling up his bedding.

"Where is the next port?"

"It's a day's travel to Aswan. We'll be able to rest there before attempting the First Cataract. After that, the river becomes... more complicated."

They gather their belongings and make their way through the temple complex, past the towering columns and eternal stone guardians, back toward the town and the river beyond. The morning sun has transformed the temple from a place of shadows and whispered nightmares into merely another ancient ruin.

At the harbour, the militia remains at their posts, a wall of bronze-tipped spears and suspicious eyes blocking access to the town proper. The citizens of Behdet have no intention of lowering their guard until these dangerous Romans are well and truly gone. As the expedition passes, Marcus and Quintus offer mocking salutes. Hands raised in exaggerated formal gestures, followed by barks of laughter. Marcus makes an obscene gesture. Quintus shouts something about Egyptian hospitality.

They board their vessel, and the crew pushes off. The Temple of Horus recedes behind them, growing smaller with distance until it becomes just another cluster of stone columns against the endless Egyptian sky.

Titus positions himself near the stern, ostensibly watching their wake but actually maintaining a clear view of the entire deck. His eyes track Sextus, who has claimed a spot near the bow where he can feel the wind and watch the river ahead. There's nothing unusual in the way he moves. The same confident stride, the same casual awareness of his surroundings, the same occasional glances back to check on his men. But Titus can't shake the memory of those black eyes, the feeling of steel punching through his ribs. Kashta materializes beside Titus, silent as shadow.

"You did not sleep well."

Titus turns to look at him fully.

"Have you ever had a dream that seemed too real to not be true?"

"The ancients believed that the gods communicated to mortals through dreams. The wiser men understood to heed their warnings."

Titus looks back at Sextus, watching him laugh at something Marcus has said, watching him clap Quintus on the shoulder with easy camaraderie. Just a dream, Titus tells himself again. Just a dream. But for a brief moment, just as Sextus makes eye contact across the ship, Titus is sure he sees his eyes flash a familiar shade of black.

Chapter 12
The Pissonian Conspiracy

Rome, 65 AD. Where fire had devoured the heart of the eternal city, the construction site of Nero's Golden House now rises from the ashes. In the merciless afternoon sun, dozens labour beneath gleaming scaffolding. Slaves bent double under stone blocks, artisans embedding tiny coloured tiles into future floors, and engineers shouting orders as they assemble the mechanisms for dining rooms that will rotate like the rings of Saturn.

Nero strides through the controlled chaos with keen interest, his imperial robes flowing as he gestures toward various architectural marvels taking shape around him. His eyes shine with the vision of completed grandeur that exists only in his mind. A group of engineers and architects accompany him, scribbling down his every word.

"This shall be the greatest domicile ever constructed in the history of the empire. It will be the beginning of my grand architectural revival. I shall be remembered not merely as Rome's greatest artist, but also as its greatest architect."

A man runs toward them across the construction site, his face flushed with panic and exertion. His naval uniform marks him as an officer, though his dishevelled appearance suggests urgent news.

"Emperor! Emperor!" he calls out.

Tigellinus steps forward like a living shield, fingers curling around his sword hilt as he positions himself between Nero and this breathless intruder. Nero tears his attention from architectural plans at this unexpected interruption.

"Who are you?"

"My name is Volusius Proculus. I command a fleet in your navy. I must tell you something of utmost urgency."

"I don't have time to deal with naval tribulations at the moment," Nero replies dismissively, beginning to turn back toward his architectural wonders.

"Senator Piso conspires to assassinate you!"

Nero stops in his tracks, his entire demeanour shifting from artistic contemplation to predatory focus as he approaches Proculus.

"What did you say?"

"Senator Piso conspires with others to make himself Emperor. They plan your death."

"How do you know this?"

Proculus catches his breath.

"A freedwoman named Epicharis approached me, trying to recruit my fleet to join the assassination plot. She spoke of multiple conspirators, of detailed plans, of timing and methods."

"Tell me everything you know."

"That's all I learned, my Emperor. I refused her immediately and came here as quickly as possible to warn you."

Nero studies the naval officer's face, searching for any trace of deception.

"If what you say proves true, you will be greatly rewarded. Thank you for your loyalty to the empire."

He turns to Epaphroditus, who has been recording architectural notes but now stands ready for imperial commands.

"Find this Epicharis. I should very much like to have a conversation with her. Bring her to the Tullianum."

Epaphroditus bows and hurries away to execute the order, while Nero remains standing among the rising walls of his golden palace.

The Tullianum squats beneath the Capitoline Hill. Built from massive blocks of volcanic tufa, the prison consists of two chambers carved directly into the rock. The upper level where prisoners await judgment, and the lower dungeon where Rome's enemies face their final hours. A narrow opening in the floor connects the chambers, through which condemned souls are lowered into darkness that has swallowed senators, kings, and rebels alike.

Nero descends the stone steps into the lower chamber with Seneca, his imperial robes incongruous in this dark, damp prison. Epicharis lies bound to an interrogation rack, surrounded by Praetorian Guards. Despite her restraints, her eyes burn with defiance that no amount of imperial power has yet managed to extinguish. Nero nods to her with false courtesy.

"Hello, Epicharis. I hope I'm not interrupting anything important."

She spits at him, though the gesture falls short and lands on the stone floor between them.

"How uncivilized."

Nero nods at the guard by the wheel. The man grunts and turns the handle, the ropes creaking as they tighten. Epicharis's body elongates against her will, joints straining beyond their design. A scream rips from her throat, raw and piercing, echoing off the stone walls. Her fingers claw at the air, her face contorting in agony as the rack stretches her joints to the brink.

Nero lifts a hand, and the guard stops. Epicharis gasps, her chest shuddering as she fights to regain her breath.

"Unfortunately, my dear, Proculus told us about your plans. Your conspiracy to make Piso emperor. Tell us your co-conspirators and we can end this unpleasantness."

"I have no idea what you're talking about," she gasps.

Nero's smile tightens. He nods again. The wheel turns, slower this time, each click of the mechanism drawing out her torment. Her scream is guttural, her body arching against the ropes as her joints strain, the sinews in her arms and legs trembling under the pressure. The guards watch, unmoving, their faces betraying nothing.

Nero raises a hand, and the stretching halts. Epicharis slumps, panting, sweat dripping from her brow onto the rack.

"We can continue this indefinitely. Why put yourself through such torment? Simply provide the names of your fellow conspirators and this will end. You might even face mere exile rather than death."

"If I had any information to give you, I would. I have nothing to say."

"So Proculus is lying for no apparent reason?"

"Maybe he just wants to make you paranoid about shadows."

“I wish I could believe you.”

He nods sharply at the guard. The wheel turns again, faster now, the ropes groaning as they pull her body taut. Her scream is deafening, a raw, animal sound that claws at the air. Her fingers curl into fists, nails digging into her palms, drawing blood that trickles down her wrists. The guards remain still, their eyes fixed on Nero, awaiting his next command.

Seneca stands in the shadows, his expression showing how unaccustomed the philosopher is to this level of brutality. Nero turns to address him.

"She is the mistress of one of your brothers, is that correct, Seneca?"

"That is correct, my Emperor."

"Do you have reason to distrust her testimony?"

"In my experience, Caesar, loyalty and betrayal often wear identical faces until the moment of crisis reveals their true nature."

Nero studies his former tutor for a long moment, reading the philosopher's face for any sign of deception.

“Perhaps you are working with her."

Seneca chooses his words with the careful calculation of a man walking across thin ice.

"Of course not, my Emperor. My loyalty belongs to you and to Rome itself."

Nero continues to study Seneca and then nods to the guards to continue their work. Despite the prolonged interrogation, Epicharis refuses to provide any information about co-conspirators, her silence as unbreakable as the stone walls that surround them. Nero taps his foot in evident boredom, then motions for the guards to stop.

"I grow weary of these surroundings. I'm certain she will eventually crack, so continue the questioning, but I would much prefer to conduct this business in the comfort of my own palace. Have her transported to my residence. I shall meet you there."

With that dismissal, the Emperor strides from the Tullianum, leaving behind the echoing sounds of an interrogation that shows no signs of yielding the information he needs to identify his enemies.

Nero strides through the marble corridors of his palace as he returns from the Tullianum. The contrast between the prison's dank depths and his golden residence feels stark. Here, sunlight streams through tall windows, illuminating walls decorated with the finest art the empire can provide.

Messalina waits in the atrium, her beauty enhanced by silk robes and precious jewels that mark her status as Empress. She rises gracefully as he approaches, reading the tension in the room with the skill of a woman who has learned to navigate imperial moods.

"My dear wife. I have discovered something terrible."

"What troubles you?"

"Senator Piso seeks to assassinate me and make himself Emperor."

Messalina studies his face with careful attention.

"Are you certain you're not allowing paranoia to cloud your judgment?"

"Proculus brought me the information directly."

"What evidence did he provide?"

"He reported that Epicharis attempted to recruit him and his fleet for the conspiracy."

"Did you question Epicharis personally?"

"Yes. I had her interrogated in the Tullianum all afternoon."

"What did she reveal?"

"Nothing. She refused to speak."

Messalina's expression grows thoughtful.

"Then you cannot know anything with certainty?"

"I feel the truth of it in my bones. I know she will eventually tell me about the conspiracy. I'm having her brought here so we can continue the questioning in more comfortable surroundings."

"Make certain you extract the truth, my husband. Sometimes I fear your own suspicions may prove more dangerous to you than any actual conspiracy."

Nero's expression softens as he looks at her.

"Why couldn't my other wives possess your wisdom?"

Seneca enters the chamber and nervously clears his throat.

"My Emperor."

"Where is Epicharis?"

"There were... complications during transport."

Two Praetorian Guards drag in a lifeless form. Epicharis, her face pale and waxy, dark bruises visible around her throat. They deposit the body on the marble floor like a sack of meat.

"What happened?" Nero demands.

"She strangled herself with her girdle in the transport wagon."

"Strangled herself?"

Nero stares at the corpse in disbelief. He steps closer to Seneca, his eyes blazing with suspicion.

"Perhaps you ensured she died before she could reveal details of the conspiracy that might implicate you."

Seneca freezes in terror, understanding how quickly imperial favour can transform into mortal danger.

"Which of you was responsible for watching her?" Nero asks the guards.

One man steps forward reluctantly.

"I was, my Emperor. She was secured, but alone. I didn't anticipate she would be able to..."

"Tigellinus. Kill him." Nero calls to his Praetorian Prefect.

Without missing a beat, Tigellinus drives his sword through the guard's chest. The man crumples beside Epicharis's body, his blood pooling on the pristine marble floor. Nero looks down at the two corpses at his feet as if bored by them.

"What is next on my schedule?" he asks Seneca.

"The Senate is in session tomorrow morning. Senator Piso is delivering an address. Will you be attending?"

Nero smiles softly.

"I wouldn't miss that for the world." He turns to Tigellinus. "Assume there is indeed a conspiracy developing. Make all necessary preparations to thwart it before it gains momentum. Hopefully they'll prove foolish enough to expose themselves."

The next morning, the Senate house erupts with voices raised in anger and accusation. Nero stands silently at the chamber's edge, studying the scene through half-lidded eyes, as if watching actors perform a tedious play he's seen too many times before. Senator Piso stands at the chambers heart, his voice carrying to every corner of the vast chamber.

"You have neglected our military while barbarians press our borders! You have murdered members of your own family in fits of paranoid rage! You have alienated the very Senate that forms the backbone of Roman governance! The people will not stand for this tyranny!"

Nero steps forward, his voice cutting through the din with trained projection.

"I may have alienated you, Piso, but I possess something you never will. The genuine love of the Roman people."

"The people know it was you who set Rome ablaze. Do you think us all fools to be deceived by transparent lies?"

"It was the Christians who started the fire, Piso. But fear not, where ash now lies, I will build Rome's greatest architectural marvels."

"You're squandering the empire's entire treasury on lavish building projects while the outer provinces collapse into ruin! The Boudican revolt was merely the beginning. Other provinces will rise in rebellion if this fiscal madness continues!"

"Tell me, Piso, do you believe you would perform better as Emperor?"

"I think a stray dog from the streets would make a better Emperor than you."

The chamber freezes as if Medusa herself had entered. Six hundred senators who moments before had been a storm of motion and noise now stand silent. A stylus drops somewhere in the gallery, the tiny sound ricocheting off marble like a catapult stone. Every man present feels the temperature of the room plummet as they realise Piso has crossed a line.

Nero stands taller, his hand moving to the gladius at his side. With deliberate ceremony, he draws the blade and hurls it so that it clatters to the marble floor at Piso's feet.

"Then strike me down, Piso. Save Rome from my tyranny."

Piso stares at the weapon, then at Nero, his gaze shifting to the Praetorian Guards who stand ready to intervene.

"Spare me the theatrical performance, son of Agrippina. If I pick up your blade, your Praetorian lapdogs will cut me down before I can take a step."

"Guards, you are hereby ordered to allow Piso to strike me down, under penalty of death for interference."

The senators watch in stunned fascination as Piso continues staring at the Emperor, the blade lying between them like a bridge between the republic's past and the empire's future.

"What are you waiting for, Piso? This is your opportunity. Why not pick up that blade and save Rome from collapse? With that steel, you will carve your name into history as the Emperor who rescued the eternal city. Take it."

Piso's heart thunders in his chest as he stares at the gladius glinting on the marble floor. His eyes flick to the Praetorian Guards, their hands resting on their swords, their faces unreadable behind polished helmets. Piso's gaze returns to the gladius, his fingers twitching. With one swift lunge he could end Nero's reign and make himself Emperor. But something flickers across his face, a look of serenity. He turns his head back to Nero and raises his chin.

"The end of your reign will be far more civilized than your reign of terror, my Emperor."

Nero smirks.

"This is precisely why you will never be Emperor, Piso. You lack what it takes to dirty your hands with the blood of your enemies."

Nero pivots on his heel and strides toward the bronze doors, each footfall cracking against marble in the chamber's unnatural quiet.

"Don't be so certain of that, my Emperor," Piso calls after him.

Nero pauses mid-stride, his shoulders tensing. For a moment, the entire Senate holds its breath. Then he continues walking without looking back, leaving behind a chamber full of men who have just witnessed either supreme confidence or fatal arrogance.

Days later, Nero walks through the smouldering ruins of central Rome among the blackened stones that mark where neighbourhoods once thrived. The great fire's devastation stretches in all directions. Collapsed walls, charred timber beams, and the skeletal remains of shops and homes that housed thousands of Roman citizens.

Epaphroditus trails the emperor like a shadow, scratching furiously at his wax tablets to capture every grandiose pronouncement. A few paces away, Tigellinus stands guard. Nero gestures toward a particularly vast expanse of rubble.

"And here is where I will construct the greatest amphitheatre ever built. It will dwarf even the Theatre of Marcellus, seating eighty thousand spectators who will witness spectacles that rival the Olympics themselves."

A man runs toward them through the ruins in a panic, stumbling over broken stones and debris. Tigellinus immediately moves to intercept him.

"Emperor! I must speak with you!" the man calls out breathlessly.

"Who is that man, Epaphroditus?" Nero asks without taking his eyes off the architectural possibilities before him.

"Milichus, a freedman of Flavius Scaevinus," the secretary replies, consulting his records.

"Go see what he wants."

While Epaphroditus approaches the agitated freedman, Nero continues his survey of the destruction. He walks toward what remains of the area where Peter's church stood. Now nothing but ash and scattered stones. Something catches his eye among the debris: a small wooden crucifix, somehow surviving the inferno that consumed everything around it.

He stares at the artifact with complex emotions, remembering the man who had challenged him with quiet courage and died for his beliefs. The crucifix's survival amongst the flames seems impossible. Epaphroditus returns with Milichus in tow, both men's faces grave with urgent news.

"My Emperor, Milichus reports that he has observed Flavius sharpening his blade as if preparing for battle. He believes the conspirators are about to make their move."

Nero's attention snaps away from the crucifix to focus entirely on this new threat.

"Who are these conspirators, Milichus?"

"Senator Piso leads them, along with Subrius Flavus, Sulpicius Asper, Faenius Rufus, and Plautius Lateranus. There may be others."

"I had wondered why Rufus failed to appear for duty today," Nero muses. He turns to his loyal Praetorian Prefect with decisive authority. "Tigellinus, I was wise to trust you over him. Assemble every guard you can muster. Round up all the named conspirators and bring them to the Tullianum. Move swiftly. If they're preparing to act, we must strike first."

"At once, my Emperor," Tigellinus replies, already signalling to his men.

"Show them no mercy. The time for subtle interrogation has passed. Rome will see what happens to those who plot against their Emperor."

As the Praetorians scatter through the ruined city to hunt down the conspirators, Nero looks once more at the small crucifix lying among the ashes.

Nero descends into the Tullianum's lower chamber with Seneca following close behind. The basement presents a grim tableau of imperial retribution. Bodies of conspirators line the walls. Men who hours before had held senatorial rank and commanded respect throughout the empire, now reduced to broken corpses bearing the marks of intensive interrogation. The ancient stones seem to drink in their blood, adding these deaths to the countless others that have sanctified this place of final judgment.

At the chamber's centre sits a man tied to a chair but notably unharmed, his clothing intact and his face unmarked by torture. He watches Nero's approach with the careful attention of one whose survival depends on maintaining imperial favour.

"Who is this?" Nero asks Seneca.

"Antonius Natalis, my Emperor. We struck an arrangement with him. In exchange for revealing every detail about every conspirator, he would be acquitted of his crimes."

Nero approaches the bound man with interest.

"And where is the ringleader? Where is Piso?"

"He remains at his villa. He has requested permission for a private death," Natalis answers quickly.

"Has he indeed? Well, who am I to disregard the wishes of such an esteemed senator?"

Nero's smile carries no warmth. He turns to Seneca.

"What do you think we should do with our cooperative friend here?"

"Release him, my Emperor. If you earn a reputation as a just and merciful emperor, it will prove much easier to thwart any future conspiracies. Mercy can be more valuable than fear."

"You are so wise, Seneca. We shall grant him freedom."

Nero moves to another figure bound nearby. Seneca's nephew, Lucan. Though bound like the others, the young man holds himself with the quiet confidence of someone who believes his family connections will spare him from the fate of his co-conspirators.

"My dear friend, Lucan. How did such a promising young artist become entangled in such a ghastly conspiracy?" Nero asks with apparent sadness.

"Uncle, please help me. I'm sorry. I was foolish," Lucan pleads, turning to Seneca, who looks at Nero.

"My Emperor, please show mercy to Lucan. He is family to me. I know he has acted wrongly, but he's merely an impressionable young man led astray. I beg for lenient punishment."

Nero steps closer to the bound poet, studying his face with the appreciation of one artist for another.

"Normally I would not be so forgiving. But I have so enjoyed your poetry, Lucan. Your verses show genuine talent. I shall spare you for now."

"Thank you, Emperor," Lucan breathes with relief.

"Thank you, my Emperor," Seneca echoes. "Your kindness and mercy honour the empire."

"Return with your uncle to his villa. I will visit later to discuss the terms of your punishment."

Seneca and Lucan exit the chamber, their footsteps fading up the stone stairs toward daylight and freedom. Nero turns to Tigellinus.

"Now let us pay a visit to our dear friend Piso. I'm curious to see how a senator chooses to meet his end."

Nero and Tigellinus climb the worn stone steps away from the dungeon. Behind them, the Tullianum holds its secrets. Dead men who nearly changed history, their ambitious whispers now silenced forever in chambers few Romans ever leave.

Nero arrives at Piso's villa with Tigellinus and a contingent of Praetorian Guards. The residence speaks of old Roman wealth. Marble columns, carefully tended gardens, and the kind of understated elegance that marks families whose power predates the empire itself.

Inside, they find Piso sitting alone in his atrium, the oil lamps unlit, shadows gathering around him like mourning clothes. He doesn't look up as Nero enters and takes the chair across from him, the two men facing each other in the growing darkness. Piso finally raises his head and shakes it slowly.

"How did a psychopath like you manage to thwart one of the most elaborate assassination plots in Roman history?"

"You have no idea who you're addressing, Piso. You should consider yourself fortunate to be even a footnote in the reign of Rome's greatest Emperor. I have barely begun telling my story. With Rome as my canvas, I shall paint the greatest masterpiece in history with the blood of my enemies. But first, I must coat my brush with your blood."

Piso deflates, his voice carries the weariness of complete defeat.

"By the gods, that's it then. There's nothing left to stop you from reducing Rome to ashes. Well, go on then. Let's finish this. I'd rather die than watch a degenerate burn our empire to the ground."

The senator exposes his neck to the Praetorian Guards in a gesture of defiant surrender. The guards remain motionless, fingers hovering near sword hilts, awaiting orders. When no command comes, Piso's eyes drift back to Nero, who watches with the sardonic smile of a cat observing a cornered mouse.

"A man who plots in secret to murder another, yet lacks the courage to do the deed himself, does not deserve a warrior's death."

Tigellinus enters from deeper in the villa.

"The bath is drawn, my Emperor."

Nero stands up and smiles at the senator.

"Walk with me, Piso."

"I don't take orders from a bastard who murdered his own mother and wife," Piso says.

"It seems you believe your family successfully fled to safety. They came so close to boarding that ship at Portus. If not for Natalis, we might never have caught them."

Piso's defiance crumbles instantly.

"My family have nothing to do with this. Let them go."

"I will give you one opportunity to save their lives. Walk with me to the bath."

Piso stands slowly, the weight of imperial coercion breaking his final resistance. They walk into the villa's bath chamber, where steaming water fills a marble basin. A small knife rests on the basin's edge.

“Get in the bath,” Nero commands.

Piso disrobes, his tunic falling to the floor in a heap. He steps into the bath, the hot water scalding his skin, but he doesn’t flinch. His eyes are fixed on the knife, his hands trembling as he reaches for it. Nero watches, his expression unreadable.

“The arteries you need to cut are on your wrist and your thigh. Make sure to cut deep.”

Piso grips the knife, his knuckles white against the polished bronze handle. The blade glints against pale flesh as he aligns the knife's edge with the delicate map of veins beneath his skin. He inhales sharply, then drags the edge across in one savage motion. A moment's resistance, then flesh parts like ripe fruit. He barely pauses before pressing the knife to his inner thigh, where the femoral artery pulses beneath taut skin. The second cut opens deeper than the first. Blood erupts in twin fountains, first trickling then gushing into the steaming water. It blooms in delicate crimson clouds, unfurling like silk scarves, before dissolving the bathwater into a murky wine.

His breath hitches in his throat, a sound halfway between a gasp and a sob, as his body begins to convulse with minute tremors. The knife slips from his fingers, disappearing beneath the darkening surface as the warmth of his life seeps away into the tepid embrace of his final bath.

“Just let my family live,” Piso says as he draws his last breath.

Nero watches intently as Piso's eyes glaze over, his head slumping forward into the crimson bath. The senator's final exhalation emerges as bubbles breaking the bloody surface, a quiet end for a man who had dreamed of saving Rome from tyranny. Nero stands to his full height.

“Wonderful. Now let's pay a visit to my dear friend Seneca."

Later in the evening, Nero arrives at Seneca's villa with Tigellinus and his guards. Inside, he finds Seneca and Lucan in the atrium, both men rising respectfully as the Emperor enters.

"Welcome, Emperor. Have you met with Piso?"

"Piso has been dealt with,“ Nero sits down in the atrium across from them, “permanently."

"That is wonderful news, Caesar. What is to be the fate of my dear nephew Lucan?"

"I have conceived the most splendid idea for a poet as talented as your nephew. I will allow him to recite his poetry with musical accompaniment from the Emperor himself."

"You are most generous and kind, my Emperor. History shall remember your mercy fondly."

Nero smiles softly as he stands up to address Seneca.

"Thank you, Seneca. Without your wisdom and guidance, I could never have achieved what we have achieved here together."

Seneca puts his hand on Nero's shoulder and smiles.

"It's been an honour, Emperor."

"Likewise, my old friend."

Nero clasps Seneca's shoulder in kind. The two men exchange a warm look before Nero finishes.

"Now, draw your nephew a hot bath."

Seneca's face pales.

"But he has already bathed today."

Nero's expression hardens as he lowers his voice.

"Draw the bath."

Tears well up in Seneca's eyes as understanding dawns. He exits without another word. Nero sits down next to Lucan.

"I so admired your poetry at the Theatre of Pompey," he says to Lucan conversationally.

"I am only accomplished because of your inspiration, Nero. You have created a culture of artistic excellence. You are a muse for Rome itself."

"Then why plot to kill me?"

Lucan's composure cracks.

"Envy, my Emperor. I knew that as long as you lived, I could never be considered Rome's greatest artist. If I helped Piso remove you, then I might have had a chance to be recognized as the empire's greatest performer."

Seneca returns, his face ashen.

"The bath is drawn."

Nero motions Lucan towards the bath chamber.

"Come, Lucan. Together we shall give Rome the greatest performance she has ever witnessed."

Lucan stands up with Nero. They enter the bath chamber, where steam rises from heated water.

"Prepare yourself, Lucan," Nero commands.

"But I have already bathed, Emperor."

Tigellinus steps into the room, his presence carrying unspoken threats. Nero's voice hardens.

"Get in the bath, Lucan."

Lucan's eyes flash to his uncle Seneca who looks on helplessly. His hands tremble as he disrobes, his tunic falling to the floor. He steps into the hot water, his jaw tight, his eyes fixed on Nero. The Emperor's smile returns, sharp and cruel.

"Are you ready to perform, Lucan? You shall recite your poetry, and I shall accompany you on the lyre."

Lucan nods, his voice barely audible.

"I am ready, Emperor."

"Perfect. Now, we shall make this performance truly historic. Something that will make the gods themselves turn their heads."

Nero hands Lucan a small knife, its blade glinting wickedly. Seneca steps forward, his voice breaking.

"My Emperor, please—"

"Silence," Nero snaps, his gaze never leaving Lucan.

Lucan stares at the knife, his hands shaking.

"Nero, please, I won't do that."

Nero leans closer, his voice a venomous whisper.

"You will, Lucan, because if you don't, I will cut out your tongue and cut off your hands. You will spend the rest of your life unable to make art, attending to my stables. Useless, mocked, and derided, until the day comes you are begging for this blade. Or you could join me right now and put on a performance so powerful we'll make Apollo himself envious."

Lucan's eyes fill with tears as he takes the knife, his hands trembling. Seneca chokes out.

"Lucan!"

"It's okay, uncle."

He drags the blade across his wrists, blood welling instantly, spilling into the water. He begins to cry, soft sobs echoing in the small room. Nero lifts his lyre, his fingers plucking a haunting melody.

"Now, begin reciting your poetry."

Lucan's voice trembles as he begins, the words faltering but clear.

"O lucent herald of the fading day,
You slip between the olive leaves,
And bathe the Tiber in your silver fire.
Rome stands eternal, so they say.
Yet marble cracks, and kings grow pale,
While still you rise, unchanged, divine."

His voice weakens, his body slumping as the blood swirls in the water. With a final, shuddering breath, Lucan falls silent. Nero stops playing his lyre. Seneca weeps openly, his hands covering his face. When the tragic performance concludes, Nero turns to console the grieving philosopher.

"I know how difficult it is when family dies. Every member of my family, from my parents to my wives to my only daughter, has perished. Trust that I did what was necessary for the empire and understand that I share your pain."

Seneca wipes away his tears.

"You are right, my Emperor."

"You are a true friend, Seneca."

Nero places his hand on Seneca's shoulder and smiles with apparent warmth. Then his expression shifts.

"Now get in the bath."

The blood drains from Seneca's face.

"What?"

"Where were you today, Seneca?"

The philosopher stands speechless.

"On the day all my enemies sought to betray me, you were nowhere to be found, and your own blood was part of the conspiracy. Do you think me a fool?"

"My Emperor, I swear by all the gods, I swear to you, I knew nothing of any conspiracy. I have always been loyal."

"My dear Seneca, I wish I could believe you. Let's not make this more difficult than necessary."

Seneca nods, tears carving glistening channels down his face as he disrobes, his movements slow and deliberate as a ritual. The fabric of his toga falls away, revealing a body once strong but now softened by age and scholarly pursuits. He steps into the bath, the water now clouded with Lucan's blood. A rusty haze that swirls around his ankles like wine in water.

He takes the knife, its bronze handle warm from Lucan's grip, and draws it across his left wrist first. The blade bites deep into papery skin, parting flesh with barely a whisper of resistance. Bright arterial blood pulses forth in rhythmic spurts, then slows to a steady stream that spirals into the bathwater, transforming it from pink to crimson.

As Seneca's life ebbs away, his breathing growing shallow and his skin turning alabaster white. Nero kneels beside the bath and watches with fascination, his golden laurel wreath catching the lamplight as he leans forward, pupils dilated with awe.

"You were always one of the few I trusted, Seneca. It breaks my heart to witness this."

"You see, then, that I am not permitted to repay your kindness with the final offerings of my devotion," Seneca whispers.

Their eyes lock as the great philosopher draws his last breath, ending a relationship that had shaped an empire.

Chapter 13
Anubis

The scorching African sun blazes on the expedition as Aswan appears over the Nile's eastern bank. The ancient trading city spreads across granite hills that glow golden in the afternoon sun, its mud-brick buildings climbing toward the sky in terraced layers. Palm trees rustling in the hot wind line the waterfront.

But it's what lies beyond the city that draws every eye and chills every heart. The first cataract stretches across the river like a barrier built by angry gods. Massive granite boulders creating a maze of churning rapids and deadly whirlpools that have claimed countless vessels over the millennia. The water crashes against ancient stone with a roar that echoes off the surrounding cliffs, sending spray high into the air that transforms the sunlight into countless glittering prisms.

They dock their boat at a wooden pier below the cataract, the relatively calm water here offering their last moment of peace before facing the river's fury. Paulinus shakes his head in dismay.

"How are we supposed to sail through that, Titus?"

"That's the wrong question, Paulinus. You should ask how we're going to sail through all five of them."

"There are four more? Wonderful. I've been practicing my backstroke."

"We'll rest in the tavern in Aswan tonight. We're going to need our energy to traverse the cataracts tomorrow."

The expedition disembarks, sandals sinking into the silty riverbank as they walk through Aswan's labyrinthine streets. Mingled aromas of cardamom and donkey dung fill the hot air. They pass vendors hawking ostrich feathers and amber beads, children with kohl-rimmed eyes chasing wooden hoops through clouds of ochre dust. Locals in indigo-dyed robes press against mud-brick walls to let them pass, their expressions a careful mask hiding thoughts behind evaluating eyes.

A tavern crouches near the waterfront, its cedar planks warped from decades of annual floods. They claim a table beneath a window framed by tattered palm-fibre curtains. Through the window they see the Philae Temple gleaming alabaster-pale on an island that splits the Nile. Titus motions towards the server. A thin man whose dark skin speaks of Nubian heritage. He says something in rapid Coptic, his tone clearly unwelcoming.

"What did he say?" Titus asks.

"He says they don't serve Romans here and that we should leave," Kashta translates.

Sextus stands slowly and walks over to the server, locking eyes with him in a stare that carries the weight of imperial authority.

"You're going to serve us, or I'll massacre every last person in this tavern and burn it to ashes."

Kashta starts to translate but Sextus interrupts him.

“Don’t translate,” Sextus says without ever breaking eye contact with the server. “He knows what I said.”

The server nods quickly and hurries away to fetch food and drink. Paulinus gazes through the window at the temple rising from its island sanctuary.

"What is that structure?"

"The Philae Temple," Titus replies.

"Let me guess, another temple we're forbidden to enter?"

"You guessed correctly."

"I must document that temple for my encyclopaedia, Titus," Pliny interjects. "The inscriptions there could provide invaluable historical context."

“Great idea, Pliny,” Paulinus replies sarcastically. “Maybe we could end up in another dungeon full of scarabs.”

"No, Pliny,” Titus replies. “We're here to rest and resupply. Do not go near any temple."

Titus stares out the window at the ancient structure, its stone walls gleaming white against the dark water. For a moment, he hears something. A whisper that seems to emanate from the temple itself, slithering across the water like a serpent. The sand-dry rasp of Anubis, calling him to cross the water, to enter the sacred hypostyle halls.

Anubis’s whispers stop when the server returns with platters of food. Flatbread, roasted meat, dates, and local wine that tastes of grain and river water. Sextus rips a chunk of bread with his teeth and fixes Titus with a hard stare.

"So tell me, Titus, how exactly do you plan to get us through those cataracts?"

"I'll tell you when we get there."

"And what happens if you die before we cross them?"

"Then you'll have to work extra hard to keep me alive."

Sextus's frustration shows as he sinks back into his chair.

"There are sleeping quarters upstairs where we can spend the night," Kashta offers.

"Try to sleep well. You're going to need your energy tomorrow," Titus says, draining his cup.

They finish their meal in relative silence, each man contemplating the challenges that await them with the rising sun.

As night falls, the sleeping chamber above the tavern lies in perfect darkness, its wooden shutters blocking even the faintest starlight. Multiple single beds fill the room, each occupied by an expedition member exhausted from their long journey. The only sounds are the gentle lapping of Nile waters against the shore and the distant rumble of the first cataract's eternal fury.

Titus tosses restlessly in his bed, sweat beading his forehead despite the cool night air. Behind his closed eyelids, visions unfold. Ancient corridors carved with hieroglyphs that seem to move and writhe, the eyes of Anubis watching from shadow, whispers in languages that predate human memory. The jackal-headed god speaks directly into his mind:

"Come to me, son of builders, leader of warriors. Your destiny awaits in the sacred chambers where judgment is rendered."

Titus's eyes snap open and he bolts upright, chest heaving as if he's been running. Sweat soaks his tunic as he struggles to separate dream from reality. The room remains dark and peaceful around him, his companions sleeping soundly in their beds.

He looks to the bed beside him. Empty. The blankets lie rumpled but abandoned.

"Pliny," he whispers into the darkness, but receives no response.

Moving carefully to avoid waking the others, he makes his way to the window and peers through the wooden slats. In the moonlight, he sees a solitary figure walking across the sand toward the island temple of Philae. The man's gait and silhouette are unmistakably familiar.

"Pliny!" he hisses, but the distant figure continues walking as if drawn by invisible strings.

Titus glances back at his sleeping companions, then at the scholar approaching the forbidden temple. He climbs through the window and drops to the sand below.

"Pliny! Stop! Don't enter the temple!" he shouts as he sprints across the desert, but his words seem to vanish into the night air.

Pliny disappears between the massive columns of the temple entrance just as Titus reaches the water's edge. Without pausing to consider the consequences, Titus plunges into the Nile and swims desperately toward the island.

"Pliny!" he calls as he rushes into the temple, water streaming from his clothes.

He runs past the colossal statues of pharaohs flanking the entrance of the temple and into its labyrinth of stone corridors. The interior of the temple seethes with darkness layered upon darkness. The echo of his footfalls ricochets off cyclopean pillars. Row upon row of them, each rising more massive than the last, carved with rows of hieroglyphs.

He calls for Pliny again, voice rasping in the chill air. It dies as if swallowed whole by the stone. Suddenly, the whisper of Anubis coils inside his skull. Barely a sound, more a sense of pressure behind the eyes.

"Down into the sanctum of Thoth. The divine scribe seeks wisdom in the Duat."

He catches a glimpse of the scholar's silhouette disappearing down a corridor lined with carved deities. Following frantically, Titus races through passages that seem to shift and change around him, until he emerges into a circular chamber lit by an otherworldly glow. Pliny stands with his back turned, motionless before a towering statue of Thoth, the ibis-headed god of writing and wisdom.

"Pliny? What's happening?"

The figure doesn't move or respond.

"Pliny?"

Titus approaches cautiously and places his hand on the scholar's shoulder, turning him around. What he sees makes his blood freeze. Pliny's eyes are as white as full moons. He speaks, but it is not his voice. It is the voice of Thoth himself, resonant and layered with the weight of ages.

"I am the scribe of the gods, keeper of words, master of the sacred script. Through writing, I have given humanity memory across the void of time. Here, where ink becomes blood and papyrus becomes flesh, our true journey begins."

The temple begins to shake violently. Ancient stones crack and groan as the ceiling starts to collapse. Titus stumbles backward as a massive boulder crashes between him and the possessed scholar.

"Pliny!"

More rocks rain from above. Titus looks up to see the roof disintegrating and breaks into a desperate sprint toward the corridor. He dodges falling stones, his heart hammering as the ancient structure comes apart around him. A wall begins rising from the floor ahead. Titus leaps over it like a hurdler, landing hard but maintaining his momentum. Further down the passage, a wide pit opens in the floor. He launches himself across the gap, his fingers scraping against the far edge as he hauls himself up.

The walls start closing in faster than he can run, threatening to crush him between tons of stone. He bursts into a full sprint just as another wall begins rising to block the exit. With a final, desperate leap, he hurdles over the barrier and tumbles out of the temple onto the sandy shore. He lies gasping on the beach, his lungs burning as he turns back to the temple.

"Pliny!" he calls into the night, but only silence answers.

Dawn begins to lighten the eastern sky as he swims back to shore and runs toward the tavern, his wet clothes clinging to his body. He bursts through the door to find Paulinus sitting calmly at a table, breaking his fast with bread and fruit.

"Titus? I thought you were upstairs sleeping."

"It's Pliny! He's trapped in the temple. We have to save him!"

"What?"

Pliny walks in from the kitchen, carrying his own breakfast. He stops when he sees Titus's wild appearance and the tension in the room.

"What's going on?" Pliny asks.

"Pliny! How did you escape the temple?"

"I've been here all night."

Titus shakes his head in disbelief, trying to reconcile what he experienced with the reality before him.

"Is everything all right, Titus?" Paulinus asks with growing concern.

"Yes... fine. Just a vivid dream."

Sextus enters with his characteristic swagger.

"Ready your breakfast and eat heartily, men. Our fearless leader is going to guide us through five cataracts today."

Marcus and Quintus laugh as they wolf down their breakfast. Titus looks out the window at Philae Temple, which stands perfectly intact on its island, showing no evidence of the destruction he witnessed. But the taste of fear remains in his mouth, and the echo of Anubis's voice still whispers in the corners of his mind.

They arrive at their boat, docked before the first cataract. Jagged granite rocks thrust through shallow, churning water that foams white with fury. The river, so peaceful upstream, has transformed into a maze of death that has claimed countless vessels over the millennia. Paulinus stares at the violent rapids.

"How do we sail through there?"

"We don't. We carry the boat around," Titus replies.

"You're not serious."

"Unpack the ship. Use ropes to tie the supplies around your necks."

“So this is your master plan, general? Carry the boats?” Sextus says, shaking his head.

“I told you the warships would be no use,” Titus smirks. “Now get to work.”

The team reluctantly follows orders, securing their provisions and equipment before lifting the boat over their heads. The vessel's weight presses down on their shoulders as they trudge across the rocky terrain, their feet slipping on loose stones while sweat pours down their faces. When they reach calmer water beyond the rapids, Titus calls out.

"Here."

They throw the boat back into the Nile and collapse on the shore, gasping for breath.

"Thank Neptune it's not my turn to row," Paulinus pants.

They resume their journey, oars dipping rhythmically into the murky waters as they pass the ancient Temple of Dedwen. As their boat glides by, Titus feels a sudden chill despite the merciless Egyptian sun. The air around him thickens, and the familiar whisper of Anubis slithers from the temple into his mind:

"Do not struggle against the inevitable. Enter my realm willingly, and together we will preside over the Duat."

Titus's knuckles whiten as he grips the oar tighter, his jaw clenches as he shakes off the whispers.

The Second Cataract materializes ahead, a writhing serpent of white foam slithering between knife-edged black rocks. Though less violent than the first, its treacherous currents conceal submerged stones that could splinter their hull like kindling. Titus gestures toward a narrow strip of sand wedged between towering granite boulders.

"Port here."

They guide the boat to shore, muscles already trembling from the morning's labour. Sweat carves muddy rivulets down their dust-caked faces as Paulinus squints upriver, his expression souring.

"How do we get past this one?" he asks.

"We carry the boat."

Paulinus delivers a slow, sarcastic clap.

"Brilliant strategy, Titus. Carry the boats. You truly are a master tactician worthy of Caesar himself."

"You all know the drill," Titus says.

They repeat the exhausting portage, shoulders raw beneath the boat's wooden hull, leg muscles quivering with each step on the blistering rocks. When they finally reach navigable water, they collapse onto the scorched sand, chests heaving, throats parched and burning.

Hours later, as the merciless sun hangs directly overhead, Titus raises his palm. The oars still, water dripping from their blades.

"Why are we stopping?" Sextus asks.

"The Third Cataract lies directly ahead."

Titus points to the deceptively calm surface. Sextus squints against the glare reflecting off the Nile.

"I don't see any rapids."

"Shallow rocks lurk beneath the surface, jagged as spear points. They would splinter our hull like dried papyrus if we struck them."

"So what do we do?"

"We get out and carry the boat."

Paulinus shakes his head.

"Why don't we carry it all the way to the Nile's source while we're at it?"

The team performs another gruelling portage, their bodies pushed to the limits of endurance. At the Fourth Cataract, Sextus doesn't even bother asking. They portage once more, each man lost in his own thoughts of exhaustion and the growing certainty that they're pushing deeper into hostile territory.

The team has time to catch their breath as they slowly row down a calm section of the river. As they row past the ruins of an ancient city, its blackened stones telling stories of conquest and destruction. Pliny breaks the weary silence.

"What happened to that city?" he asks Kashta.

"That was Napata, my birthplace. Your people destroyed it when Rome tried to conquer the Kingdom of

Kush forty years ago. This was once our capital, where my ancestors ruled for generations. My family fled to Meroe when the legions came. We thought all was lost. But the Fifth Cataract proved too much for Roman engineering. We fortified ourselves in Meroe, and when they tried to siege us, they couldn't get their supply ships through the rapids. Eventually, they gave up and withdrew."

The fifth cataract looms ahead, its waters more treacherous than any they've yet encountered. Beyond it stands the Kingdom of Kush. Massive walls of mud-brick and stone stretch along the riverbank, decorated with colourful murals depicting warrior-kings and protective gods. Towers rise at regular intervals, their peaks crowned with stone parapets.

"What is that?" Sextus asks, though his soldier's eye already recognizes a military stronghold.

"The Kingdom of Kush," Kashta replies.

"Are they friendly?"

Archers appear between the parapets. Warriors in leather armour carrying bronze-tipped spears and powerful composite bows. They nock arrows and draw their bowstrings, the arrowheads glinting as they aim at the Roman boat.

"No."

Chapter 14
Olympic Champion

Rome, 67 AD. The Domus Aurea stands completed in the heart of Rome. Three hundred acres of imperial excess. The palace complex gleams with walls sheathed in gold leaf, transforming ordinary sunlight into scattered fragments of captured flame. The main banquet hall rotates slowly on bronze mechanisms. Artificial lakes reflect facades decorated with precious stones and ivory inlays.

In the palace's octagonal dining room, frescoes cover every surface. Scenes of mythological splendour where gods feast alongside mortals, where Apollo himself seems to approve of earthly artistic endeavours. The ceiling opens to reveal painted stars that mirror the real constellations above, while fountains spray perfumed water into marble basins carved to resemble divine chalices.

Nero reclines on a silver couch, his imperial robes flowing around him like liquid purple. At twenty-eight, he has achieved what he considers the perfect fusion of political power and artistic expression, ruling an empire from within a palace that serves as his masterpiece.

Epaphroditus stands ready with his tablets and scrolls. Tigellinus stands at attention at the door. Empress Messalina sits nearby, her beauty enhanced by silks and jewels. Since their marriage, she has learned to navigate Nero's moods with the skill of a diplomat, providing the admiration and support his artistic ego requires. Nero gestures toward the golden splendour surrounding them.

"Do you appreciate our new home, my darling wife?"

"Of course, my Emperor. Your vision and generosity continue to astound me."

Nero turns to Tigellinus.

"Have all the conspirators been accounted for and dealt with?"

"Yes, my Emperor. Every last one has been eliminated."

"Then no obstacles remain to impede my greatest ambitions. Epaphroditus, arrange my schedule."

"What would you like me to organize, my Emperor?"

"I shall tour Greece soon to treat the Greeks to my artistic performances. I will compete in the Olympic Games while there."

Epaphroditus hesitates slightly.

"My apologies, Caesar, but the Olympics are not scheduled for another three years."

"Then send word to Greece immediately. Tell them to reschedule the Games to coincide with my tour."

The secretary pauses, understanding the impossibility of the request but recognizing the futility of argument.

"Yes, my Emperor."

"Furthermore, I shall add new events to the Olympics. Musical contests, poetry recitation, lyre performance, and tragic acting. The Games should celebrate all forms of human excellence, not merely physical prowess."

"Of course, my Emperor."

"I will demonstrate my incredible equestrian skills by entering the chariot race, where I fully expect to claim victory."

"Indeed, Caesar."

"There is one final matter. I am not impressed with any of the accommodations available in Greece. None are suitable for Rome's greatest artist. Have them construct a palace in Olympia specifically for my residence during the Games."

Olympia, Greece, 67 AD. In the sacred valley beneath Mount Kronos, the hippodrome stretches nearly two stadia in length. Forty thousand spectators fill the marble terraces, their voices creating a thunderous roar that echoes off the surrounding hills. At the starting line, magnificent four-horse chariots await the signal. Each team represents the finest breeding and training the Greek world can offer. Sleek Arabian stallions with coats like polished copper. Reins wrap around the wrists of charioteers as they prepare for the most dangerous race in the ancient world. The herald takes his place at the podium to address the crowd.

"Citizens of Greece and honoured guests! Welcome to the tethrippon, the four-horse chariot race around the sacred hippodrome! When the gates open, each contestant will complete twelve laps around the course!"

The crowd erupts in anticipation as the chariot horses kick up dust. Betting tablets change hands rapidly while spectators shout encouragement to their favoured riders.

"Today truly is a special day because we have a surprise final contestant. Our glorious Emperor Nero!"

A chariot emerges from the imperial pavilion, but gasps ripple through the crowd as they see what approaches the starting line. Where every other contestant drives four horses, Nero's chariot is pulled by ten horses. White stallions from the imperial stables, their harnesses decorated with gold and precious stones.

The crowd's murmur grows disapproving, understanding immediately that this is no fair competition. Throughout the stands, spectators begin to voice their displeasure at this blatant violation of Olympic tradition.

Praetorian Guards positioned throughout the audience suddenly stamp their feet in unison, the sound like thunder. As one, they raise their spears and point them directly at the crowd. The disapproval transforms instantly into feigned enthusiastic cheering for Nero.

"Competitors, take your positions! On your marks... get set... Go!"

The bronze gates swing open and chaos erupts. Eight chariots surge forward in a cloud of dust and pounding hooves, but Nero's ten-horse team immediately pulls ahead with overwhelming power. The other charioteers struggle to match his pace, their four-horse teams straining against the impossible disadvantage.

Nero maintains his lead through the early laps, his imperial purple cloak streaming behind him as the crowd cheers under armed guard. By the second lap, he's extended his advantage dramatically, raising one hand to acknowledge the forced adulation.

But on the fourth lap, disaster strikes. Distracted by applause, Nero takes the far turn too aggressively. His outside horses, unable to navigate the tight corner in their cumbersome ten-horse configuration, stumble over each other. The chariot lurches violently, tips, then flips completely, throwing the Emperor into the dust as his horses tangle and thrash in their traces.

The crowd falls silent. Nero lies motionless before struggling to his feet, covered in dust. The other charioteers complete their twelve laps while Nero limps from the track. A Greek charioteer from Corinth claims victory, though few pay attention to the actual winner.

At the medal ceremony, the winners podium stands in three tiers at the centre of the hippodrome. The actual race winners, genuine athletes who completed their events, stand uncertainly to one side, while two Praetorian Guards flank the herald, their presence containing a veiled threat. The herald's voice carries forced enthusiasm across the stadium.

"Ladies and gentlemen. I am thrilled to announce your gold medallist and new Olympic champion! Emperor Nero!"

The crowd offers scattered, uneasy applause. Nero ascends the podium, his torn and dusty racing attire hastily cleaned. He waves to the audience with the confidence of a man who believes his own propaganda, as the herald places the gold medal around his neck. He nudges the heralder, who clears his throat nervously.

"Ladies and gentlemen, we are delighted to announce a new event at this year's Olympics. Lyre playing."

A young slave boy runs across the arena floor, carrying a magnificent lyre inlaid with ivory and precious stones. As he hands the instrument to Nero, their eyes meet and both smile, a moment of genuine warmth that seems oddly innocent amid the surrounding theatrics.

The Praetorian Guards gesture for silence. Nero positions his fingers on the strings. When he begins to play, the melody that emerges is hauntingly beautiful. The same song he performed while Rome burned three years earlier. Despite the circumstances, his musical talent is undeniable.

The crowd erupts in genuine applause this time, their appreciation for artistry overcoming their disgust at the political manipulation. Even those who despise the man can recognize the skill of his performance. Nero bows with the grace of a natural born performer, basking in the warmth of the applause. The herald awes at Nero with what seems to be sincere amazement.

"I can honestly say that was the finest lyre playing I have ever heard. I am pleased to introduce your two-time Olympic champion, Emperor Nero!"

A second gold medal is placed around Nero's neck as the slave boy returns to collect the instrument. Again, emperor and slave exchange warm smiles. Nero nudges the herald once more.

"Now?" the herald whispers.

Nero stares at him without responding, the silence stretching until the announcer capitulates.

"Ladies and gentlemen, we are honoured to announce yet another new event at this year's Olympics. Poetry! I present to you, Rome's greatest poet, Emperor Nero!"

Nero steps forward, his voice carrying with the trained projection of a natural performer. He begins reciting his poem:

"O bright-shod Helios, rider of the morning sky,
Whose golden reins pull forth the day,
Witness thy servant crowned in laurel green,
And let no shadow dim the fire of Rome.
I have sung of Ilium's fall and the sorrow of kings,
Of seas that swallowed the proud,
Of swords whose clang was the music of destiny.
Yet sweeter still is the roar of the crowd
That hails me, Caesar, victor in word and deed.
Let Olympus know my lyre has rivalled their thunder,
That the Muses, once daughters of Greece,
Have found a new home by the Tiber's banks.
And you, fair Fame, carve my name in marble,
So it endures when stars grow cold."

The crowd erupts in thunderous applause, genuinely moved by the delivery of the poetry. The herald's jaw drops in genuine surprise at the artistic quality.

"That was truly magnificent! Ladies and gentlemen, I give you your Olympic champion and three-time gold medallist! Emperor Nero!"

Nero stands up on the podium and bows his head to accept his third gold medal, breathing in the applause.

The announcer looks at Nero, who nods expectantly. With growing dread, the herald nervously clears his throat.

"Ladies and gentlemen, I am delighted to announce yet *another* new event at the Olympics—"

A collective groan emanates from the crowd, forty thousand voices expressing their exhaustion with this endless parade of imperial ego. Immediately, the Praetorian Guards stomp their feet in unison and raise their spears toward the spectators. An audience member stands to leave, but guards block his path.

"I must use the latrine," he says desperately.

"Back in your seat!" the guard barks.

"But I really must go—"

"Back in your seat now!"

The guard kicks the man forcefully backward, sending him tumbling into his seat. Throughout the stadium, other spectators who had hoped to escape find their way blocked by armed soldiers who refuse to allow anyone to leave. The herald motions for the audience to settle down.

"Emperor Nero shall compete in our final new Olympic event. Tragic acting."

Nero steps forward to the centre of the arena, his imperial bearing transforming as he prepares to embody one of Greece's most devastating myths. The first syllable bursts from his throat like Apollo's arrow, striking the farthest seats with such clarity that even those straining to see him can suddenly feel his presence:

He becomes Niobe, the proud Queen of Thebes, mother of fourteen children. Seven sons and seven daughters. His portrayal captures her fatal arrogance as she boasts of being more blessed than the goddess Leto, who bore only Apollo and Artemis. The audience watches transfixed as Nero embodies her hubris, mocking the worship of the divine mother and claiming superiority in motherhood itself.

Then comes the transformation as divine vengeance strikes. Nero's performance shifts to show Leto's rage, calling upon her children for retribution. His voice becomes both Apollo and Artemis as they descend from Olympus, raining arrows upon Niobe's children. Apollo slaying the sons, Artemis the daughters.

But it is in Niobe's grief that Nero's performance reaches its peak. He portrays a mother's devastation with such raw emotion that tears stream down faces throughout the stadium. His body conveys the weight of unbearable loss as Niobe watches her children fall one by one, powerless to protect them.

The climax comes as the gods transform Niobe into stone, yet even as a statue, she continues to weep for her lost children. Nero stands motionless, tears flowing down his face like water from eternal rock, embodying grief so profound it even moves some of the Praetorians to pity.

The crowd erupts in thunderous applause, many spectators openly weeping at the performance's emotional power. Even the guards seem moved by what they've witnessed. The herald approaches Nero.

"I must confess, Emperor, I thought this was all pretence. I believed you were a megalomaniac forcing people to pretend you were a great artist. I can say now that you truly are the greatest performer I have ever witnessed. Ladies and gentlemen, I present your Olympic gold medallist and four-time Olympic champion! Emperor Nero!"

Nero accepts his fourth gold medal to sustained applause, the crowd's appreciation clearly genuine. He basks in the adulation, his face flushed with genuine pleasure. This is what he has craved since boyhood, not merely submission through fear, but true recognition of his talents. For a precious moment, he seems almost childlike in his joy, drinking in the applause as though it were divine ambrosia. He addresses the crowd.

"Today you have witnessed true greatness. The rebirth of Apollo himself. Go and tell all of Greece what you have witnessed today."

The spectators rise and begin filtering out, their conversations animated with what they've seen. Some shake their heads in disbelief at the manipulation of the chariot race, but many speak in hushed, reverent tones about the Emperor's artistic prowess.

As the stadium empties, Nero notices the slave boy who brought his lyre standing quietly at the edge of the performance area, watching him with undisguised admiration.

"By the gods, that boy bears a striking resemblance to my late wife Sabina," Nero says to Tigellinus

"I suppose he does, my Emperor."

"The gods must have sent him here as a gift to reward my artistic triumphs."

He approaches the boy, his medals clinking softly with each step. The slave looks up, his eyes wide with fear and awe, his face pale under the grime of his station. Nero towers over him, his presence overwhelming, his smile both warm and predatory.

“How would you like to accompany me to my quarters?”

The boy’s hands tremble, his voice barely above a whisper.

“But I’m just a slave, my Emperor. I have nothing to offer a man of your stature.”

Nero’s smile widens, his eyes gleaming with something fervent, almost manic.

“That’s where you are wrong. You have everything to offer me, and I have everything to offer you. I shall show you a world you could only dream of, if you would just take my hand.”

The boy takes the Emperor’s hand with uncertainty about what this imperial attention might mean.

"What is your name?" Nero asks.

"Sporus”

Chapter 15
The Kingdom of Kush

At the walls of the Kingdom of Kush, the archers maintain their deadly aim from the parapets, stone-tipped arrows nocked and ready to loose. Their leather armour gleams with sweat, while painted shields bearing the symbols of Kushite gods rest against the stone walls. Sextus's hand moves to his gladius.

"If you have led us into a trap, Kashta, I swear by the gods I will cut your head off before those arrows can reach us."

Kashta calls out to the archers in the melodic tones of the Kushite language. The archers shout back angrily, their words sharp with suspicion and hostility. Kashta responds in reassuring tones, gesturing toward his companions while speaking rapidly. After a tense moment, the archers slowly lower their weapons and disappear from the walls. The massive wooden gates begin to swing open with the groan of bronze hinges.

The expedition enters Meroe, and the sight takes their breath away. Towering pyramids dominate the skyline, smaller than those at Memphis but no less impressive, their steep sides decorated with colourful murals depicting Kushite Kings and Queens. Palm trees line wide boulevards where merchants display goods from across Africa: ivory from the interior, gold from Nubian mines, exotic feathers from southern kingdoms.

The architecture blends Egyptian grandeur with distinctly African elements. Mud-brick buildings rise three and four stories high. Stone statues of lion-headed gods guard temple entrances. As they walk through the streets, Kashta's wife and daughters rush forward to embrace him, crying joyfully. The reunion brings tears to the guide's eyes as he holds his family close after years of dangerous travel.

Members of the royal guard approach. Tall warriors in bronze armour decorated with golden sun discs, their spears bearing the symbols of Kushite authority. They speak briefly with Kashta before stepping back respectfully.

"Queen Amanitore seeks an audience with you," Kashta translates.

Titus nods cautiously, understanding the significance of such an invitation.

"Tell her we are honoured to accept."

They follow the royal guard through the city's heart, past markets where spices from lands Rome has never conquered fill the air with exotic aromas. Citizens pause their activities to stare at the foreigners. Some with curiosity, others with undisguised hostility. Children point and whisper behind cupped hands while elders mutter prayers to ancient gods for protection against these pale intruders.

They make their way to the royal temple, a massive structure that rivals anything in Rome or Egypt. Columns carved to resemble date palms support a roof painted with images of ancient deities, while walls depict the conquests of Kushite rulers over Egyptian Pharaohs. Inside, the air carries the scent of frankincense and myrrh, the walls are covered with hieroglyphs that tell stories of African glory.

Queen Amanitore sits upon a throne of ivory and gold at the temple's far end. She appears to be in her middle years, her regal demeanour enhanced by elaborate jewellery and robes of finest silk. A crown bearing the symbols of both Upper and Lower Nubia rests upon her head, while the traditional uraeus serpent marks her divine authority. She addresses the group in her native Kushite tongue.

"This is the first time Romans have entered our capital city. The last time your people entered our previous capital, Napata, you burned it to the ground."

Kashta translates her words for those who don't understand, then conveys Titus's response.

"That was long ago, Queen Amanitore. We mean you no harm. We seek only passage through your lands."

"Are the stories I hear of your new Emperor true?"

Paulinus can't resist responding.

"I can assure you, there is no tale about Nero too outrageous to be true."

"Tell me then, why are you here?"

"Emperor Nero has sent us on an exploratory mission. He wishes to discover the source of the river Nile," Titus says.

"You mean sources," the Queen corrects.

“You mean there is more than one?"

"The Nile divides into two rivers beyond Meroe. One runs blue, the other white. The Blue Nile flows toward the Aksum Empire. The White Nile continues into the heart of our ancestral lands."

"Can you guide us there?"

"No. We cannot travel the Blue Nile. The Aksum Empire seeks to devour our Kingdom. They would kill us on sight."

"What of the White Nile?"

"Impossible. Our kingdom weakens since your empire destroyed our capital, forcing us to relocate here. We only have a handful of guards left. Barely enough citizens to repopulate. If the enemy ever breached our walls, we would be slaughtered. We cannot spare resources to satisfy the whims of a mad Emperor."

Sextus steps forward aggressively.

"Tell her that if she speaks ill of the Emperor again, I will personally ensure Meroe meets the same fate as Napata."

Kashta refuses to translate the threat.

"Say it!" Sextus demands.

"Look around you, Roman," Kashta replies firmly. "You are hopelessly outnumbered. They already distrust you. One wrong word and you are all dead."

Sextus looks around and backs down with frustration. He looks to Marcus and Quintus and the three Praetorians share an imperceptible nod.

"We wish to rest and resupply for our journey. Will you grant us safe passage?" Titus asks.

"If you are to make this journey, you must first consult the gods. However, most have fled these lands."

"What do you mean?"

"The gods have abandoned us," The Queen begins. "Isis, goddess of motherhood, fled to Nazareth sixty-six years ago. Osiris, god of resurrection, followed her to Jerusalem thirty-three years later. Amun-Ra was mummified to return again. We believe he hides in Thebes. If you wish to travel the Nile, be warned: Horus, god of kingship, fled down the Blue Nile. Set, god of chaos, chose the White Nile. Each hopes to find the river's source. If Horus succeeds, he will bring order. If Set prevails, chaos will reign."

"What if both find their respective sources?" Titus asks.

"Then this kingdom is doomed to fluctuate between order and chaos for eternity."

Paulinus whispers to Titus.

"This is a bigger load of nonsense than that sect worshipping the carpenter. At least he actually existed."

Queen Amanitore suddenly speaks in perfect Latin:

"You think it false, Roman, but observe our artwork spanning thousands of years. Artists paint what they witness."

She gestures toward hieroglyphs depicting gods with animal heads and human bodies, their forms consistent across millennia of artistic tradition.

"In thousands of years, perhaps people will look at your Roman sculptures and claim you never existed."

"You speak Latin?" Titus asks with surprise.

The Queen returns to her native tongue.

"You have overstayed your welcome in my throne room."

Kushite guards begin escorting them toward the exit, but Titus calls out desperately.

"Tell me about Anubis!"

The Queen raises her hand, stopping the guards mid-step.

"What do you know of Anubis?" She asks.

"He has been whispering to me."

"Where?"

"At every temple throughout the river."

The Queen's expression grows serious.

"That means he follows you. You will need all assistance you can gather. Go now and rest. When you have eaten, visit our temple. There you will meet our shaman, who will help you find the answers you seek. Leave now."

The expedition exits the royal palace and trudges through the sun-scorched village, dust clinging to their sandals, before stepping into the tavern. The tavern's interior provides welcome relief from the desert heat, its thick mud-brick walls keeping the air cool while wooden shutters filter the harsh sunlight. They sit in the relative privacy of a corner alcove, their voices low as they discuss the challenges ahead.

A server brings a food platter and a jug of wine to their table. Paulinus pours himself a cup of wine and offers Sextus a mock toast.

"Thanks for not crucifying any innocent civilians so far, Sextus. I know restraint must be really difficult for you."

"No one who threatens the empire with that carpenter's sect is innocent," Sextus replies without humour.

"Right, of course. The gods forbid they listen to a man who preached peace."

"What is the desire for peace other than admission of weakness?"

Marcus and Quintus raise their cups in agreement.

"Hear, hear!"

Sextus leans forward and stares at Titus.

"What are we going to do about the split in the Nile?"

"We'll need to divide into two teams. I will lead one group down the White Nile. Paulinus will command the other down the Blue Nile. Sextus and Pliny come with me. Marcus and Quintus accompany Paulinus."

Sextus eyes Pliny with disdain.

"Do we really need this scholar to accompany us? He's dead weight. We might increase our chances of success if he were to have an unfortunate accident."

"Our mission is to report our discoveries to the Emperor. Pliny is the only one who can interpret what we find. Do you think you could explain hieroglyphics to Nero? As long as Pliny returns safely, our mission succeeds."

"And what is my team supposed to do?" Paulinus asks

"Think on your feet."

"You know I never think. That's what I have you for."

"We'll rendezvous back here in Meroe if both teams succeed."

"What if one team succeeds and the other doesn't?" Paulinus asks.

"If a month passes without the other team's return, venture back to Rome. Now, if you'll excuse me, I must visit the temple."

Titus stands from the table and leaves.

Titus walks across the village and enters a Meroe temple where walls are covered in hieroglyphs depicting the journey of souls through the afterlife. Incense burns in bronze braziers, filling the air with the scent of frankincense and myrrh. The ceiling arches overhead, painted with stars that seem to move in the flickering light, while carved columns stretch upward like palm trees reaching toward the cosmos.

At the temple's heart stands a shaman draped in leopard skin and wearing a headdress of ostrich feathers. Two other shamans sit cross-legged nearby, their hands moving rhythmically over traditional drums and rattles that create a hypnotic percussion echoing off the stone walls.

"Your Queen has sent me here," Titus announces as he approaches.

The shaman gestures for him to sit on a woven mat placed before a small altar decorated with carved ivory figurines of animal-headed gods. Without speaking, he offers

Titus a clay cup filled with a dark liquid that tastes bitter and earthy, like roots ground with honey.

Next comes a clay pipe filled with burning herbs. Leaves that produce thick, sweet smoke. The shaman motions for Titus to inhale deeply, and the Roman obeys despite his soldier's instincts warning him against unknown substances.

The drumming grows louder, more insistent, as the temple begins to shift around him. The walls seem to breathe, the hieroglyphs begin writhing, and suddenly Titus finds himself transported beyond the physical realm. Visions unfold before his eyes with crystalline clarity:

He sees Horus, the falcon-headed god, soaring down the Blue Nile with wings spread wide against a brilliant sky. The god-king follows the water to its source deep in the Ethiopian highlands, where a golden chest rests in a sacred grove surrounded by ancient trees. The chest pulses with divine light, and Horus bows before it.

The vision shifts, and Titus sees Set, the god of chaos, stalking along the White Nile. Set carries a vial of poison that gleams like liquid night, and his destination becomes clear. He arrives at a black temple of impossible proportions at the source of the White Nile. There, he stands on the balcony of the temple and pours the black liquid into the lake, poisoning the sacred source that gives life to all of Egypt. But more terrifying still, Titus watches as Set's shadow falls over Sextus, merging with the Praetorian Prefect until the Roman's eyes glow with the god's malevolence.

The vision shimmers and transforms. Now Titus sees Sextus, eyes glowing black with Set's malevolence, escorting Titus's father through marble corridors to the imperial baths. Steam rises in ghostly tendrils around them as Agrippina's whispered commands echo from unseen corners. Sextus presents his father with a gleaming blade. Blood mingles with bathwater, spreading like crimson ink across the surface while Sextus stands impassive, a statue carved from cruelty, watching as the life drains from his father's eyes.

Then the vision changes again, and Titus sees his peaceful cottage in Britannia where his wife tends their garden while their sons play in the yard. The scene fills him with warmth and longing until the cottage door opens to reveal a figure silhouetted against the light. Nero, his imperial robes soaked in blood, a gladius dripping red in his hand as he steps across the threshold toward Titus's family.

Titus jerks awake on the temple floor, his body drenched in cold sweat and his heart hammering against his ribs. The shaman watches him with knowing eyes while the drumming continues its steady rhythm.

He staggers to his feet and exits the temple into the cool night air, his mind reeling from the visions that felt more real than the stones beneath his feet. The implications of what he witnessed weigh heavily as he makes his way back through Meroe's quiet streets.

At the tavern, he climbs the wooden stairs to the sleeping chamber where his companions rest peacefully. Titus lies down on his simple mat, but sleep comes slowly as the shaman's visions rattle around in his head.

Titus, Paulinus, and Pliny wake to find their sleeping chamber half-empty. The beds where Sextus, Marcus, and Quintus had slept stand abandoned, the sheets folded military neat. The sound of screaming erupts from the streets below, followed by the clash of bronze on bronze and the roar of flames consuming wood and thatch. They bolt upright and rush outside to witness a scene of systematic destruction.

Meroe burns around them. Houses collapsing in showers of sparks, dead Kushites sprawled in the dusty streets, survivors fleeing in terror as Roman steel cuts down anyone too slow to escape. The hut where the Kushite guards had been sleeping lies burned to the ground, the pile of corpses at the door indicating it had been locked from the outside. Along the parapet walls, sentries slump at their posts, dark stains spreading beneath their severed necks, their weapons still sheathed. Titus shouts as he spots the Praetorian prefect directing the carnage.

"Sextus! What are you doing?"

"Destroying enemies of the empire, Titus," Sextus replies with a satisfied smile.

"We told them we came in peace! They gave us food and shelter. They trusted us!"

"Then this will serve as a valuable lesson about trusting your enemies."

"The Queen will send her royal guard to kill us all!"

Marcus and Quintus laugh while Sextus smiles with sinister pleasure. Titus sprints through the burning streets toward the royal palace, dodging falling debris and stepping over bodies that litter his path. When he reaches the palace courtyard, he stops dead in his tracks.

Queen Amanitore hangs crucified before her own palace gates, her royal robes torn and bloodied, her crown lying broken in the dust below. The woman who had shown them hospitality and wisdom now dies the death Rome reserves for rebels and criminals. Titus falls to his knees, overwhelmed by the magnitude of this betrayal. Sextus walks up behind him.

"Perhaps she should ask Anubis to mummify her as well."

Marcus and Quintus burst into laughter at their commander's wit before following him away from the scene. Paulinus approaches Titus, his face grim.

"Are you really sending me alone down the river with these mad dogs?"

"What choice do we have?"

The sound of girls screaming draws their attention toward the harbour. They run toward the boats to find Kashta kneeling beside their vessel, tears streaming down his face as he embraces his wife and daughters. Sextus strides up and holds a knife to the guide's throat.

"What should we do with you, Kashta?"

"Let him go, Sextus." Titus commands.

"Why should I spare this barbarian?"

"Have you considered our return journey, you damned psychopath? We have no idea how long the Nile extends.

We may need to stop here and resupply on our way back to Rome."

Sextus considers this practical concern before slowly removing the blade from Kashta's neck.

"You're right, Titus. Perhaps I've been a bit blood-drunk lately. It appears to be your lucky day, Kashta. You're coming with us. Tell your wife to wait here for our return and ensure sufficient supplies are ready." Sextus moves the blade to Kashta's wife's throat. "Or do I need to remind you how much you have to lose?"

"No, please," Kashta begs. "I'll come with you for as long as necessary. My family will have supplies ready for our return, and fresh boats if needed. Just please don't harm them."

Sextus looks at Titus and for a brief moment, his eyes flash that familiar shade of black. He sheathes his blade with a calculated slowness that makes Kashta's family flinch.

"Say your goodbyes, then. We leave within the hour."

Kashta embraces his wife and daughters, whispering frantically in their ears as he presses his forehead against theirs. The youngest girl clutches at his tunic, her small hands leaving dusty prints on the fabric as tears cut clean tracks through the soot on her face. He gently pries her fingers loose, planting a kiss on her palm before closing it into a tiny fist, as if sealing the gesture inside.

Two boats wait at the harbour with fresh supplies loaded aboard. The expedition divides as planned. Titus, Sextus, and Pliny in one vessel, while Paulinus, Kashta, Marcus, and Quintus take the other.

As they sail away from the burning capital of Kush, Titus looks back at the smoke rising from what had been a magnificent African city. The vision from the temple haunts him. Set's influence over Sextus now seems terrifyingly real.

The boats approach one of nature's most remarkable phenomena. The point where the mighty Nile splits into two distinct rivers that have shaped the destiny of empires. Here, at the convergence near ancient Khartoum, the waters literally divide before their eyes, creating a sight that seems almost supernatural.

The Blue Nile flows from the east, its waters carrying the deep azure hue that gives it its name. This river runs swift and clear, fed by the highland rains of distant Ethiopia, its current strong enough to power the seasonal floods that have made Egypt's agriculture possible for millennia. Rocky outcroppings line its banks, while acacia trees provide patches of green against the desert landscape.

The White Nile stretches toward the south, its waters a milky pale colour from the sediments it carries from the heart of Africa. This river moves more slowly, broader and more mysterious, winding through vast papyrus swamps and marshlands that extend beyond the horizon. Its banks teem with wildlife. Hippos wallowing in shallow pools, crocodiles basking on muddy shores, and countless species of water birds that depend on its life-giving flow.

Between the two rivers lies a narrow island of sandy soil, creating a natural harbour where boats can easily separate to follow their chosen paths. Palm trees cluster around freshwater springs, while ancient stone markers carved with hieroglyphs suggest this confluence has been recognized as sacred for thousands of years.

"This is where we part ways," Titus announces as their boats reach the division point.

Titus, Sextus, and Pliny point their vessel toward the White Nile, while Paulinus, Kashta, Marcus, and Quintus point their vessel towards the Blue Nile.

"I'll meet you back here soon," Paulinus calls across the water, though his usual humour carries an undertone of uncertainty.

"I hope so," Titus replies.

As the boats begin to separate, Paulinus notices Marcus and Quintus in the stern of his vessel. Both guards sit sharpening their gladii as they stare at Paulinus like wolves studying their prey.

Chapter 16
Sporus

Olympia, Greece, 67 AD. Nero and Sporus walk towards the palace built specifically for Nero's Olympic sojourn. The structure sprawls across several acres with marble columns imported from Carrara. Gardens surround the complex, featuring roses from Damascus, cypress trees from Lebanon, and fountains that spray perfumed water into basins carved from precious stones. Sporus awes as they approach the magnificent entrance.

"Oh, wow."

"Do you like it, Sporus? I had it constructed specially for my journey to Greece."

"I've never seen such a beautiful home before."

"I'm delighted you appreciate it. Come, join me for dinner."

They enter through bronze doors decorated with scenes of Apollo leading the Muses, stepping into an interior that rivals anything in Rome itself. The floors gleam with intricate mosaics depicting Olympic victories, while the walls display masterworks of Greek art acquired through imperial conquest.

The dining hall features a table that could accommodate fifty guests, though tonight it's set intimately for two. Platters overflow with delicacies from across the Mediterranean. Peacock tongues, honeyed dates, wine from the Emperor's private vineyards, and fruits that have travelled from the furthest reaches of the empire.

"Would you join me for dinner?" Nero asks.

"I would be honoured."

They recline on silk-covered couches as slaves serve course after course. The conversation flows as smoothly as the wine, punctuated by Nero's stories of his artistic achievements and plans for future performances. Sporus twirls his hair as he admires Nero.

"My Emperor. I couldn't help but notice at the Olympic Games that you are truly the greatest artist who ever lived."

"Thank you for your honesty, Sporus. If only my late wife had mirrored both your appearance and your kindness."

"I live to serve my Emperor."

Nero smiles softly as he observes Sporus across the table.

"You know, I have something for you."

He motions for Epaphroditus to approach and whispers something in his ear. The secretary exits and returns carrying an elaborate silk gown decorated with pearls and gold thread.

"This belonged to my late wife Sabina. It would mean everything to me if you would put it on."

"Of course, my Emperor. I will do anything you ask."

Sporus begins to walk away with the dress, but Nero stops him.

"No. Change here."

Sporus nods and silently disrobes in the dining hall as Nero watches with growing emotion. When he dons Sabina's gown, the transformation is remarkable. The silk emphasizes his figure, making him appear more like Nero’s late wife.

"You look exactly like her," Nero whispers, tears beginning to well in his eyes.

Sporus holds up his hair to create a more feminine silhouette, and Nero's expression transforms from grief to something approaching joy. He stands up and approaches Sporus.

"I know how sudden this is, but I wish to make you my wife and Empress."

"Yes! A thousand times yes!"

“You have made me the happiest Emperor in Roman history!”

Nero lifts Sporus onto the table, stroking his hair while gazing into his eyes with adoration.

"There is just one difference between you and Sabina that we need to address."

Nero nods to Tigellinus, and suddenly two guards pin Sporus to the table.

"What are you doing?" Sporus cries in panic.

Tigellinus moves to the fireplace, where flames lick at a blade glowing red-hot. He lifts it, the metal hissing in the air, and Sporus’s eyes widen with terror as he sees it.

"Emperor, please," he pleads, his voice a desperate tremor.

Nero takes the blade, his expression serene, almost loving.

"Don't worry, my love. This will help you be a better wife for me."

The red-hot blade descends. Nero's eyes glint with excitement as the blade castrates Sporus. Sporus's screams reverberate against the marble walls. He collapses to the floor, writhing in agony, clutching the wound at his crotch as blood seeps through his fingers. Nero observes him writhe before he turns to Epaphroditus with the satisfied smile of an artist who just completed a masterpiece.

"We shall marry in Athens with full imperial ceremony. Deconstruct this palace and rebuild it there. We'll stage a wedding that would make Eros herself blush with envy."

Epaphroditus bows his head.

"As you command, Caesar."

Nero crouches beside the writhing figure on the marble floor and begins running his fingers through Sporus's hair.

"I know it's painful, my darling fiancé, but pleasure and pain are two sides of the same coin; without one, the other loses meaning."

Sporus continues to roll on the floor, clutching his wound and screaming in pain. Nero leans in to whisper, his lips almost touching Sporus's ear.

"Fear not, my love. Our glorious wedding will make you forget all about this."

Athens, Greece, 67 AD, one week later. The House of Nero stands resplendent, a monument of decadence reborn for an imperial wedding. Rebuilt by Greek slaves, two of whom perished under the weight of its marble slabs. The palace gleams under the Athenian sun, its columns draped in garlands of roses and myrtle. Golden tapestries shimmer from the porticos, woven with scenes of gods blessing mortal unions, while braziers burn with frankincense.

Inside, the atrium is a riot of colour: crimson and saffron fabrics cascade from the ceiling, and mosaics of Venus and Cupid glitter under torchlight. Servants scatter rose petals across the marble floors, their fragrance mingling with the scent of spiced wine and roasted lamb. The air hums with anticipation, musicians plucking lyres and blowing flutes, their melodies weaving through the chatter of Rome's elite, gathered to witness an Emperor's nuptials.

The wedding unfolds in Roman splendour, a ceremony veiled in tradition and magnified by Nero's flamboyance. Sporus stands at the centre, a vision of imperial grace, his bridal veil of sheer saffron silk cascading over his shoulders, embroidered with gold thread that sparkles light like a halo. His hands, trembling slightly, clutch a bouquet of orange blossoms, symbolising fertility and eternal love.

Nero, resplendent in a purple toga edged with gold, stands beside him, his eyes gleaming with possessive pride. The augur, clad in white, invokes Juno and Jupiter, offering a libation of wine to the gods as the couple's hands are bound with a woollen cord, their union sealed with sacred vows. Guests toss walnuts for good fortune, their laughter echoing as the couple exchanges rings, the golden bands glinting with promises of eternity. Nero steps forward, raising a goblet, his voice commanding the hall's attention.

"My beloved Sporus, my Empress, and my heart. Today, we are not merely joined as husband and wife, but as rulers of Rome, destined to shape her golden future. Together, we shall weave a tapestry of glory, our love a beacon to rival the sun. Sporus, your grace and devotion will guide our empire to new heights, your beauty a mirror to Rome's splendour. We shall rule not as tyrants, but as artists, crafting a world where every citizen basks in the light of our union. Let our enemies tremble, for with you at my side, Rome will be eternal, her name sung by poets for a thousand years!"

The crowd applauds nervously, goblets raised, as Sporus's eyes shimmer with tears, his smile radiant yet fragile. Nero's voice softens, a mischievous glint in his eyes.

"In celebration of our marriage, I have prepared the most wonderful light show for my new Empress. I'll ask you all to join me in the garden."

He takes Sporus's hand, leading him through the throng, the guests trailing behind in a wave of silks and murmurs. The garden is a labyrinth of beauty, its paths lined with jasmine and laurel, fountains sparkling under the moon's gaze. But at its heart, a chilling tableau awaits: dozens of figures, bound to tall poles, their bodies glistening with honey, their faces contorted in fear. Nero pauses, his arm encircling Sporus as he gestures to the captives.

"This is everyone in Greece who was caught worshipping the carpenter from Nazareth. They even dared to speak ill of our beautiful union."

He nods to Tigellinus, and the Praetorian Guards move with torches in hand. Flames leap to life, licking at the honey-soaked bodies, the fire catching slowly, deliberately, as the captive's screams pierce the night, a cacophony of anguish that drowns the garden's serenity. Nero puts his arms around Sporus.

"The honey makes them burn slower. I call it a 'Roman candle'."

Sporus leans into him, his veil fluttering, and Nero's arm tightens around his waist. They stand together, bathed in the flickering glow of the burning Christians, their silhouettes entwined as the screams fade into crackling embers, a symphony of light and pain sealing their union under the Athenian stars.

Rome, 67 AD. Nero and Sporus return from Greece. Nero strides through the golden halls of the Domus Aurea, his Olympic victories having inflated his already considerable ego to new heights. Four gold medals gleam from chains around his neck while Sporus follows behind, still adjusting to the elaborate imperial robes and jewellery that mark his transformation from slave to Empress.

Messalina waits in the main atrium, her composed demeanour betraying no surprise at the unprecedented situation unfolding before her. Years of marriage to Nero have taught her to navigate even the most shocking developments with diplomatic grace.

"My darling wife Messalina. I wish to introduce you to the latest addition to our family. This is my new wife, Sporus."

Messalina maintains her calm composure despite the historical significance of this moment.

"Lovely to meet you, Sporus."

"Doesn't she bear a remarkable resemblance to Sabina?" Nero asks.

Messalina studies Sporus intensively, shocked by the genuine semblance.

"They are almost identical."

"Our family, and our empire, have just become more complete."

"Husband, while you were celebrating your artistic triumphs in Greece, there has been considerable turmoil throughout the empire. Citizens struggle to afford basic necessities like food and housing. There aren't enough dwellings for Roman citizens, while hostile foreign tribes simply walk into the city and occupy entire neighbourhoods. The provinces lack funding for essential public services, and there are rumours of another revolt brewing."

Nero waves away these concerns with imperial indifference.

"Let's not burden ourselves with tedious political matters. It's time to introduce Rome to my new wife."

"Are you certain that's wise, my Emperor? The citizens have not responded favourably to news of your new union."

"Once they lay eyes on Sporus, they'll fall in love just as I did. I shall present him to the people at the chariot races."

Nero takes Sporus by the hand and leads him toward the palace doors, leaving behind Messalina.

Later that evening, Nero and Sporus arrive at The Circus Maximus, Rome's beating heart of spectacle and blood sport. Marble seats rise in tiers toward the sky, filled with citizens from every level of society. Senators in their purple-striped togas occupying the prime positions, while plebeians pack the upper levels in a sea of rough wool and leather. The roar of conversation creates a thunderous din that echoes off the surrounding walls.

At the track's centre stands the spina, the long barrier decorated with bronze dolphins, golden eggs, and towering obelisks that mark the laps. The starting gates stand ready to release the chariots that will thunder around the seven-lap course in a display of speed, skill, and mortal danger.

Nero stands on the Emperor's viewing platform, elevated above the crowd to display his imperial majesty. Sporus remains beside him, adorned in the silk robes and precious jewellery that mark his unprecedented status as Empress. The crowd's reaction to this sight is immediate and hostile. Hisses and boos rise from the packed seats like the sound of angry serpents.

"Pay no attention to the rabble, my dear Empress. They are merely jealous of your divine beauty."

He raises his hand for silence, and gradually the crowd settles into sullen quiet.

"Citizens of Rome! Welcome to the chariot races of the Neronian Games! I know many of you have complained about the difficulty of seeing evening races in darkness. During my glorious wedding to Sporus in Athens, I devised an ingenious solution to illuminate our spectacles. I present to you, Roman Candles!"

At his signal, the Praetorian Guard ignite rows of prisoners bound to poles along the track's edge. The captives, Christians drenched in honey, scream as flames lick their bodies, the honey ensuring a slow, torturous burn. Their agonised cries pierce the air, mingling with the crackle of fire and the crowd's uneasy murmurs, the arena bathed in a ghastly, flickering glow. Nero's smile is radiant

"Let the games begin!"

The crowd's attention turns to the track as twelve chariots line up at the starting gates, their horses pawing the sand with eager energy. When the gates spring open, the race explodes into motion. Wheels spinning, hooves thundering, dust clouds rising as the charioteers fight for position around the first turn.

The race unfolds with spectacular intensity. Chariots crash in sprays of splintered wood and screaming horses, drivers are thrown from their vehicles to be dragged by their reins, and the crowd roars its approval for each moment of danger and skill.

One charioteer distinguishes himself above the others. A man whose driving shows both courage and tactical brilliance. He navigates the chaos with steady nerves, taking calculated risks while avoiding the reckless moves that claim other competitors. As the final lap approaches, he edges into the lead and maintains it through sheer determination.

The victor guides his foam-flecked horses to a stop before the imperial platform, leaping down with the confidence of a man who has conquered both speed and death. When he removes his bronze helmet, he reveals rugged features and intelligent eyes that meet Nero's gaze without flinching. Nero turns to Epaphroditus.

"Who is that man? I should like to meet with him."

"A freedman, my Emperor. His parents named him after their favourite Greek philosopher."

"What is his name?"

"Pythagoras."

Chapter 17
The Ark of the Covenant

The Blue Nile cuts through the Ethiopian highlands like a sapphire ribbon, its waters carrying the deep azure hue that gives the river its name. Dense jungle crowds both banks, creating walls of green that rise dozens of feet into the sky. Ancient trees with trunks wide enough to house entire families stretch toward the canopy, while vines thick as ship cables hang between them like natural bridges. Exotic birds call from above while monkeys move noisily through the branches in lively groups.

Paulinus and Kashta pull at the oars while Marcus and Quintus occupy the boat's stern, their gladii moving rhythmically across whetstones with the methodical scraping that has become the expedition's most ominous sound. The foliage seems to breathe, expanding and contracting like the chest of some vast living organism. Kashta's eyes remain fixed on the jungle that presses in from all sides as he whispers.

"We are being watched."

Marcus follows Kashta's gaze, scanning the dense wall of vegetation.

"By who?" Marcus asks.

"Or what?" Paulinus adds.

"Many eyes. They move with us."

"I don't see anything," Quintus mutters.

Marcus thumbs through the boat's food supply, and then flashes a look to Quintus, who nods.

"I'm not so sure we have enough rations for all of us to survive this trip. Remind me, Paulinus, why do we need you?" Marcus asks.

"For my charming personality," Paulinus replies.

"We don't know how long this journey will take. We might not have sufficient supplies for the return trip," Quintus adds.

"Maybe you should consider going on a diet," Paulinus says.

Both guards rise simultaneously, their swords singing as they clear their scabbards. They advance on Paulinus with their gladii drawn. Marcus lowers his sword and points it at Paulinus's heart.

"Consider this food rationing. Goodbye, Paulinus."

Marcus lunges forward, but Paulinus swings his oar upward, knocking the gladius from the guard's grip. The sword spins through the air before splashing into the blue water. Marcus pulls a dagger from his boot, but Paulinus begins rocking the boat violently from side to side. The small vessel pitches wildly on the current, and both guards lose their footing, tumbling into the Blue Nile with surprised shouts.

"Row for shore!" Paulinus commands.

Kashta pulls desperately at his oar while Paulinus steers toward the muddy bank. They reach the shallows and leap from the boat onto solid ground.

"Where is your sword?" Paulinus asks urgently.

"I don't have one," Kashta replies.

"For the love of Mars!"

Paulinus looks back at the two guards swimming steadily toward shore, their butterfly stroke cutting through the cerulean water. A nervous smirk twitches at the corner of his mouth as sweat beads on his upper lip.

"Don't worry. One of those giant crocodiles will eat them any moment now," Paulinus says with forced optimism.

The guards continue swimming, their faces contorted with rage, eyes fixed on Paulinus.

"Any second now," Paulinus mutters.

Marcus and Quintus reach the shore and drag themselves onto the muddy bank, water streaming from their ornate armour in rivulets. They draw short backup daggers.

"I didn't realize it was the crocodile's day off. Run!"

As they turn to flee into the jungle they are blocked by a wall of stone-tipped spears. Dozens of native tribal warriors emerge from the treeline pointing spears at the group. Their dark skin bears intricate scarification, while their bodies are adorned with feathers, bone jewellery, and paint that makes them seem part of the jungle itself.

They shout in a language that sounds like music mixed with thunder, their voices rising and falling in complex harmonies that echo through the trees. The Praetorians drop their daggers, recognizing the hopelessness of their situation.

"Who are they?" Paulinus whispers to Kashta.

"The Mbenga tribe. They have lived in these jungles for thousands of years."

"What are they saying?"

"They say we are trespassing on sacred ground."

"Tell them we're just passing through. Let us go and we'll leave peacefully."

Kashta translates, but the response is immediate and hostile. Angry shouts and spear points moving closer to their throats.

"They say that decision belongs to their chief," Kashta translates.

The warriors bind all four men with ropes made from jungle vines, then begin dragging them through the dense undergrowth. Thorns tear at their clothes while insects swarm around their faces, but their captors move through the jungle with the ease of people born to this environment. Paulinus turns to Kashta as they're hauled deeper into the green maze.

"Look on the bright side. If they wanted us dead, we'd be dead already."

They emerge from the dense jungle undergrowth into a clearing that takes their breath away. Before them lies a pristine mountain lake, its waters reflecting the sky like a mirror of polished silver. Springs bubble up from the earth around its edges, feeding the lake that gives birth to the Blue Nile. The water flows out in a clear stream that will eventually join the White Nile and become the mighty river that has sustained civilizations for millennia.

"By the gods, there it is. The source of the Nile," Paulinus breathes.

The lake nestles in a natural amphitheatre of ancient trees and moss-covered rocks, while mist rises from its surface in ghostly tendrils. The air carries the pure scent of mountain water and wild flowers that bloom in impossible profusion around the sacred pool.

Beside the lake sits a small tribal village of huts with conical roofs made from woven grass and mud walls painted in earth tones. Smoke rises from cooking fires while children play near the water's edge under the watchful eyes of their elders.

The warriors escort their captives toward the largest hut, where an elderly man waits with the bearing of natural authority. Behind him, visible through the hut's open entrance, stands an ornate golden chest that seems almost to glow with inner light. The artifact measures roughly four feet long, two feet wide, and two feet high, crafted from what appears to be solid gold and decorated with intricate carvings of winged creatures.

"What's in that golden chest?" Paulinus asks quietly.

Kashta poses the question to the chief, who responds with reverent tones.

"He says it contains stone tablets handed down by God himself. His tribe has been given the divine mission to guard these tablets and ensure no one ever opens the chest. He has brought us here to participate in a ceremony honouring them."

The four prisoners are forced to kneel on the hard-packed earth before the hut, their hands still bound behind their backs. Tribal shamans begin playing traditional instruments, drums made from hollowed logs, rattles crafted from gourds, and flutes carved from bone. Dancers emerge wearing elaborate costumes of feathers and animal skins.

They burn herbs that create sweet-smelling smoke while chanting in harmonies that seem to resonate with the very earth beneath them. The ceremony builds in intensity, drawing the entire village into its rhythmic embrace. The chief addresses the captives, speaking in a language that predates the pharaohs. Kashta translates.

"The ark has been in our care since time beyond memory. It was entrusted to our ancestors by beings who descended from the sky in chariots of fire."

Paulinus studies the ornate golden chest, his eyes narrowing with recognition.

"That looks like the sacred chest the Hebrews talk about."

"The chief says that one of you will be chosen for a higher purpose, but you must volunteer. The rest will not be so fortunate." Kashta translates with growing unease.

"Me! Me! It should be me!" Marcus shouts desperately.

The chief smiles at Marcus's eagerness and nods to his warriors. Two tribal dancers pull the Roman guard into the ritual circle, seating him on a wooden table positioned directly in front of the golden chest.

They perform an elaborate shamanistic ritual around him, painting symbols on his face and body while chanting invocations. They offer him a clay cup filled with dark liquid, followed by a wooden pipe containing burning herbs. Marcus drinks and inhales as directed. His demeanour shifts from his usual military bearing as he waves his hand in front of his face and laughs at it.

"By the gods, I feel invincible. I can see the cosmos in my palms." He starts laughing, staring at his own hands in wonder. He touches his face experimentally. "I can't feel anything."

The chief approaches carrying a large ceremonial blade, its edge gleaming in the firelight. Marcus looks at the blade, his smile beaming from ear to ear.

"What's that for?"

Without a word, the chieftain swings the blade, severing Marcus's leg at the thigh. The captives scream, their voices a raw cacophony of horror. Marcus throws his head back in hysterical laughter, seemingly oblivious to the dark pool spreading beneath what remains of his leg.

“I can't even feel that!” he cackles, his eyes glassy with delirium.

Paulinus, Kashta, and Quintus struggle against their bonds, shouting, but tribesmen hold them back with iron grips. Dancers tie a tourniquet around Marcus's stump, their movements ritualistic. They catch the spurting blood in a chalice, pouring it over their bodies in streaks of crimson reverence. The severed leg is carried to a fire, skewered on a spit, and roasted, the air filling with the nauseating scent of charring flesh. Paulinus turns to Kashta.

"I know why they're keeping the rest of us alive."

"Why?"

Paulinus nods towards the spittle where Marcus’s leg is roasting above a campfire.

"They don't want their meat to spoil."

The tribesmen drag the captives to wooden poles staked deep into the dirt, their hands rebound tightly behind their backs, the ropes biting into their skin as the village’s chants grow louder, the golden chest looming like a silent judge over the unfolding nightmare.

Night falls across the village, bringing no mercy with its shadows. The tribal dancers have retreated to their huts, leaving only two guards to watch over the captives. Marcus's delirious laughter has faded into unconscious moans, his body slumped against the ropes that hold him upright. Blood continues to seep from his bandaged stump, drawing flies that buzz incessantly around the wound.

Paulinus tests his bonds again, feeling the rough fibres bite deeper into his wrists.

"How are you doing over there, Quintus?" he whispers.

The Praetorian's face is a mask of barely controlled rage.

"When I get free, I'm going to massacre every last one of these godless savages," Quintus says through gritted teeth.

"That's the spirit. Always think positively."

Kashta's eyes scan the clearing, tracking the movements of the guards. He whispers to Paulinus, his voice barely audible above the night insect's chorus.

"They will come for more meat soon. They believe consuming the flesh of enemies transfers strength."

"Wonderful. I'd prefer to keep all my limbs attached, if possible," Paulinus replies, wincing as he shifts position against the wooden post, before realising any attempt to break the bonds is futile.

"That chest. Is that what I think it is?" Quintus whispers to Kashta.

"My people have stories of the chest that brings death. It travelled south along the Nile generations ago, carried by priests fleeing a great conquest. They said it should never be opened under any circumstances."

Quintus whispers, his earlier rage giving way to a reluctant awe.

"I heard tales from Jewish prisoners in Rome. They claim it contains immeasurable power. The very voice of their God captured in stone."

"Fascinating," Paulinus mutters, watching as one of the guards shifts position. "But I'm a little more concerned with being served as the main course right now."

Two tribal guards walk towards them, bare feet slapping against the packed earth, faces contorted with rage beneath their white and ochre war paint. The tallest one brandishes a barbed spear inches from Paulinus's throat, spittle flying from his lips as he screams words in their ancient tribal language.

"What's he saying?" Paulinus asks Kashta.

"They're telling you to stop talking."

"And here I thought we were starting to become friends."

The guards scream and inch the spear closer to Paulinus's neck. He swallows hard, feeling the point dig deeper with the movement of his Adam's apple. His lips press into a tight line as he meets the guard's wild-eyed stare. The guards exchange guttural words before retreating.

The night air grows heavy with moisture as a distant rumble of thunder rolls across the jungle canopy. The guards glance skyward, exchanging words before one disappears into a nearby hut, seeking shelter from the approaching storm.

The next morning, Paulinus wakes to find himself still sitting on hard-packed earth, his back against a wooden pole with his hands bound tightly behind him. The morning air carries the scent of wood smoke and cooking fires, while tribal voices drift from the nearby huts. He surveys their situation carefully, then closes his eyes and pretends to sleep. Kashta stirs beside him, beginning to lift his head.

"Psst," Paulinus whispers without moving his lips. "Pretend to be asleep."

Kashta immediately closes his eyes again.

"Unless you want to become breakfast, we need to escape." Paulinus whispers.

"And go where? We don't even know our location or which direction leads home," Kashta responds quietly.

"I'd rather take my chances in the jungle than over a cooking fire."

A third voice joins their whispered conversation.

"I'm free," Quintus whispers.

"What?" Paulinus whispers, surprised.

"It took me all night, but I cut through my ropes," Quintus explains softly.

Paulinus risks a glance and sees that Quintus has indeed freed himself using a sharpened stone that lies hidden beside him.

"There's strength in numbers. I'll free you as well. At the very least, you can serve as my temporary human shield."

"Thank the gods. When?"

"The guard watching us has digestive issues. He constantly visits the latrine area. Perhaps human flesh isn't the most nutritious diet. Next time he leaves, I'll cut you loose and we make our escape."

"Understood," both Paulinus and Kashta whisper.

"Just don't do anything to attract attention," Quintus warns.

At that moment, Marcus begins to stir. He looks around groggily.

"By the gods, my head. What happened last night?"

He looks around confused, wondering where he is. His expression shifts from confusion to horror as he looks down, realizes his leg has been severed, and begins screaming at the top of his lungs.

"My leg! Where is my leg!"

"Shut up! Shut up!" Quintus hisses desperately.

"My leg! Help me!" Marcus continues shrieking.

Tribal guards rush over, shouting angrily at the disruption Marcus is causing to the peaceful morning.

"That must be a hangover fit for Hades," Paulinus mutters.

The tribesman continue yelling at Marcus to shut up until one of the guards clubs him unconscious with a wooden staff, blood trickling down his cheek as he slumps forward. He begins examining the other prisoners more carefully, noticing that Quintus's restraints have been severed. He shouts an alarm that brings the entire village running.

Quintus springs to his feet and shoves the nearest tribesman to the ground, then sprints towards the jungle treeline. Spears fly through the air around him, but he dodges with desperate agility, weaving between the projectiles until he reaches the safety of the dense undergrowth.

"The fool actually made it," Paulinus says with grudging admiration.

Night falls over the tribal village like a dark shroud, bringing with it the sounds of nocturnal hunters and the distant roar of waterfalls cascading into the sacred lake. The three remaining prisoners sit bound to their wooden posts, exhaustion and fear etched on their faces.

Marcus weeps quietly, his condition having deteriorated significantly since the morning's traumatic awakening. A tribesman approaches carrying the ceremonial blade, studying all three prisoners before focusing on Marcus.

"No, no, no, no," Marcus pleads desperately.

The tribesman's face remains impassive as he raises the machete high. The blade descends with a sickening thud, biting into Marcus's thigh. Marcus screams so loud he causes the others to shut their eyes. The tribesman hacks again, and again, and again. Blood sprays, dark and viscous, pooling beneath Marcus as his cries weaken to ragged gasps. Finally, the leg gives way, severed with a final, brutal chop. Marcus's head lolls, his body slumping as consciousness flees.

The tribesman kneels, deftly tying a crude tourniquet around the fresh wound, his movements mechanical, as if he's performed this ritual a hundred times. Paulinus watches, his stomach churning, the metallic scent of blood clogging his nostrils.

"I guess the drug cocktail was a one-night-only deal," Paulinus mutters to Kashta, "What do you think they'll do when they run out of his extremities to harvest?"

Kashta looks at him with terror-filled eyes, understanding the implication. Paulinus nods.

"I wish I hadn't asked. We need the gods to intervene if we want to escape."

A soft whisper of "psst" emanates from the treeline. Both men look toward the sound to see Quintus's head poking out from behind a large tree trunk.

"What are you still doing here?" Paulinus whispers urgently.

"I'll never survive the jungle alone," Quintus admits.

"So you returned to become tonight's main course?"

"I need Kashta to guide me back to civilization."

"Then come and free me," Kashta hisses.

"Impossible. I've been observing their guard patterns all day. There are always eyes watching you. You'll have to engineer your own escape."

"How?"

"You figure it out."

"I'll create a distraction large enough to give us time to flee," Paulinus declares.

"What are you planning to do?"

Paulinus's gaze fixes on the Ark of the Covenant visible through the chief's hut entrance.

"I'm going to open that golden chest."

Chapter 18
Neropolis

Rome, 68 AD. The Senate house thrums with tension as six hundred senators occupy their marble benches. Many are new, appointed to replace those executed after the Pisonian conspiracy. They watch with clenched jaws and carefully neutral expressions, their compliance born from witnessing the brutal purges that followed. Fear has replaced debate, survival has superseded principle, and the republic's ghost haunts these halls where free men once spoke their minds.

Nero stands at the chambers heart while Sporus reclines at his feet like a favoured pet, adorned in silk and jewels.

"Furthermore, Rome shall be renamed Neropolis to better reflect the glory of our current age," Nero announces.

The senators nod in agreement, afraid of meeting the same fate as the conspirators. One figure steps forward from the provincial representatives. A weathered man whose bearing speaks of years spent governing distant territories where Roman authority still means something practical rather than theatrical.

"Emperor, if I might interject—"

Tigellinus immediately steps forward, clutching his sword hilt.

"Silence while the Emperor is speaking!"

"It's quite all right, Tigellinus. Let him speak," Nero says.

"My name is Servius Sulpicius Galba, governor of Hispania Tarraconensis. With all due respect, Emperor, the outer provinces are collapsing. While your decision to abolish taxes may have proven popular with urban workers, we no longer possess the funds necessary to maintain basic imperial infrastructure."

Nero smirks and waves his hand dismissively.

"When you become Emperor, you shall be free to change tax policies as you see fit. Now, as I was explaining, the month of April shall be renamed Neroneus."

"You've gone completely mad!" another voice shouts from the provincial delegation.

"And who might you be?"

"Gaius Julius Vindex, governor of Gallia Lugdunensis. I came here to inform you that your empire is collapsing."

Nero laughs with genuine amusement.

"A non-Roman governor lecturing an Emperor about his own empire. This should prove entertaining if nothing else. Please, my dear provincial, enlighten me."

"Your citizens can no longer afford basic housing. Rome's borders stand wide open while barbarian tribes simply walk into imperial territory and establish settlements. They contribute nothing to society while attacking and robbing Roman citizens with impunity."

"What makes these so-called barbarians any different from Romans? Over time, they will learn to love me as much as everyone else does," Nero says.

"We lack sufficient housing for existing Roman citizens. We have no resources to accommodate new populations until we've properly cared for the people we're already responsible for governing."

Nero yawns theatrically.

"Provincial politics remain eternally tedious. I have another wedding to prepare for, which requires my immediate attention."

"Don't tell me you're abandoning imperial duties to make another slaveboy your bride," Vindex says.

"Of course not. How boring would that be? This time, I shall be the bride."

The Senate chamber falls into stunned silence. Even the most seasoned politicians, men who have witnessed decades of imperial excess, cannot mask their shock. Vindex's face contorts with disgust while Galba's expression hardens into granite. Nero's smile becomes radiant with anticipation.

"Yes. I shall wed the charioteer Pythagoras in a ceremony that will redefine what it means to be divine. He shall take me as his wife, and I shall demonstrate the ultimate artistic transformation. Emperor to Empress, man to woman, mortal to goddess."

A senator in the third row vomits onto the marble floor. The sound of his retching echoes through the chamber, followed by nervous coughs and the shuffling of sandals. Sporus looks up at Nero, his kohl-lined eyes widening with confusion.

"But husband, what will become of me?"

"You shall remain my Empress, of course. I will be Pythagoras's wife while you remain mine. The beauty of imperial power is that it transcends all conventional limitations."

Vindex steps forward, his voice trembling with barely contained rage.

"This is an abomination against nature itself. The gods will not stand for this."

"The gods? I am the living embodiment of Apollo on earth. When I speak, it is with divine authority. When I sing, the Muses themselves fall silent in awe. I have surpassed the boundaries of mortal artistry. Why should I not transcend the petty constraints of gender as well?"

"You claim to be Apollo while Rome burns around you. While you parade in women's clothing, Germanic tribes cross the Rhine unopposed. While you marry slaves, our legions go unpaid. The provinces are starving, Nero."

The metallic rasp of Tigellinus's blade partially clearing its scabbard echoes through the chamber. Several senators nearest the sound flinch visibly.

"I would advise careful speech when addressing the Emperor," Tigellinus says.

“So this is how Rome ends then? Through unfettered degeneracy.”

Nero stretches his arms wide, his imperial robes catching the light streaming through the high windows.

"That's where you are wrong, my dear provincial. This is not how Rome ends. This is how Rome becomes Neropolis."

The next day, Nero and Pythagoras prepare for their wedding. The gardens of the Domus Aurea have been transformed into a wedding venue that defies every tradition of Roman marriage. White silk pavilions stretch across manicured lawns while thousands of white roses create an atmosphere of bridal innocence that contrasts sharply with the unprecedented nature of the ceremony about to unfold.

Dignitaries from across the empire fill golden chairs arranged in precise rows. Senators who dare not refuse imperial invitations, provincial governors summoned from distant territories, wealthy merchants eager to curry favour, and foreign ambassadors whose presence legitimizes this spectacle in the eyes of international politics.

At the altar stands Pythagoras, the victorious charioteer whose rugged features now bear the uncertainty of a man who has discovered that imperial favour comes with prices he never anticipated. His simple freedman's toga has been replaced with silk robes that mark his elevation to unprecedented status.

But it is the bride who draws every eye and stops every conversation. Nero approaches wearing a traditional Roman bridal gown of pristine white silk, complete with the flame-coloured veil that Roman brides have worn for centuries. Pearls and gold jewellery adorn his neck and arms while a crown of myrtle leaves, sacred to Venus, rests upon his head. Behind him walk his bridesmaids: Sporus and Messalina.

The wedding guests sit in rigid silence, their faces carefully neutral as they witness the complete inversion of Roman tradition. Fear of Nero's wrath, demonstrated so thoroughly during the Pissonian conspiracy's suppression, keeps any expression of disapproval locked behind diplomatic masks.

"Citizens of Rome," the officiant declares, "we gather today to witness the union of Emperor Nero Claudius Caesar Augustus Germanicus and the freedman Pythagoras."

As the ceremony proceeds according to ancient Roman custom, though with roles reversed, Nero glows with happiness that appears genuine despite the bizarre circumstances. When invited to exchange vows, his voice carries across the garden:

"Pythagoras, my beloved husband, I pledge to honour and obey you as a dutiful Roman wife should, bringing you the joy and devotion that marriage requires."

The crowd maintains its nervous applause throughout the ceremony, understanding that their reactions are being carefully observed by the Praetorian Guard. The wedding feast commences with a lavishness that borders on obscene. Golden platters bear exotic delicacies from every corner of the empire. Flamingo tongues from Egypt, bear paws from Germania, peacocks glazed in honey.

Nero reclines at the head table in his bridal attire, feeding morsels to Pythagoras with delicate fingers. Nero turns to his new husband, his voice carrying a feminine lilt that makes several nearby senators study their wine with sudden fascination.

"Is my husband pleased with his bride?"

"Very pleased, my Emperor,"

"Not Emperor. Tonight, I am simply your wife."

The feast stretches into evening hours as lanterns illuminate the gardens. Musicians play increasingly sensual melodies while dancers perform mythological tales. Nymphs pursued by satyrs, Leda embracing the swan, Europa carried away by the bull. As night deepens, Nero rises from his couch, swaying slightly from the effects of wine.

"The time has come for the bride to be escorted to the marital chamber. My husband and I shall retire to consummate our union. Hopefully the gods will bless us and I will conceive his child."

The wedding reception applauds nervously, as the Praetorian Guard watches them like hawks ready to swoop on their prey. Vindex leans close to Galba's ear.

"I'm going to bring this madness to an end."

Galba's hand clamps around Vindex's forearm, his grip surprisingly strong for a man his age.

"Not here. Not now," he whispers.

Vindex's jaw clenches, a vein throbbing at his temple.

"Then when? While he dresses as a woman and marries a horse next?"

Galba's eyes scan the Praetorian Guards positioned throughout the garden, their hands never straying far from their weapons.

"Patience. Rome wasn't built in a day, and neither will her salvation be. Meet me at my villa after midnight. Come alone."

A procession forms of senators and nobles bearing torches to light the couple's path toward the imperial bedchamber. Their faces glow amber in the flickering light, masks of dutiful participation hiding thoughts that dare not surface.

Later that night, the golden walls of the Domus Aurea capture the dying light of evening, In the opulent bedchamber, three figures lie entwined upon silk sheets the colour of spilled wine. Nero still wears his wedding dress, one arm draped possessively around the slender form of Sporus, his beloved bride, while he rests against the shoulder of his new husband, Pythagoras.

From her chair beside the bed, Messalina observes the scene with calculating eyes. Nero looks at her as his fingers trace lazy patterns on Sporus's bare arm.

"That was a most beautiful wedding, wasn't it, Messalina?"

"It was magnificent, husband, The Senate seemed particularly moved by the ceremony," Messalina replies, her voice measured like a physician administering precise drops of medicine.

Nero squeezes Pythagaros and laughs.

"How lucky those old bores were to have experienced true culture for an evening."

Heavy footsteps echo in the marble corridor beyond, growing closer until they halt at the chamber doors. Without ceremony, Tigellinus enters, his battle-hardened intensity cutting through the intimate atmosphere like a blade through silk.

"Emperor, The Praetorian Guard found Paul. We've brought him here to see you."

Nero's brow furrows with confusion, his wine-clouded mind struggling to place the name.

"Who?"

"The man who was helping Peter build his church."

"Ah yes, of course. Send him in."

The doors open wider, and Paul enters the chamber. His sun-leathered face, marked by years of persecution and travel, immediately contorts in shock at the scene before him. He makes the sign of the cross. Nero smirks.

"Funny, your friend Peter did the same thing with his hands."

“And where is Peter now?" Paul asks.

Nero motions towards the window.

"Go see for yourself."

Paul walks over to gaze at the gardens of Palantine Hill, where Peter’s corpse festers on an upside-down crucifix. He makes the sign of the cross again. Nero laughs.

"Shouldn't you have done that upside down?"

Paul turns to face Nero, unamused. Nero disentangles himself from Sporus, the white silk of his bridal gown whispering across the mosaic floor as he rises.

"Tell me, Paul, why did you come to Rome?"

"I come bearing witness to the truth of Jesus Christ. Even in this hive of corruption, his light can reach."

Nero laughs as his fingers play with his collection of swords hanging on the wall.

"Truth? The only truth in Rome, is power. Beliefs mean nothing to the sharp end of a Roman sword."

"Power is finite. You are just a man, sooner or later, another man will take your power, and you will end up like Peter out there. But Christ's reign is eternal. He watches empire's rise and fall. Only through him can you gain the wisdom to understand that short term power on earth is meaningless."

Nero smirks at the bed where Sporus and Pythagoras lay.

"It may be meaningless. But it sure is fun."

"You build palaces of gold while Rome's poor starve in darkness. You murder innocents for sport while calling it justice. But we... we are building something eternal."

"What could you possibly build? You have no armies, no gold, no power."

"For every Christian you crucify, ten more rise to take their place. Your persecutions only strengthen our resolve; they forge us in the fire of faith, making our community unbreakable. While your empire crumbles under its own weight of decadence and tyranny, the Kingdom we build endures beyond stone and sword. Eternal, invisible to those blinded by earthly power. You may be Emperor for a few more years, but he is King of Kings for eternity."

"Your imaginary Kingdom will never change the fact that I am Emperor. I am more powerful than your so-called God."

"You are a psychotic megalomaniac in women's clothing. You will never be a god."

"Enough. I'll show you what a god can do!"

Nero screams, his wedding dress billowing around him as he seizes a sword from the nearby wall. He swings the sword down in a perfect arc, separating Paul's head from his shoulders. The bright red spray of blood contrasts sharply against the pure white of Nero's flowing wedding gown, staining it like a violent painting. The drops of blood create a pattern on the fabric, resembling delicate rose petals scattered on a snowy ground. Paul's head tumbles across the mosaic floor before coming to rest at Pythagoras's bare feet.

Pythagoras screams, scrambling from the bed and fleeing the chamber in terror. Sporus presses himself against the wall, eyes wide with shock, while Messalina remains perfectly still, her expression unchanged. Nero turns to his Praetorian Prefect, his face stained with the blood of Paul.

"Tigellinus! Find every last Christian in Rome and crucify them. They cannot be persuaded. I will never be able to have true power as long as they worship someone above me."

Before Tigellinus can respond, the chamber doors burst open again. Epaphroditus enters in a panic.

"Emperor! The provinces are revolting! They are marching on Rome!"

Nero's grip tightens on his sword, Paul's blood still dripping from its edge.

"Vindex..."

"No, Emperor. Vindex committed suicide after his rebellion was defeated by Rufus."

"So, Rufus seeks to replace me as Emperor."

"No emperor, Rufus's army revolted against him."

Nero raises both eyebrows and blinks theatrically.

"Well they have certainly been busy. So who is marching on Rome to supplant me?"

"Governor Galba."

Nero's face goes pale beneath his bridal makeup.

"Galba... Thank you, Epaphroditus. You have saved me from rebellion again. Tigellinus, gather the Praetorian Guard, fortify the walls, quash this rebellion as you did the last one."

But Tigellinus remains perfectly still. He stares at the Emperor with his hand on his sword hilt.

"Tigellinus!" Nero's voice cracks like a whip.

Slowly, the Prefect reaches up and removes his helmet, letting it fall to the marble floor with a resounding clang.

"I'm sorry, Emperor. This has gone too far."

The betrayal hits Nero like a physical blow. Around them, the golden walls seem to close in, the very foundations of his world crumbling.

"They are approaching this house. Nero, we must flee." Epaphroditus says.

Nero's eyes dart wildly around the room, seeking something, anything, to anchor him in this dissolving reality.

"Come, my wives."

Sporus, still trembling from witnessing Paul's decapitation, runs into Nero's arms, pressing his face against the blood-stained wedding dress. But Messalina remains seated, her eyes reflecting the lamplight like cold stars.

"Messalina, we must leave now."

She doesn't move.

"You will obey your eEmperor!"

Nero steps toward her, his hand still gripping the bloodied sword. But Tigellinus moves between them, his massive frame blocking Nero's advance. The Emperor stops, understanding in that moment that even this last vestige of power has abandoned him. Nero nods slowly, a broken smile twisting his painted lips. He pulls Sporus closer, breathing in the scent of his hair.

"I always loved Sporus more anyway. Come, Sporus."

The sound of splintering wood echoes through the palace. Heavy fists pounding against the great doors of the Domus Aurea.

"They are here. Quickly, we must flee out the back door," Epaphroditus says.

"Where are we going?"

"The last place in Rome we can find sanctuary. Phaon's villa."

Chapter 19
The Temple of Set

The White Nile glides before Titus, Pliny, and Sextus like a liquid mirror, its surface gleaming under the relentless Nubian sun. The papyrus boat slices through the current with a soft hiss, creaking under the weight of its weary passengers and their scant supplies. At the stern, Sextus grips the steering oar, his scarred visage locked in a scowl as he guides the boat through the river's gentle bends. Titus rows at the bow, his eyes scanning the shoreline where shadows flicker beneath the jungle canopy. Pliny sits amidships, hunched over a tattered scroll as he scribbles notes.

"Titus, what happened at the temple in Meroe?"

"The shamans there showed me visions, possibly of what we'll find at the source of the river."

Pliny lifts his gaze from his scroll.

"What did you see?"

"In the visions I saw a temple of impossible scale. The Temple of Set. Although in all my years in Egypt I've never seen it. Does such a temple exist?" Titus asks.

Pliny sets his scroll aside and reaches for the Book of the Dead, its ancient papyrus crackling as he opens it with reverent care.

"According to the book, it does. The charts show an image of Set standing in front of a black temple. Although, I don't see a specific location of the temple on any of the maps"

A sudden jolt stops the boat as it slams into a hidden rock.

"What was that?" Sextus snaps.

Titus peers over the side.

"Another cataract. The rocks are just beneath the surface. We'll need to portage around it."

Sextus's scarred face twists in frustration.

"Damn this river."

They guide the boat to the shore, their feet sinking into the soft, black mud of the bank. The jungle presses close, its canopy a mosaic of green where sunlight filters through in golden shafts. The air is thick with the scent of wet moss and wild jasmine, pierced by the shrill cries of hornbills and the distant roar of some unseen beast. As they trudge along the shore, the boat balanced between them, a rustling stirs from the jungle. Sextus halts, his hand hovering near his sword.

"Did you hear that?"

The trio freezes, the silence swelling. The rustling fades, swallowed by the jungle's hum. Pliny exhales.

"Maybe it was nothing."

They resume their march, muscles straining under the boat's weight. Suddenly, a spear hisses from the jungle, grazing past Titus's ear with a whisper of death. His heart lurches.

"Ambush!"

Another spear arcs from the green shadows, its stone tip gleaming. Titus uses the boat to parry the incoming spear.

"Run! Get to the water!" he bellows.

They sprint toward the river, the boat bouncing between them as spears rain down, thudding into the mud at their heels. A tribesman bursts from the undergrowth, his machete raised, his body painted with swirling ochre patterns, muscles gleaming with sweat.

Sextus, gripping the boat with one hand, unsheathes his gladius with the other and thrusts it into the warrior's chest, the blade punching through sinew and bone. The man collapses into the reeds, blood pooling in the mire. Pliny's voice cuts through the chaos.

"We passed the cataract! Throw the boat in!"

They heave the vessel into the deeper water, the current seizing it with a surge. Pliny scrambles aboard, grasping the steering oar as the boat begins to drift. Titus pauses at the water's edge and draws his sword.

"I'll hold them off."

The tribesmen charge, their machetes flashing like shards of sunlight. Pliny shouts from the boat.

"Get in!"

But Sextus turns and stands shoulder to shoulder with Titus. He snarls as he looks at the tribal warriors with disgust.

"I'll die before I let these spear-chuckers take glory from the Roman Empire!"

Together, they face the onslaught. Titus's gladius dances through the air, parrying crude machetes with lethal precision, each stroke finding flesh. A throat slit here, a chest pierced there, blood spraying across the muddy bank.

Sextus fights with perfect technique, his blade snapping a machete in half before driving into an attacker's gut, the warrior crumpling with a gurgling cry. A tall tribesman lunges at Titus, his machete arcing toward his skull. Titus sidesteps, his sword sliding along the weapon's edge before slashing open the man's arm, sending him staggering into the shallows. Pliny calls from the boat, paddling frantically, battling the current to hold position.

"I'll keep it close to shore!"

Titus and Sextus retreat step by step, their blades a blur as they carve through their foes. But more tribesmen emerge from the jungle, their war cries echoing like thunder, their painted faces twisted with rage.

"There's too many! Get in the boat!" Titus gasps, his sword arm burning.

They turn and sprint for the water, splashing through the shallows as spears whistle overhead. With desperate strength, they hurl themselves onto the boat, landing in a tangle of limbs and clattering steel.

A tribesman pursues too closely, his feet slipping on the muddy bank. He tumbles into the deeper current with a splash. A crocodile surges from the depths, its jaws snapping shut with a crack like breaking timber. The warrior's scream is cut short, swallowed by the river as crimson ripples spread and vanish. Before the crocodile submerges, it turns to look at Titus with its one remaining eye.

The boat glides downstream. Titus, Sextus, and Pliny sit in stunned silence, the jungle receding behind them like a curtain falling on a stage of blood and survival.

As the days go by, time has become their enemy. Days bleeding into weeks into what seem like months. The relentless sun bakes their skin to leather, and the endless green walls of the upper Nile begin to feel less like a journey and more like a tomb. Their papyrus boat, once sturdy and reliable, now groans with every gentle wave, its bindings loosened by the constant moisture and the weight of three increasingly desperate men.

The leather satchels that once bulged with provisions now hang limp and nearly empty. What remains of their food supply fits in a single pouch. Hardtack bread gone stale and bitter, a precious flask of olive oil, and dried meat that has developed an alarming green tinge around the edges.

Pliny sits hunched in the middle of the boat, his scholarly frame now gaunt with hunger. With the care of a man savouring his last meal, he breaks off a piece of bread and dips it into their dwindling supply of olive oil. The golden liquid soaks into the stale crust, transforming the meagre meal into something almost palatable. He chews slowly, his eyes distant as he contemplates their increasingly dire circumstances. Sextus watches this simple act with the intensity of a hawk.

"Do you know what you just ate, Pliny?"

"Bread?"

"Not just bread. That was the point of no return. There is now not enough supplies for all three of us to make a return journey alive."

Titus, who has been scanning the shoreline for any sign of civilization, turns to face his companions with forced optimism.

"We can hunt if we need to."

Sextus laughs as he gestures toward the impenetrable wall of green that presses close to both banks.

"In that jungle? Be my guest, Titus."

"We could fish for one of the crocodiles."

"And which of us would you like to use as bait?"

Titus scans the dense jungle before them.

"It's entirely possible there is a port around the next bend."

Sextus fixes him with a stare that could freeze the river itself.

"A port? This is a rough neighbourhood, Titus. The locals don't seem too friendly."

Their boat glides around a sweeping curve in the river, revealing nothing but more endless water stretching toward the horizon and an unbroken wall of jungle that mocks their hopes with its verdant indifference.

"Well look at that," Sextus drawls. "It appears there isn't a luxurious palace waiting for us. But I'm sure there will be one around the next bend."

More days pass in grinding monotony, each sunrise bringing them closer to starvation. The bread grows harder, the oil more precious, and the silence between them more oppressive. Sextus watches as Pliny eats another piece of bread

"Only two of us are going to make it home," Sextus says.

Pliny doesn't look up from his meagre meal.

"That sounds optimistic to me."

"Every minute we allow this farce to continue, we lessen the chances of two of us surviving."

Pliny finally raises his eyes.

"You sound confident that it won't be you who dies first."

"Enough!"

Sextus explodes upward like a striking viper. The boat rocks dangerously beneath them. Titus, who had been dozing in exhaustion, has no time to react before Sextus shoves his limp body out of the boat. The splash comes with a desperate gasp as Titus hangs on to the boat's edge.

"Sextus!"

Titus's voice carries desperation as he grips the gunwales, his legs kicking frantically in the dark water. The sound of steel leaving its sheath rings across the river as Sextus draws his gladius and points it at Pliny.

"I promise you, Pliny, your corpse won't go to waste. I'll use you as bait."

Pliny's eyes widen as he scrambles backward, nearly capsizing the boat. His soft hands find his stylus, clutching it like a pathetic weapon against Sextus's gleaming blade.

"You won't make it without me. I'm the only one who can read the hieroglyphs, the only one who can interpret what we find!"

Sextus advances, the boat rocking dangerously beneath his feet. Behind him, Titus's fingers slip on the papyrus hull, the current tugging at his legs with hungry persistence. He tries to pull himself up but the force of the river is too strong. He looks at Sextus, whose pupils start to dilate so wide they eclipse the iris, his eyes turning jet black as he approaches Pliny.

"What good are hieroglyphs to starving men? What use is knowledge when our flesh rots from our bones?"

Sextus inches his blade towards the scholar, but just as he raises it, the boat crashes into solid ground. The force of the crash hurls Sextus forward, tumbling onto the bank. Pliny falls face down in the bow of the boat. Titus crawls onto the shore from the side of the boat as Pliny looks up to see what they hit.

Before them stretches an inland lake so vast that its far shores disappear into a haze, its crystalline waters reflecting the African sky like a mirror. Gentle waves lap against rolling green hills, while tropical vegetation cascades down from verdant hills that ring the enormous lake. Pliny stares at the lake in awe.

"By the gods, I never knew a lake this big could exist. Can you believe it, Titus?"

Titus stares at the banks of the lake, mouth agape in disbelief.

"That's not what I can't believe."

Pliny turns his head and follows Titus's gaze. He gasps when he sees it.

A jet-black temple of impossible proportions stands at the lake's edge like a fever dream carved in obsidian. The temple's scale defies reason. Its pylons dwarf anything they have seen on the Nile or in Rome. Giant statues of Set flank the entrance. Hieroglyphs spiral and fracture across the walls in patterns that refuse to settle into order, depicting Set in his myriad forms: the strange dog-headed god, the desert storm, the dismemberer of Osiris.

But the most arresting feature thrusts out from the upper levels: a balcony of black stone that juts over the lake's still surface, forty feet or more from the water below. It has no railing, no wall, no protection whatsoever. Just a broad platform that ends in empty air above the lake.

Suddenly, a rustling disturbs the jungle canopy above the beach, as if someone has crashed through the undergrowth with desperate haste towards the temple. Branches sway and leaves flutter to the ground like green snow. Titus looks to where Sextus had been lying a moment earlier.

"Sextus?"

He looks at Pliny and then towards the temple.

"Sextus!" Titus's voice echoes across the sacred waters.

Titus and Pliny exchange a look and then plunge into the tropical forest, following the trail of broken vegetation up the steep hillside. Thorns tear at their tunics and vines catch their feet as they climb through the emerald maze, their breath coming in ragged gasps in the humid air.

They break through the final wall of vegetation, and the temple reveals itself all at once. It is the size of a mountain that has chosen its own shape. Statues of Set, massive beyond reason, guard the doorway with their strange angular heads tilted as if considering these intruders. The Romans pause at the threshold, feeling the temperature drop, feeling something older than their empire watching from within. They hear fading footsteps echoing through the temple.

They step forward through the massive doorway. Inside, the scale is truly incomprehensible. The ceiling vaults so high above that darkness claims it entirely, lost somewhere in that black stone vastness. Braziers burn with flames that seem reluctant, their light barely pushing back the shadows. The air tastes of stone and incense and something older, something that predates Rome, predates Greece, predates memory itself.

Their footsteps echo and re-echo, multiplying until it sounds like an army marches with them. Columns rise on either side, each one wider than five men standing fingertip to fingertip, their surfaces alive with carved reliefs of Set that spiral upward into shadow.

As they move upwards through the temple, the walls tell Set's story in stone. Here, the god of chaos tears apart his brother Osiris, limbs scattering across Egypt in fourteen pieces. There, he commands the desert winds, sand and chaos bending to his will. Further on, he battles Horus for the throne of the gods, their divine war rendered in such exquisite detail that individual feathers show on the falcon god's wings. Titus is not sure if he is dreaming or still feeling the effect of the Shaman's ceremony.

"Pliny, are you seeing this too?"

Pliny looks around in disbelief at the sheer scale of the temple.

"I see it, Titus."

They begin their ascent up a spiral staircase that curves along the temple's inner wall. Each step stands as high as a man's waist, designed for someone, or something, at least three times their size. They climb the steps rather than walk. As they reach the top of the stairs, there on the walls, they see something they cannot believe.

Carved into the black stone with impossible precision, they see an unmistakable image of Emperor Nero, his face rendered with such detail that his madness seems etched into the stone itself. Around him lie the bodies of those he destroyed: Britannicus twisted in death by poison, Agrippina stabbed and bleeding, Octavia drowned in her bath, Seneca with opened veins, Sabina broken beneath his kicks. They sprawl across the lower portion of the relief like an offering, a foundation of corpses upon which the emperor stands.

Then the carving depicts Nero handing Set a vial of liquid. Then the carving shows the god striding down the Nile, temple after temple, city after city, all the way to where the great river begins. Then, Set tips the vial of black liquid into the lake, spreading like ink through water, like corruption through an empire. Titus stares at the depiction of the Emperor in disbelief.

"Is that who I think it is?"

Pliny stares at the carvings, shaking his head as his rational mind refuses to let him believe his own eyes.

“It’s not possible. It can’t be.”

Suddenly, a malevolent laugh cuts through the eerie silence of the temple, snapping the two Roman’s out of their trance. They sprint towards the sound. The corridor seems to stretch forever, then suddenly opens onto the balcony. A platform of polished black stone jutting out over the lake, boundless and bare. At the very edge of the precipitous ledge stands a solitary figure with his back to them, motionless as a statue carved from living rock.

"Sextus?" Titus gasps, his chest heaving.

The figure pivots with unnatural slowness. It wears Sextus's flesh like borrowed clothing. His scars still map campaigns across his cheeks, his skin still bears the leather texture of years under foreign suns, his jaw still juts with Roman stubbornness. But where Sextus's eyes once held the calculating gaze of a soldier, now two black wells drink in the daylight without reflection. In his right hand, he holds a vial of jet-black liquid.

"Sextus?" Pliny whispers.

Sextus’s lips part and form a crescent that has never graced a mortal face. A smile ancient as the Nile itself. Titus straightens to his full height, drawing upon every ounce of imperial authority in his bloodline.

"Hello Set."

Chapter 20
Qualis Artifex Pereo

The modest villa of Phaon feels like a tomb compared to the golden splendour Nero has known all his life. The furniture consists of simple stools and a wooden table that bears the scars of countless humble meals. Through the single window, the distant glow of Rome flickers like a dying star, while closer at hand, the sound of the approaching mob grows ever louder. A tide of vengeance that will not be turned back.

Nero sits hunched on a rough wooden bench, still wearing the remnants of his wedding dress, though the silk is now torn and stained with sweat, tears, and the blood of Paul. Beside him, Sporus trembles like a frightened bird, his painted eyes never leaving his beloved Emperor's face. Epaphroditus paces near the door, his secretary's robes wrinkled and his usually composed demeanour cracking under the weight of their desperate circumstances.

"Where is my husband Pythagoras?" Nero asks.

Epaphroditus stops his pacing and turns to the Emperor.

"He has abandoned you."

Nero's smirks as if unsurprised, then turns to Sporus.

"I never truly loved him anyway. In fact, I never knew what true love was until I met you, Sporus."

Sporus takes Nero's hand in both of his own, tears streaming down his painted cheeks like rain on marble. His touch is warm and desperate, clinging to these final moments as if love alone could hold back the approaching storm. Through the window, a column of black smoke rises against the evening sky, emanating from the direction of the Domus Aurea. Nero's eyes follow its dark ascent.

"I was hoping they would let my golden palace stand in honour of me."

"They already have plans to replace it," Epaphroditus says quietly.

"With what?"

"A Colosseum, my Emperor. The largest colosseum Rome has ever seen. They say it will host gladiator battles that will echo for thousands of years."

Nero's eyes grow distant, as if he can see across time itself.

"I wonder what they have planned for the inaugural ceremony."

Epaphroditus nervously clears his throat.

"Your crucifixion. They intend for the colosseum to symbolize the end of your reign and the beginning of Rome's new golden age."

Nero turns to Sporus with a smile that mingles tenderness with infinite sadness.

"All this for little old me. What do you think, Sporus? Should we give them the satisfaction?"

Sporus throws his arms around Nero's thigh, his slender body wracked with sobs that shake them both. His tears soak into the silk of the wedding dress. With theatrical flourish, Nero reaches for a simple iron dagger that lies on the wooden table. A tool meant for cutting bread.

"Goodbye, my love."

He brings the weapon toward his throat with the same grace he once used to tune his lyre, but his hand freezes mere inches from the pale skin of his neck. His muscles tremble with effort, as if invisible chains bind his wrist, preventing the final act.

He tries again, his face contorting with concentration and desperation, but again his hand refuses to obey. With a cry of rage and frustration, he hurls the dagger across the room, where it clatters against the stone wall and falls to the floor.

"I cannot! To kill Rome's greatest artist would be a true crime. You will have to help me, Epaphroditus."

The secretary's face goes ashen.

"What do you mean, Emperor?"

"Pick up the blade and plunge it into my neck."

"My Emperor, I could never."

"Hush." Nero's voice becomes gentle, almost paternal. "It's alright, Epaphroditus. I will forgive you."

Epaphroditus retrieves the fallen dagger, his hands shaking as he approaches his master. The blade trembles against Nero's throat, its cold metal a whisper away from ending an empire.

"It's okay, Epaphroditus. I would rather it be you than the hordes who never understood my art."

Epaphroditus's hands begin to shake violently, and the dagger slips from his nerveless fingers to clatter on the floor between them.

"I cannot."

Nero reaches out and touches his faithful secretary's cheek with infinite gentleness.

"It's okay. We still have some time left."

Sporus cries at Nero's feet as the sound of the approaching mob gets louder.

Deep in the jungle at the source of the Blue Nile, Paulinus, Marcus, and Kashta remain bound to weathered pillars. Quintus continues to hide in the tree line, watching from a distance.

"Marcus?" Quintus whispers from the trees.

Paulinus shifts against his bonds and nudges Marcus with his foot. Marcus's body responds with the lifeless flop of dead meat, his head lolling at an unnatural angle.

"Deceased," Paulinus mutters. "Which means they'll be looking for fresh meat."

The tribal chief approaches the captured prisoners, machete in hand.

"When I give the signal, throw a spear at the guards, and Kashta, run for it," Paulinus hisses to his companions.

"What's the signal?" Quintus calls softly.

"You'll know it when you see it," Paulinus replies.

The chief reaches Marcus's corpse and prods it with his spear tip, confirming what he already suspected. His gaze shifts to Paulinus's leg, and he raises his machete like a butcher preparing his work. Before he can swing the blade, Paulinus interrupts.

"I wish to participate in your ritual," he declares.

The chief freezes, his blade suspended in mid-air. He turns to Kashta with questioning eyes. Kashta's voice trembles as he renders the Roman's words into the local dialect.

After a moment of consideration, the chief nods and gestures to his men. They swarm forward, cutting the bonds that hold both prisoners to their wooden pillars. They seize Paulinus and drag him toward the large ceremonial hut, where the golden chest sits upon a raised platform. Kashta is restrained between two powerful warriors, forced to watch the ritual unfold. The same ritual that took Marcus's leg

The ritual begins with the rhythmic beating of hide drums that seem to resonate with the rustling of the wind. Warriors dance in a circle around the altar, their movements hypnotic and primal, while their voices rise in chants that predate the written word. Smoke from burning herbs creates a haze that makes everything seem dreamlike and unreal.

The chief approaches Paulinus with reverent ceremony, offering first the carved cup. The Roman takes it, noting the bitter scent that rises from its depths. A mixture of fermented fruit and something far more dangerous. He brings it to his lips and drinks from it.

Next comes the pipe, its ivory surface carved with intricate spirals. Paulinus draws on it as instructed, letting the smoke fill his mouth while keeping his throat closed, then releases it in a convincing exhale. He sways slightly, letting his eyes grow heavy-lidded as if the sacred substances are taking hold of his senses.

The chief watches with interest as the Roman appears to succumb to the ritual intoxicants. He raises his machete high above his head, as he prepares to complete the ceremony with blood sacrifice.

In that moment, Paulinus spits the bitter liquid directly into the chief's eyes. The warrior chief staggers backward, clawing at his eyes as the unknown substance burns his vision. Paulinus drives his fist into the chief's solar plexus, doubling him over, then tears the machete from his weakened grip and brings it around in a devastating arc that separates the chief's head from his shoulders in a spray of crimson.

"Now!" Paulinus roars.

A spear comes whistling from the jungle and finds the heart of one of Kashta's captors with deadly accuracy. The Kushite wrestles free from his remaining guard.

The camp erupts into chaos. Warriors howling war cries, spears whistling past Paulinus's ear close enough to stir his hair, bare feet pounding the earth in pursuit. The ceremonial fire scatters into embers as bodies collide, sending sparks spiralling upward into the canopy where startled birds take flight in an explosion of colour and sound. A tribesman lunges at Paulinus with a bone dagger, missing his throat by inches as he twists away.

Paulinus turns and races toward the golden chest, but suddenly, a spear pierces his calf, the stone tip grinding against bone. He crashes to the jungle floor, his scream of pain echoing off the ancient trees. Rolling onto his back, he looks up to see a painted warrior standing over him, spear raised for the killing thrust.

Before the spear reaches Paulinus, steel bursts through the tribal warrior's chest in a spray of blood and bone, the point of a blade emerging like a deadly flower. He looks down in shock, then crumples to the ground, revealing Kashta standing behind him.

"Let's go!" Kashta shouts as he tries to pick Paulinus up.

"No!" Paulinus gasps through gritted teeth, his leg useless beneath him. "Go now! I'll create the distraction!"

Kashta hesitates for only a moment before sprinting toward the tree line where Quintus waits. The remaining warriors pour after him like a flood of painted death, their war cries splitting the jungle air.

Alone now except for the dead, Paulinus begins the agonizing journey toward the golden chest, dragging himself forward on his elbows while his wounded leg leaves a trail of blood on the sacred ground. Each movement sends lightning through his shattered calf, but his eyes remain fixed on the ancient artifact.

On the balcony of the Temple of Set, Titus and Pliny face Sextus. The Praetorian Prefect's eyes have turned obsidian black, his veins darkening beneath skin as his lips curl into an unnatural smile. Both men feel the primordial dread crawling up their spines as they realize what stands before them is no longer their companion but a vessel for Set, the ancient Egyptian god of chaos.

The vial of black liquid in Sextus's grip seems to absorb the very light around it, creating a sphere of darkness in his pale hand.

"I suppose I don't need to ask what that is," Titus says.

Sextus speaks in a language that predates Rome, predates civilization itself.

"What's he saying?" Titus asks Pliny.

Pliny frantically flips through the Book of the Dead.

"He says he is fulfilling the prophecy. He is going to usher in an era of chaos. The end of all order, all life."

"Tell him to hand over the vial."

"I'm afraid I can't speak that language. I can only roughly translate it."

Titus raises his gladius and points it at the vial of liquid night.

"You aren't pouring that poison into the lake, Sextus. Hand it over."

Sextus draws his sword, the steel singing as it leaves its sheath. He speaks again in that ancient tongue, his malevolent tone dripping with mockery. Pliny continues rifling through the book of the dead to translate, but Titus waves him off.

"You don't need to translate that. I know what he said." Titus raises his weapon fully and begins to circle Sextus. "Unsheathe your sword, Pliny."

The scholar draws his blade with unpractised hands, his grip awkward but determined. Sextus's lips curve in a smile that belongs in nightmares, and without warning, he tilts back his head and drinks the entire contents of the vial. The black liquid disappears down his throat like liquid shadow, and for a moment, his eyes flare with darkness deeper than the abyss. Titus and Pliny stare in shock.

"Why did he just poison himself?" Pliny gasps.

"He's going to jump into the lake. His corpse will spread the poison. We have to kill him first."

The three men stand frozen in a triangle of tension, each waiting for the other to make the first move. The sacred lake stretches below them, its pristine waters reflecting the sky like a mirror of the heavens themselves.

"Now!" Titus roars.

Both Romans charge simultaneously, their feet pounding against the black stone of the balcony. Sextus parries Titus's thrust with perfect technique before driving his boot into the general's chest, sending him staggering backward. In the same fluid motion, he seizes Pliny's wrists, his grip like iron manacles.

The scholar's eyes widen in terror as Sextus draws back his head and drives his forehead into Pliny's skull with the force of a battering ram. The crack of bone on bone echoes throughout the temple like breaking timber. Pliny's eyes roll back, showing only white, and his body goes limp as a discarded doll. Without releasing his grip, Sextus pivots and hurls the unconscious scholar through the air. In the same moment, Sextus tears the sword from Pliny's nerveless fingers, now wielding two blades that gleam like twin fangs in the afternoon light.

Pliny's body arcs in a parabola before crashing to the floor twelve feet away, rolling to a stop against the wall beneath an ancient carving of Set torching the library of

Alexandria. He lies motionless, blood trickling from his scalp to pool on the stones beneath his head.

"Pliny!" Titus struggles to his feet, his chest aching from the kick.

Sextus turns to face Titus, and when he speaks, two voices emerge from his throat simultaneously. His own familiar tone layered with something infinitely older and more malevolent.

"I have waited five thousand years for this moment. The old gods will reclaim what is theirs."

Titus circles warily, his gladius held in the defensive position taught to every Roman officer. The being before him moves with unnatural fluidity, as if Sextus's body has become liquid shadow given human form.

"You don't have to do this, Sextus," Titus says, buying time as he searches for an opening.

A laugh erupts from Sextus's throat. A sound like desert winds scraping across ancient tombs.

"Sextus was merely a vessel waiting to be filled. His unwavering loyalty to his master, his ruthlessness, these made him perfect for my purpose."

Titus lunges suddenly, a feint followed by a swift diagonal slash. Sextus parries with both blades, the impact sending sparks cascading through the air. The weapons lock momentarily, steel grinding against steel as the two men strain against each other. Sextus's black eyes bore into Titus's, and in their obsidian depths, the general glimpses something ancient. A consciousness that has witnessed the rise and fall of civilizations, that has fed on chaos since the dawn of creation.

With supernatural strength, Sextus breaks the blade-lock and launches a flurry of attacks that drives Titus backwards onto the ground.

"I'm going to enjoy watching you die, more than I enjoyed watching your father die."

Sextus charges, both swords weaving deadly patterns in the air. Titus scoops up a handful of loose stone chippings and flings them directly into Sextus's black eyes. The Praetorian staggers, momentarily blinded, and Titus rolls past him with the agility that has kept him alive through countless battles.

When he comes to his feet, he stands between Sextus and the sacred lake, his back to the edge of the balcony. Sextus wipes the dirt from his eyes and fixes his terrible gaze on the Roman general. Titus glances over his shoulder at the deadly fall, then back at the Praetorian Prefect. He exhales forcefully, steeling himself for what must come.

They charge each other simultaneously, their war cries echoing across the sacred waters. Steel meets steel in a shower of sparks, but momentum carries them forward, and all blades find their mark. Titus feels the hot punch of metal through his abdomen, not once, but twice, as both of Sextus's swords pierce his body. At the same moment, his own gladius slides between Sextus's ribs, the tip grinding against bone as it seeks the heart beyond.

Both men fall, their blood mingling on black stone beneath. Titus looks down at the two sword hilts protruding from his midsection, dark blood already soaking through his tunic. He turns his head to see Sextus struggling to his feet, the gladius still buried to the hilt in his chest.

"No," Titus whispers, trying to rise but finding his body no longer obeys his will.

Sextus limps toward the balcony's edge, each step leaving a crimson footprint. The black poison courses through his veins, visible now as dark lines spreading beneath his skin like veins of night.

The air above Titus shimmers and Anubis materializes. The jackal-headed god of death, his form translucent yet terrifyingly real. Golden light emanates like smoke from his eyes as he gazes down at the dying Roman.

"*It is time to join me in the Duat, Titus,*" Anubis whispers.

"Sextus! Stop!" Titus calls out desperately.

At the balcony's edge, Sextus turns to face Titus one final time. The possessed warrior spreads his arms wide, mimicking the position of crucifixion.

Anubis lifts Titus from the ground, his divine power raising the general into the air as his mortal form begins to fade. Visions flood Titus's fading consciousness. His wife's gentle smile, his sons playing in the fields of their farm in Britannia. Blood bubbles from Titus's lips as he reaches out with his last strength toward the figure at the balcony's edge.

"Stop..."

Sextus's voice rings out across the lake, but now it carries only Set's tone, as if Set's presence has finally burned away everything that made Sextus human.

"I am Set, the mighty one of strength, lord of the desert and of the red land. It is I who am the eldest, the son of

Nut, the strength of Ra himself! The kingship is mine by right."

He begins to fall backward toward the pristine waters that have given life to Egypt for millennia, his arms still spread in that terrible parody of crucifixion, the black poison ready to flow from his wounds into the source of the White Nile.

At the source of the Blue Nile, Paulinus's blood seeps into the earth as he drags himself across the ground, each movement sending lightning through his shattered calf. His fingers claw at roots and stones, propelling his broken body toward the golden chest that sits like a beacon.

Behind him, the sounds of pursuit echo through the village. War cries growing more distant as Kashta sprints from the painted warriors towards the jungle maze. The Kushite dodges spears, while Quintus waits at the tree line with an outstretched hand.

Paulinus reaches the base of the Ark, his breathing ragged with pain and exhaustion. The golden chest looms above him, its surface blazing with reflected light that seems almost alive with divine fire.

With tremendous effort, he hauls himself up onto the stone platform, his wounded leg leaving a crimson trail across the sacred surface. His hands find purchase on the chest's ornate edges, feeling the strange warmth that emanates from within.

Through the jungle canopy, he catches a glimpse of Kashta bounding between the trees. the pursuing warriors catching up to him with each desperate leap. The sight fills

Paulinus with a fierce determination that cuts through his agony.

His palm presses against the lid of the Ark, feeling the subtle vibration that seems to pulse with the rhythm of creation itself. The golden surface burns against his skin, not with heat but with a presence so pure it seems to sear his very soul. He takes a deep breath.

"I hope you made it, Titus," he whispers.

With the last of his strength, he shoves the lid aside.

Light explodes from the opened chest. Not the yellow glow of lamp or sun, but something infinitely more primal. It is the light that blazed at the moment of creation, the radiance that divided darkness from day, the light brought to the life by the light bringer himself. The beam erupts skyward like a pillar connecting earth to heaven, its brilliance so intense it turns the green jungle white as bone.

Around the camp, the painted warriors freeze mid-stride as the light washes over them. Their stone weapons melt like ice, their ritual paint evaporates like morning mist, and their bodies are reduced to shadow and memory in an instant that stretches into eternity.

Through his dissolving vision, Paulinus sees Kashta reach Quintus at the safety of the tree line, the Kushite's form silhouetted against the jungle as he turns back one final time. Their eyes meet across the blazing clearing. Roman governor and African warrior, bound together by shared struggle and mutual respect.

Paulinus feels his flesh begin to burn away, not with pain but with a sensation of overwhelming purity that dissolves everything mortal about him. As the divine fire consumes every atom of his being, he looks up and sees Horus, the falcon headed god of kingship standing above him. Horus reaches out his hand toward the Roman governor. In his last moment, Paulinus reaches out and takes the hand of Horus.

The light from the ark takes them both completely, and Paulinus feels his consciousness expand beyond the boundaries of flesh and bone, becoming one with the eternal radiance that has slept within the golden chest since the world began.

As Sextus begins to fall backward toward the sacred waters, his arms still spread in a mocking crucifixion pose, the distant jungle suddenly erupts in brilliant radiance. A pillar of pure light blazes skyward from somewhere far beyond the lake's eastern shore. Light so intense it turns the night sky white as bleached bone, so powerful it seems to shake the very foundations of the earth.

The shockwave hits like the fist of an angry god.

Sextus's backward fall becomes a forward tumble as the divine force slams into him, driving him to his knees at the balcony's edge. His possessed form writhes against the sacred ground, the black poison in his veins seeming to recoil from the purifying radiance that washes over the entire landscape.

The temple starts to shake as if struck by an earthquake. Dust falls from ceiling as statues of Set begin to collapse. Massive blocks that have stood for millennia wrench free from the walls, grinding against each other as they fall.

Above Titus, Anubis's grip falters as the light strikes his divine form. The jackal-headed god staggers in mid-air, his golden essence flickering like a candle in hurricane wind. Titus crashes back to the balcony, the impact driving fresh agony through his pierced body.

But something has changed. The nearness of death that had been dragging him toward darkness now retreats, pushed back by the same divine force that blazes from the distant jungle. With strength he should not possess, Titus struggles to his feet, his hands finding the hilts of the two swords that still protrude from his abdomen.

He grips the leather-wrapped handles and pulls both blades free from his body. Dark blood flows from the wounds, but not the arterial spray that should herald his death. Instead, the flow seems measured, controlled, as if some greater power has decided he has work yet to finish.

Sextus kneels at the precipice, his head hanging low as he fights against the purifying light that continues to blaze across the landscape. The thing that wears his face looks up as Titus approaches, and for just a moment, the darkness in his eyes flickers, as if the real Sextus peers through the supernatural veil that has claimed him.

Titus raises both swords above his head, their steel catching the divine radiance and reflecting it back like mirrors of judgment.

"God wills it," he whispers.

The blades sweep down in unison, meeting at Sextus's neck. His head separates from his shoulders cleanly, rolling across the ancient stones to come to rest at the very edge of the balcony. The black poison that had coursed through his veins evaporates like smoke in the brilliant light, leaving only the mortal remains of the Praetorian prefect who had been claimed by forces beyond his understanding.

Titus staggers backward, the effort of his final blow draining what little strength the divine light had granted him. He collapses onto the ground, his breathing shallow and laboured as his life begins to ebb once more. The wounds in his abdomen resume their steady flow, and darkness creeps in at the edges of his vision.

Through fading sight, he sees movement at the far side of the balcony. Pliny struggles to his feet, blood matting his hair but consciousness returning to him. The naturalist looks around wildly and sees Titus lying in a pool of his blood.

"Titus!" Pliny yells.

He runs over to Titus as the temple shakes and crumbles around him. Titus's vision blurs as Pliny kneels beside him, tearing strips from his own tunic to stanch the flow of blood from the general's wounds. The scholar's hands move with deftness, pressing against the twin punctures where Sextus's blades had entered.

"Leave me," Titus gasps, each word a struggle against the tide of darkness rising within him. "Save yourself."

"I'm not going anywhere," Pliny replies as he presses his bandages against Titus's chest.

A large status of Set crashes to floor, narrowly missing them. Titus coughs up blood.

"Rome needs to know what happened here. Go home. Write your book."

"I can save you!"

"Look where my wounds are, Pliny. I won't even make it back to the boat."

Tears well up in Pliny's eyes, as he looks at the blood pouring from Titus's midsection.

"If you make it back to Britannia, tell my sons of my sacrifice. And tell them I was wrong about their grandfather. He died a hero, saving my life."

Pliny straightens, mastering his grief.

"It was an honour, General."

"The honour was mine."

Pliny rises and flees into the collapsing temple, the unearthly beam of light carving his path through the darkness.

Above Titus, Anubis reforms his divine presence, the jackal-headed god's golden eyes fixed upon the dying Roman with something that might be respect. The god of death extends his ethereal tendrils once more, but this time there is no force in his grip, only the gentle inevitability of a harvest whose time has finally come.

As Anubis lifts Titus from the ground, the temple under him collapses entirely. Columns thick as ancient oaks snap at their bases and topple inward, crushing the floor beneath them. The temple descends into the depths of the lake like a landslide of obsidian, leaving nothing behind on the surface.

As the divine light from the distant jungle radiates the sky, Titus feels his consciousness slip away. The sacred lake stretching before him in all its pristine beauty. Unmarked, unpoisoned, eternal as the God who made it.

Nero paces the small chamber in Phaon's villa, his wedding dress rustling with each agitated step. Sporus sits huddled in the corner, tears still streaming down his painted cheeks, while Epaphroditus maintains his vigil by the shuttered window. The sounds of the approaching mob grow ever closer. A tide of vengeance that cannot be turned back.

Then the night sky erupts in radiance.

A pillar of pure light blazes upward from somewhere south, far beyond the seven hills of Rome, its brilliance so intense it transforms darkness into day. The divine radiance pours through every crack and crevice of the humble dwelling, banishing shadows and filling the air with an otherworldly glow that seems to pulse with the rhythm of creation itself.

Nero rushes to the window, throwing open the wooden shutters to stare in wonder at the celestial phenomenon. His face, still bearing traces of cosmetics from his wedding celebration, is illuminated by the supernatural light. For a moment, all thoughts of pursuit and death flee from his mind, replaced by the pure aesthetic appreciation that has always been his greatest gift and his greatest curse. His voice becomes filled with the same reverence he once reserved for the finest poetry or the most exquisite music.

"By the gods, it's beautiful."

The moment of transcendence shatters as the sound of splintering wood echoes through the villa. Heavy fists pound against the front door with increasing violence, and voices raised in anger penetrate even the divine light that bathes the world. Epaphroditus calls urgently, his face pale with terror.

"My Emperor, they're here."

Nero turns from the window, the celestial light still blazing behind him like a backdrop painted by the gods themselves. His eyes find the simple iron dagger where it lies on the rough wooden floor. The same blade he could not use before, the instrument of his liberation that his hands had refused to grasp.

He picks up the dagger with steady hands, feeling its familiar weight as he has felt the weight of the imperial purple, the weight of a crown, the weight of an empire's expectations.

The blade gleams in the supernatural light as he raises it to his throat. Through the window, the pillar of radiance continues to blaze across the heavens like a bridge between Earth and Olympus, beautiful beyond all mortal comprehension.

As Nero awes at the illuminated sky and inches the blade towards his neck, he speaks his final words:

"What an artist dies with me."

www.ingramcontent.com/pod-product-compliance
Ingram Content Group UK Ltd.
Pitfield, Milton Keynes, MK11 3LW, UK
UKHW040757220426
12011UKWH00014B/16

9 781068 477355